# Death in
# Saratoga Springs

Books by Charles O'Brien

DEATH OF A ROBBER BARON

DEATH IN SARATOGA SPRINGS

Published by Kensington Publishing Corporation

# Death in Saratoga Springs

## A GILDED AGE MYSTERY

### CHARLES O'BRIEN

KENSINGTON BOOKS
www.kensingtonbooks.com

KENSINGTON BOOKS are published by

Kensington Publishing Corp.
119 West 40th Street
New York, NY 10018

All Kensington titles, imprints, and distributed lines are available at special quantity discounts for bulk purchases for sales promotion, premiums, fund-raising, educational, or institutional use.

Special book excerpts or customized printings can also be created to fit specific needs. For details, write or phone the office of the Kensington Special Sales Manager: Kensington Publishing Corp., 119 West 40th Street, New York, NY 10018. Attn. Special Sales Department. Phone: 1-800-221-2647.

Kensington and the K logo Reg. U.S. Pat. & TM Off.

ISBN-13: 978-0-7582-8638-3
ISBN-10: 0-7582-8638-4
First Kensington Trade Paperback Printing: June 2014

eISBN-13: 978-0-7582-8639-0
eISBN-10: 0-7582-8639-2
First Kensington Electronic Edition: June 2014

10 9 8 7 6 5 4 3 2 1

Printed in the United States of America

*For Elvy*

# Acknowledgments

I wish to thank Andy Sheldon and Jennifer Krouse for helpful computer services. I am grateful also to Gudveig Baarli for diligently assisting with the maps, and to the editors and other professionals at Kensington who produced this book. My agent, Evan Marshall, and Adam Braver of the NY State Summer Writers Institute at Skidmore College, Saratoga Springs, read drafts of the novel and contributed much to its improvement. The librarians of the Saratoga Room at the Saratoga Springs Public Library generously offered skillful guidance into the rich historical sources of their Gilded Age city. Finally, my wife, Elvy, art historian, deserves special mention for her keen editorial eye and her moral support.

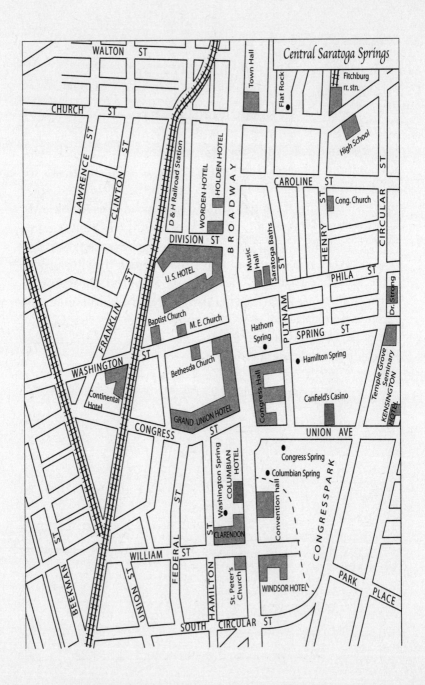

Central Saratoga Springs

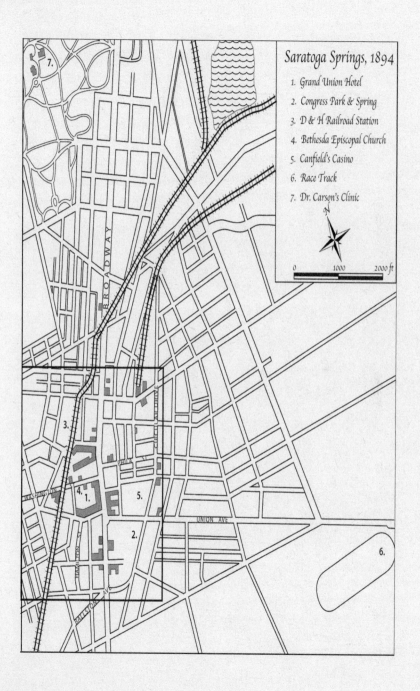

Saratoga Springs, 1894

1. Grand Union Hotel
2. Congress Park & Spring
3. D & H Railroad Station
4. Bethesda Episcopal Church
5. Canfield's Casino
6. Race Track
7. Dr. Carson's Clinic

N

0      1000      2000 ft

# CHAPTER 1

## A New Case

*New York City*
*Monday, February 5, 1894*

On a freezing Monday morning, Pamela Thompson shuffled over an icy patch on Irving Place, balancing on her steel-tipped walking stick. At the sign on the door, PRESCOTT AND ASSOCI-ATES, COUNSELORS-AT-LAW, she was reminded that, two years ago, she had come here, a desperate woman seeking counsel. A year ago, the law firm employed her as an investigator, and soon Prescott himself became her mentor and friend.

She stepped into the warm reception room and left her stick by the door. Peter Yates, the firm's retired librarian and Pamela's friend, took her coat and hat. "The receptionist is ill. I'm helping out today. Mr. Prescott would like to see you in his office. You are to meet a visitor."

A hint in Yates's voice made Pamela glance in a mirror and touch up her hair. He showed her into the room. A slim, elegant gentleman about fifty, a cane by his side, was sitting with Prescott. They rose to greet her. Prescott introduced the visitor as Mr. Virgil Crawford, the butler to the Crawford family.

Pamela assumed from the family name that he was a relative. They gathered around the writing table.

Mr. Crawford addressed her politely in cultivated English with a Southern accent. His skin was fair in color; his eyes, almond shaped and a deep golden brown. His thick, curly hair was receding and turning gray, adding to an already strong impression of high intelligence. Pamela suddenly realized that this man was black and very likely once a slave.

Crawford took note of her surprise with the flicker of a smile, then said to her, "I have a problem: Our housekeeper's niece, Ruth Colt, disappeared a month ago. Without evidence of a crime, the police won't spend time or money to look for her. The detective in charge of missing persons, Larry White, recommended hiring a private investigator. So, I've come here. I'm acting on behalf of Mr. James Crawford, head of the family, and am prepared to contract with you for the search."

"She's been gone a month?" Pamela asked. "By now, she might be in California or halfway to Hawaii. A search could be expensive."

His eyes seemed to tease her, "The Crawfords have enough money."

Prescott asked her, "Are you willing to look for the young woman? Our firm would place its resources at your disposal."

"I am, indeed," Pamela replied. "It's the kind of work I feel called to do." She turned to Crawford. "Tell me more about the housekeeper and her niece."

He leaned back in thoughtful reflection. "Martha Colt and Ruth are light-skinned black people who could pass for white. A widow, Martha has served the Crawford household for many years and is much respected. Ruth is fifteen and an orphan. A few months ago, she went to work as a chambermaid in a cheap hotel. When she disappeared and the police did nothing, Martha approached me for help."

The girl's story both moved and intrigued Pamela. As far

back as she could remember, she had felt compassion for poor, neglected, or abandoned children. For years she had helped provide them with food and clothing, shelter and counseling through St. Barnabas Mission on Mulberry Street. Having become a private investigator a year ago, she could now find them if they were lost.

As the meeting drew to an end, Crawford said to Pamela, "You should visit Mrs. Colt at our home on Washington Square. Enter from the rear at the service entrance."

He also gave her an address on a side street near Washington Square. "That's my private office, where I do sensitive projects. Henceforth, we'll meet there." He raised a cautionary finger. "Our investigation *must* be secret. We could encounter a murderer."

Pamela left the room with the impression that Virgil Crawford was no ordinary butler who spent his day polishing the family silver or keeping track of household accounts. He acted like a secret agent dealing with issues of life and death. Why conceal the family's interest in this case? Did he have a hidden objective? She felt as if she was becoming a pawn in a dangerous game.

That afternoon, Pamela approached the Crawford town house on the north side of Washington Square, a simple, elegant brick residence from the 1840s. She followed a walkway around the building to the service entrance and rang a bell. While waiting, she glanced at a tall brick shaft attached harmoniously to the rear of the building.

"Master James's elevator is inside the shaft, ma'am," said the male servant who had opened the door. "The contraption runs on vertical rails with a system of ropes and pulleys and counterbalances. Ingenious, isn't it? He's crippled and uses a wheelchair. But his arms are very strong, and he manages the ropes by himself."

The servant led her into a parlor and left to call Mrs. Colt. While waiting, Pamela studied a series of oil paintings that depicted sleek sailing ships. On a table below them stood a detailed model of a modern steamship. All the ships bore the same name, *Savannah Line.*

"The Crawfords have been in the shipping business for fifty years," Mrs. Colt remarked as she stepped into the room. "These days, Master James is in charge."

Martha Colt was a wiry, older woman with a stern cast to her face, but she smiled graciously and showed Pamela into her room in the rear of the house. It had a view of the garden and the stable beyond. To judge from faint, savory odors rising from the kitchen below, dinner was being prepared.

On the wall hung a simple, naïve painting on wood of a Southern plantation. Asked about it, Martha brightened. "We were slaves. Daddy painted coaches, walls, and anything else that needed color. One of the Crawford family's tutors taught him how to sketch a scene and prepare a canvas and mix paints. He did this one in his spare time."

In the middle of the picture was a large, square white house with wide verandas. To the left were farm buildings and a cluster of small slave cottages. To the right, Spanish moss dripped from the outstretched branches of giant live oaks. In the foreground, flower gardens encircled an ornamental pond. In the background were fields and orchards. Tiny black and white figures populated the scene.

"What a charming picture, its colors rich and strong," Pamela exclaimed. "Your father had a delightful imagination. Is this a real place?"

"Yes, it's the Crawford plantation before the war. I was born there and worked in the kitchen with Virgil Crawford. He was the chef then, and his wife was the housekeeper." She gestured to a tea table. "Please sit down."

Over tea, Pamela asked about Ruth, the missing young woman.

"She was less than a proper Christian and difficult to raise," said her aunt with a sigh. "She sassed me whenever I gave her a piece of advice. She would have her own way and live by herself."

"Do you have a picture of her?"

"No, I don't, but she's petite, light skinned, and attractive enough to interest men. As a child, she broke her left leg. It healed badly and is a little shorter than the right one. She walks with a slight limp."

Mrs. Colt didn't know her niece's friends but recalled a certain Aaron, a young black handyman at the Royal Hotel, where she worked. "I'll show you her room and the things she left at the hotel."

The young woman's room was barely large enough for a chair, a table, and a bed. From beneath the bed the housekeeper pulled a small, battered suitcase. Inside were underclothes, a woolen skirt, a pair of working shoes and stockings, and a few pieces of cheap jewelry. Among scraps of paper were brief messages from the housekeeper and reminders of various duties in the hotel.

"Did she have any fancy clothes or valuables?"

"Indeed, she did. For her confirmation she got a pink silk dress and matching bonnet, and a gold bracelet with her initials. I can't find them. She was probably going to meet a man and was wearing them when she disappeared."

Pamela suggested, "Perhaps she was."

As Mrs. Colt was closing the suitcase, a small notebook, hidden in the lid, fell out. Pamela fingered through it.

Ruth had entered several names followed by dates, perhaps referring to the men she met. The next to last reference was to a Mr. Johnson with an address on Madison Square. The last entry was merely five numbers in a row, *14414,* hurriedly written and barely legible. Possibly a street address? Pamela would check them later. In the meantime, she would speak to Aaron, the girl's friend at the hotel.

The Royal Hotel on Twenty-third Street in Chelsea was far from regal. The foyer reeked of stale tobacco, and its floor was grimy. Traveling salesmen in threadbare suits seemed to be its chief patrons.

At the reception desk, Pamela asked for Aaron, the handyman. Ten minutes later, he showed up, a harried look on his face. Pamela had caught him on the run. With a gentle smile and a small tip, Pamela persuaded him to sit with her in the foyer and talk.

He was a tall, slender, awkward young black man, gentle in his manner. A few sentences into their conversation, she realized to her surprise that he was speaking cultivated English.

He read her mind. "I don't want to be a handyman for the rest of my life in rat holes like this, so I'm attending night school."

Pamela complimented him. "It must be hard to balance work and study. I hope you persevere. If you have time, would you tell me about Ruth Colt?"

"We were friends," Aaron said shyly. "I thought we might get married. But when I asked her, she turned me down. 'Too poor and too black,' she added, and then laughed at me."

"That's cruel. I'm sorry."

He shrugged. "She was a bright, lively girl, but quick with hurtful words, heedless more than mean. She liked to mimic people and sometimes she mocked them."

"Were there other male friends?"

"Yes, she went out with several men and allowed herself more liberties than she should."

"Do you mean, like a loose woman or a prostitute?"

"Oh no. When we were going together, Ruth was a good girl. Later, she seemed to trust men too much and was trying to get married to a rich one."

"Can you describe the last man who showed interest in her?"

"He was white, older than the others, broad shouldered and tall, bearded, and walked with stiff legs. I hadn't seen him before. Called himself Mr. Johnson. When he registered, he gave us a business card that claimed he sold stocks and bonds at an address on Madison Square. His rough ways seemed to fascinate Ruth. I think he was a fraud."

At Madison Square, Pamela checked Mr. Johnson's address. As she suspected, it was fictitious. A clerk in Prescott's office determined that Johnson's business credentials were bogus: No reputable broker had ever heard of him. The so-called Johnson was clearly an imposter or worse. Pamela's fears for Ruth Colt grew. She might have fallen into a predator's hands.

The next day, Pamela woke in her bedroom to the sound of workmen clearing the street. She shuffled into the parlor and looked out a window. It had snowed during the night and covered Union Square with a soft, white blanket. She gave a wake-up call at the door of Francesca Ricci, the young woman living with her, and went through the apartment pulling up the shades.

During breakfast, the two women discussed the day's agenda; then Francesca went off to school. While lingering at the table with a cup of coffee, Pamela mulled over her investigation. Her thoughts came together in the imposter, Mr. Johnson, an older, lame man, but nonetheless strong enough to prey on young women. She telephoned Virgil Crawford for a meeting that afternoon.

His private office was located in a nondescript apartment building. At the door a concierge studied Pamela with a sharp eye. As Crawford had instructed, she asked to see Scipio Africanus, a fake name that showed off Crawford's grasp of ancient Roman history. The concierge replied, "Go to the top floor and down the hall to the back of the building. Last door on the right."

The door lacked a nameplate, but she knocked anyway. A few seconds later, Crawford showed her into a small, tight room, and she sat facing him at his writing table. The telephone and several maps hung on the wall behind him. Through an open door she could see into a small parlor. His office was probably part of a full, compact apartment. File boxes and bookshelves covered the wall to his left. A window to his right admitted natural light and offered a view into a small garden enclosed by adjacent buildings.

"This is my den," he said, pouring water for her and himself from a carafe. "I'm a butler with a wide range of duties. From here I protect the Crawford family's name and its business. For example, I check the credentials of every candidate for an upper-level position in the firm." He raised his glass to her. "Now, tell me what you've learned thus far."

She summarized her investigation and concluded that the disguised Mr. Johnson had caused Ruth Colt to disappear. She had probably never left the city.

When she finished, he remarked, "I agree that the man you've described is an imposter. Our next step is to determine his true identity. Have you heard of Captain Jed Crake, a distinguished cavalry officer under Sherman in the war and now the owner of a meatpacking business on West Fourteenth Street?"

"He's notorious," replied Pamela. "When he laid workers off in a labor dispute, he impoverished several of our families at St. Barnabas Mission, on Mulberry Street."

"Strange as it may sound, I suspect that Crake might be our disguised, predatory imposter."

"Strange indeed!" Pamela exclaimed. "Crake may be flint-hearted, but he's surely not foolish. Such a rich, prominent, and successful person wouldn't risk everything for a brief sexual adventure with a chambermaid." She felt uneasy about this conversation's direction. "Why have you suspected Crake?" she asked. "Surely Mr. Johnson's description could fit many men."

"I know Captain Crake." He spoke with an assurance that startled Pamela. "One of my duties in the Crawford family enterprise is to serve as my cousin James's eyes and ears in the jungle that is American business. In a sense, like you, I'm a private investigator. Years ago, when we expanded our shipping company and moved from Georgia to New York, I began to investigate Captain Crake and certain other cutthroat entrepreneurs with whom we had to deal. My search aimed especially at their hidden vices.

"A certain police inspector's unguarded remark led me to suspect Crake of a deeply flawed character. At stake was a contract to transport his company's meat all over the East Coast in refrigerated cargo ships. In our conversation over drinks, the inspector assured me that Crake's competitors exaggerated his faults. True, he drove a hard bargain, but he was at least as honest as they were. Then the inspector added offhandedly, 'But let young women beware. He's a wolf in sheep's clothing.' A few seconds later, he suddenly looked embarrassed and said, 'Forget I ever said that.' "

Pamela was skeptical. "Like other men, Crake may have a wolf's instincts. Still, most of them never abduct a woman."

"You're right about men," Crawford quickly agreed. "Nonetheless, from the inspector's remark I sensed that Crake might have a deeper problem. I hired spies to follow him at night. Over several years, in various disguises and aliases, he left a trail of bruised and battered prostitutes. A young female employee also accused him of assaulting her. The police were paid off and didn't charge him. I've concluded that Crake is prone to episodic violence, primarily toward women." He met Pamela's eye. "Is it farfetched to believe that Mr. Johnson and Crake are possibly the same person?"

"Perhaps not," she replied. "So my task is to prove or disprove their identity, beginning with Captain Crake, and find out what happened to Ruth Colt."

"Correct. But don't confront him or let him know that you're investigating him. His thugs could harm you. Also keep the Crawfords entirely out of the picture. And don't go to the police unless you have a case that would hold up in court."

"You've prescribed a very challenging investigation. I'm flattered that you believe I can do it." She glanced toward the file boxes. "May I assume that you've checked my credentials as thoroughly as the others?"

"Yes, of course." He smiled kindly but seemed reluctant to say more. She asked him to continue even though he would stir up painful memories from her past.

With a shrug, he complied. "When I asked Prescott for an investigator, he highly recommended you. However, the gossip concerning your husband's embezzlement of bank funds and his suicide had cast a shadow over your reputation. So, first I had to clear that up in my own mind. I concluded you were innocent of any wrongdoing and went on to learn about you helping poor families at St. Barnabas Mission. After the loss of your home and inheritance, bruised but unbowed, you ran a boardinghouse for a year. Then Prescott hired you to fight theft at Macy's. And last summer you successfully investigated murders at a great estate in the Berkshires. In brief, your story is touching and fascinating, and it reassured me that you are an intrepid and resourceful detective. I'll stop there; I could say more to your credit."

She took a moment to digest his remarks. Though they had only met twice, he probably knew her as well as almost anyone alive. She knew next to nothing about him. Still, he seemed utterly sincere. She felt good about working with him.

As she rose to leave, an afterthought came to her mind. She showed him the mysterious numbers from Ruth Colt's notebook.

For a long moment he studied them, then suddenly glanced up at Pamela. "That could be an address near Crake's meatpacking plants. Why should the missing woman have it?"

"I'll try to find out," replied Pamela.

"Then report your progress directly to me at this office. I'll cover your expenses and your stipend. Good luck and be careful."

# CHAPTER 2

## *War Hero*

*Sunday, February 11*

The sun was shining, the temperature mild for winter on this Sunday morning. Pamela waited across Fifth Avenue from the Crake mansion, a square brick building with a mansard roof. She impatiently shifted her walking stick from hand to hand. Finally, a servant came out and threw salt on icy patches on the steps. The housekeeper, Mrs. Kelly, would soon go to church.

Yesterday, Pamela had studied the mansion for what it could tell her about its rich owner. She had expected a palace but found it to be one of the older, smaller, less impressive buildings in the neighborhood. Crake apparently drew more satisfaction from amassing wealth than from displaying it. The mansion had belonged to his wife, a rich widow he married in the first flush of his success in the meatpacking business. She died five years ago, leaving him also a large fortune in railroad investments. He married again a year later.

At last, Mrs. Kelly, a stout, cheerful, middle-aged woman, emerged in a black silk dress and a matching fancy bonnet. Pamela followed her at a distance into St. Patrick's Cathedral and sat near enough to observe her with a side-view opera glass.

She met a few other servants and carried on a whispered conversation until the Mass began. After the service, Pamela followed them to a café where they drank tea, played cards, and chatted for a couple of hours.

Finally, they dispersed and the housekeeper walked alone in Central Park. Appearing to tire, she sat down on a bench and laid her purse loose in her lap. Her eyes half-closed, she didn't notice a thief sneak up to her and snatch the purse. The sudden movement woke her up, but he was already speeding away.

Pamela had observed the scene. The thief ran toward her and flashed a knife to warn her off. As he passed by, she deftly poked her walking stick between his legs and he crashed to the stone walkway. Blood streaming from his brow, he glanced up at her with a curse on his lips. But she brought the steel point of her stick to within an inch of his eye and held him in a steady gaze. "Drop the purse and the knife or I'll shove this stick into your brain."

With shaking hands, he laid the purse and knife on the walkway.

"Now, get out of my sight."

He scrambled to his feet and ran away.

Pamela picked up the purse, threw the knife into the bushes, and approached the housekeeper. She was trembling and on the verge of tears. Pamela returned the purse and introduced herself, then sat on the bench and said, "The thief is gone and you are safe now."

"Thank you, dear. I'm most grateful to get my purse back." She had a strong Irish accent.

"Do you need help? I could call your husband or your son."

She shook her head. "I'll be all right. My husband and I married late and had no children. But we were best friends. He died ten years ago, and I still miss him."

"Then it's hard being alone. A few years ago, I lost my husband and my only child, a lovely daughter."

Mrs. Kelly gazed at Pamela with sympathy and interest. "How could you cope with the grief?"

"I have companions, my foster children, one at a time. Last year, an Irish girl lived with me. This year, it's an Italian girl. They keep me young and happy."

Mrs. Kelly was listening attentively and clucking her approval.

"May I walk you home?" Pamela asked.

The housekeeper replied hesitantly, "I don't want to be a bother." Still, the tone in her voice said she welcomed the offer.

"No trouble at all," said Pamela cheerfully. "The sun is still up. I can use the walk." Pamela helped the housekeeper to her feet. They set off together for the Crake residence.

Mrs. Kelly invited Pamela into the kitchen of her small apartment on the ground floor in the rear of the building. The house was very quiet, except for a canary in a cage and a clock ticking on the wall.

"Is anyone home?" Pamela asked. "I don't hear anyone stirring."

"Not a soul but me," Mrs. Kelly replied easily. "The servants have the day off while Mrs. Crake visits a friend's country house."

"And Mr. Crake?"

"He left in the middle of January and will be back in a few weeks. His arthritis got so bad that it nearly crippled him, so he went to a hot springs spa in Georgia. He writes that the treatment relieves the pain."

Pamela quickly calculated. Crake was still in New York at the time of Ruth Colt's disappearance. She asked, "If he's a sick man, can he go alone?"

"His nurse, Birgitta, actually one of our maids, goes along to massage him, administer his medicines, and help him move about."

A look of surprise must have crept onto Pamela's face at the thought of a young female, probably blond and blue-eyed, traveling alone with Crake. She must be made of steel.

"Birgitta is Swedish, mature beyond her years, and has a way with the captain." Mrs. Kelly smiled indulgently. "She knows how to keep him calm." Putting a kettle on the stove, she added, "Would you like tea?"

"That would be lovely." Pamela took off her coat, set aside her stick, and began to survey the room. It had a sleeping alcove, a small kitchen, and decent, plain furniture. A variety of photographs and shelves of mementos covered the walls. Her gaze fixed on a framed photograph of a young Union army officer.

"That's my Dennis during the war," said Mrs. Kelly. "He served three years in the New York Sixty-ninth and won a medal for bravery, but his health suffered. After the war, he couldn't lift heavy things and tired easily. No one would hire him. Fortunately, Captain Crake has a soft spot in his heart for wounded veterans and hired Dennis anyway as butler—and hired another man as assistant for the heavy work."

In Pamela's image of Crake there were no "soft spots," certainly none in his heart. He was commonly said to be a pitiless man, especially toward anyone who stood in his way or showed disrespect. Thanks to Mrs. Kelly, his image had just become more complicated.

Mrs. Kelly must have read Pamela's mind, for she remarked, "Yes, I know what people say about the captain, but they don't know him like I do. Do you have time? I'll show you his study."

"Yes, of course." Pamela was eager to learn whatever she could about this house and its master.

Her hostess added tea leaves to the pot, poured in hot water, and let the tea steep. They climbed the servants' stairway to the next floor and entered a room that could hardly be called a study. The shelves held mainly mementos of the war: Union and Confederate weapons and insignia of rank. On a library table were fancy snuffboxes, gold bracelets, and other expensive jewelry probably looted from Georgia plantations. On the walls hung Union and Confederate battle flags, sabers, and pistols. Only one shelf was devoted to books, most of them dealing with military history. The most prominent was a richly bound edition of Buel's popular history of the war.

"The captain calls this the War Room," said Mrs. Kelly. "He has a proper office on Fourteenth Street in the meatpacking factory."

A framed document hung above the mantel. "That's the captain's certificate of heroic service near Savannah at the end of the war," said Mrs. Kelly. "And this is his Medal of Honor." She reverently opened a small green velvet–covered case. Inside lay the medal, its ribbon in pristine condition.

Photographs of men in uniform covered one wall, some taken during the war, others at veterans' encampments. "The captain calls it the Grand Army wall." She pointed to a picture of two men in uniform. "That's the captain and my Dennis twenty years ago."

Crake was a big, powerful man, clean-shaven and erect. He leaned protectively toward his smaller comrade. Pamela recorded in her mind every detail of Crake's features.

"Years ago," Mrs. Kelly went on, "they raised money for pensions and relief of wounded veterans."

Next, they passed through a richly furnished parlor. On the mantel stood a photograph of Crake in formal attire. His expression was lusty, with a touch of the wild. "That's the captain, four years ago, just before the wedding."

Next to the captain's photograph was one of a beautiful young woman. "Mrs. Crake," remarked Mrs. Kelly, a distinct note of reproach in her voice. Pamela hoped for a revealing or candid comment, but Mrs. Kelly's lips were drawn tightly together.

Back in the kitchen, they sat down to their tea. With an afterthought, she went to a cabinet and came back with a bottle of whiskey. "Will you have a nip of this juice in your cup?"

"Yes, as insurance against the cold." She took a sip, then remarked, "Captain Crake must be a very busy man. Does he find time for anything besides meatpacking and investments?"

"He and Dennis used to go regularly to the Phil Kearny Post of the G.A.R. After Dennis passed away, the captain joined a gentlemen's club. These days, he goes out by himself to their meetings and other events."

"But not with Mrs. Crake?"

Mrs. Kelly shook her head. "The club is for men only. I'll not speak ill of her, but she's much younger than he. They have different interests."

On his desk in the study Pamela had noticed an ashtray from the Union League Club, which catered to wealthy, distinguished Union veterans like Crake. She needed to find a discreet way to determine if and when Crake was at the club. Prescott might be able to help. Though not a member, he might have contacts there.

The tea finished, Mrs. Kelly followed Pamela to the door and waved a friendly good-bye. Pamela waved back, carrying in her mind a sharp, disturbing picture of Captain Crake.

# CHAPTER 3

# *A Secret Villain*

*Sunday, February 11*

"So you've sneaked into the lion's den, have you?" Prescott smiled at Pamela, a twinkle in his eye. It was Sunday evening. He was at the University Athletic Club resting after an hour of racquetball. His face had a fresh, scrubbed look that took a decade off his fifty-odd years. Pamela met him in the visitors' parlor. Women weren't allowed elsewhere in the building.

"No need to worry, sir. The lion is still in Georgia, warming his aching body. I could safely inspect his lair."

"And what did you learn?"

"Thirty years after the war, he's still a common soldier at heart, most at ease with old comrades drinking whiskey from a tin cup during G.A.R. encampments. But he goes out alone at night, dressed like a gentleman, and says he's going to his club."

"How is that suspicious?"

"He apparently belongs to the Union League Club through his wealth and business connections, but I can't imagine him dining or conversing evening after evening with gilded pluto-crats like J. P. Morgan. So, does he have a secret life at night that might account for the disappearance of Ruth Colt?"

"Really? Would he tell Mrs. Kelly, 'I'm on my way to a brothel'? Still, you might have a point."

When she suggested that he check Crake's alibi at the Union League Club, Prescott stopped her. "The Union League Club wouldn't open its attendance records to a stranger and would bring my request to Crake's attention. You wouldn't want that. Nonetheless, I'll privately ask an acquaintance how frequently Crake attends club functions, if at all."

When Pamela left the parlor, Prescott immediately telephoned Donald MacDonald, the chairman of the club's membership committee and a former comrade in arms. He was among the first to volunteer at the outbreak of the war. Four years later, having lost a leg in Virginia, he left the army with the rank of major. Now a wealthy corporation lawyer, he worked with Prescott pro bono for veterans on pension cases.

"I have a few questions related to the Union League Club," said Prescott. "Could we meet?"

"How about lunch at the club tomorrow?" MacDonald said heartily. "Be my guest."

The next day, Prescott arrived a few minutes early and waited in the visitors' parlor. MacDonald came on crutches but without apology. A lively man with silver hair and a ready smile, he had canny eyes and could not be fooled.

They sat at a table in an alcove off the main dining room. "For greater privacy," MacDonald said. "From our conversation I sensed that your questions might be delicate."

"Possibly, but they will be appropriate."

The waiter arrived and took their orders. Both ate lightly at lunch and chose the soup of the day: corn chowder. When the waiter left, they exchanged personal remarks. MacDonald was considering retirement.

Prescott showed interest. "Are you thinking of quiet country life? Try the Berkshires, where I have a cabin."

"Tell me more. I understand that Anson Phelps Stokes, investment banker, will build a cottage there."

"Yes, he'll call it Shadow Brook. When finished, though still a 'cottage,' it will be the largest private residence in the country." Prescott went on, briefly describing the area's lovely landscape, its charming villages, and the congenial society of its wealthy, cultivated summer visitors. "Take your pick. In the Berkshires you'll find something to your taste, from a cabin in the woods to a mansion that rivals anything on Fifth Avenue."

With the coffee, MacDonald offered a cigar and a brandy. Prescott politely declined the smoke. MacDonald put his away.

"A brandy, then?" he asked.

"Gladly," Prescott replied.

"Now, my good friend, what are your questions?"

Prescott took a sip of the brandy. "A client of mine is considering a sensitive, personal relationship with Captain Crake. While looking into his credentials, she was told that he belonged to this select club. May I ask, is he in fact a member? And, if so, is he in good standing?" He raised a warning finger. "I must add that my client doesn't want Crake to know that she is asking about him."

MacDonald smiled. "You speak circumspectly, Prescott, as you should in this case. The captain is hard on people who talk about him with disrespect. I also must choose my words carefully. He is a member of the club and technically in good standing—that is, he pays his dues and hasn't been convicted of a felony."

Though he soon might be, thought Prescott. "Is he active?"

MacDonald shrugged. "He attends two or three major events per year, such as the annual banquet and a royal or presidential visit."

"So he never simply drops in for an evening drink or game of cards."

"That's right. In that regard, Crake is typical of a majority of our members." He gazed at his companion, a wry look on his face. "Have I been helpful, Prescott?"

"You have indeed, sir." Prescott raised his brandy glass in a toast.

Late in the afternoon, Pamela was in her office and heard Prescott return. She called out to him. "What happened at the Union League Club?"

"Crake has apparently misled his housekeeper, the good Mrs. Kelly. He doesn't go there in the evening."

"Where does he go?"

"Perhaps Harry can tell us. He's speaking to a former companion in the NYPD detective department and should return soon."

Harry Miller, the other investigator in Prescott's firm, was Pamela's age and a former NYPD detective. Slim, plain in his features, with thin, sandy hair, he was easily overlooked in a crowd. At first Pamela resented his cool, opaque gray eyes and his searching gaze into her mind. His remarks to her were curt and almost rude. But, working together, she discovered his sterling compassion and integrity. He mellowed, and they became friends.

When Harry arrived late in the afternoon, Pamela and Prescott went to his office.

"I was amused," he began. "The detective department is like a cage of scared rabbits. The state government in Albany is questioning them about corruption. Most of them are guilty, but they try to shift the blame to each other and suspect that I spy for the reformers. The clean ones are afraid to talk to me for fear of reprisals. Fortunately, I found an old friend who would speak in strict confidence.

"He said that when the Crawfords first reported the Colt

girl missing late in January, Inspector Williams told him to look into the matter. His initial search of refuges, jails, brothels, and the morgue yielded no sign of her."

Pamela remarked, "Isn't it strange that she would disappear without a trace, as if she'd fallen off the edge of the earth?"

"My friend thought so," Harry agreed. "He's a conscientious detective, so he checked the files on other missing children for similar patterns of place, time, and other circumstances. A few petite young women, apparently prostitutes, vanished without a trace on the city's West Side between Fourteenth and Twenty-third streets. He also found a similar pattern of attempted abductions. One of those girls worked at Crake's meatpacking plants and claimed that Crake, wearing a false beard, had tried to seize her in the evening near the plants. His voice and arthritic gait gave him away. My friend reported his findings to Inspector Williams, who saw Crake's name and said, 'Leave this affair to me. You're off the case. Don't speak about it to anyone or I'll have your hide.' "

Pamela knew and disliked Alexander Williams. From his brutal methods of interrogation, he had earned the nickname "Clubber." He had also become rich from the blackmail of gambling dens and brothels in Chelsea's notorious Tenderloin district. Last year, she had quarreled with him over the custody of Brenda Reilly, one of her foster children.

She asked Harry, "Would the inspector obstruct my investigation of Crake?"

"Crake pays Williams for protection. Enough said."

"Why do you suppose your friend confided in you?" Prescott asked Harry.

"He finally realized that the inspector had walked away from the problem, perhaps because Crake had paid him off. Now that reformers are investigating the department, my friend fears that the inspector might shift the blame for corruption in the Colt case onto him. I think he's also bothered that Crake walks about at night, still free to prey on young women."

Pamela asked, "Have you found a room that Crake might have secretly used?"

"No, I haven't. In the packinghouse area there must be hundreds of possibilities."

She pressed on. "The address might be a combination of 14414, the mysterious numbers I found in the missing Colt girl's room."

"Then begin on Fourteenth Street," said Prescott to Pamela. "Harry will help you."

"Let's hope this isn't a fool's errand," said Harry.

Thursday morning, after a tedious search of the area, Pamela and Harry approached number 414 on West Fourteenth Street, a decrepit, five-story brick building. At the street level was a small butcher shop. A bald, shriveled old man was behind the counter, sharpening a knife.

Pamela asked, "Do you have rooms to rent upstairs?"

The old man studied her and Harry with a cynical eye. "By the hour?"

Pamela replied evenly, "It's not for us but for a friend and for a longer period. Could we see a room on the first floor?" With his arthritis, Crake wouldn't have wanted to climb any higher.

"I can't leave the shop." He turned toward a back room. "Peter," he shouted. "Come here."

A young man appeared at the door, wiping his hands on a blood-smeared apron.

"Show these people the first-floor room."

Peter took off his apron, pulled a ring of keys from a rack on the wall, and beckoned the visitors to follow. They climbed a rickety stairway to the first floor into a dark, narrow corridor.

At the far end was another stairway. Crake could use it to come and go unobserved. Harry asked where it went.

"Down to the alley behind the building where they haul the trash." Peter opened the door to the room and let them in. "It's the only room we rent on this floor."

It was surprisingly large, furnished with a table and a couple of chairs. A bed was fitted into an alcove. There were no obvious signs of Crake. A clothes cabinet stood against a wall.

"I want to look inside," said Harry.

"It's locked," said Peter.

"I can open it. I just want to look." Harry held out a coin and gazed at the young man.

For a few moments, he just stood there, his eyes dancing between Harry and the money. Finally, he took the coin and mumbled, "Yes."

Harry quickly picked the lock and opened the cabinet door. Pamela looked over his shoulder. A businessman's suit hung on a hanger. A workman's clothes hung on a hook. The beard was in a box on a shelf. A small traveling bag stood on the floor. Pamela fingered through underclothing until she came to a small, loaded pistol and a sheathed knife. She held up the weapons.

Harry turned to the young man, who had begun to perspire. "Tell us about the man who rents this room." Harry offered him another coin.

He took it with a trembling hand. "He's tall, broad in the shoulders, walks like he's stiff in the hips, and calls himself Mr. Anderson. He's used to bossing people. From time to time, he comes in the evening dressed up like a gentleman, changes his clothes, and goes out again. He comes back late and sometimes brings a young woman with him." He hesitated. "Are you police?"

Pamela spoke gently to him. "We're only private investigators asking questions, not police. Just forget we were here and you won't get into any trouble."

She put the traveling bag back in order. Harry locked the cabinet. As they were leaving, Pamela went back for a closer look at the bed. Nothing was hidden in the mattress. But when she pulled the bed from the wall, she found a fancy pink purse.

"Crake could have overlooked it when he was leaving," said Pamela, opening the purse. Inside were coins, a kerchief, and a photograph of a young, light-complexioned black woman.

There was writing on the back side of the photograph. Harry read aloud, " 'Ruth Colt, Christmas 1893.' It proves she's been here after she left the Crawford household."

"We'll take the purse with us," said Pamela to the young man. "It belongs with her aunt."

He started to object, then thought better of it.

On the way out, Harry told the old man downstairs that their friend wouldn't be interested in the room.

In a quiet coffee shop nearby, Pamela remarked to Harry, "That dressed-up gentleman who calls himself Mr. Anderson is certainly Crake. In his business clothes he is also the Mr. Johnson of the fictitious Madison Square address."

"And Ruth Colt was with him in that room." He shook his head. "But we saw no blood, no other signs of struggle."

"Crake could have used his hands to strangle her or kill her with a single blow," Pamela insisted.

Harry looked irritated. "We need to find a body, or at least solid evidence of her murder. Otherwise, we have no case to give to the police. Where could she have gone?"

Pamela offered a likely scenario. "Late at night, Ruth and Crake quarreled in the secret room and he strangled her. He wrapped her in a bedsheet, carried her down the back stairs to the alley, threw her into a cart, and pulled it through the alley to a side street off Fourteenth."

"Plausible, so far," Harry agreed. "But, to avoid a police investigation, he had to permanently hide or destroy the corpse."

"That would be difficult," agreed Pamela. "He was alone, short of time, and probably unprepared—he might have killed Ruth on an impulse. Wouldn't he go to a familiar place that was nearby?"

"Right," Harry replied. "I think he'd pull the cart west on Fourteenth Street, perhaps to his meatpacking plants or, a little farther on, to the Hudson River at the Fourteenth Street ferry to Hoboken."

"Let's test that theory," said Pamela. "Karl Metzger, the German butcher, might help us. I know him from St. Barnabas Mission. He worked for years in Crake's plants on West Fourteenth Street until he opened a small shop nearby. As the union's business agent, he protested against dangerous working conditions, low wages, arbitrary hiring and firing, and other abuses in Crake's plants. The management ignored him. The union then began a strike."

"I recall the strike," said Harry. "Crake fired the union members and hired scabs, mostly penniless Italian immigrants willing to work for low pay and in poor, unsafe conditions. The strike collapsed. What happened to Metzger?"

"Crake's thugs harassed Metzger's employees and spread false rumors that his meat was bad. The police closed his shop. Crake blackballed him from the New York meatpacking business. Destitute, he came to St. Barnabas Mission. I found part-time work for him and his wife, Erika."

"Metzger owes you a favor, Pamela, and should be hungry for justice. Pay him a visit."

# CHAPTER 4

## The Missing Body

*Friday, February 16*

The next morning, Pamela met the Metzgers in their tiny room near the mission. They seated her at a table and served her coffee and German sweet bread. Karl had a broad smile on his face and could hardly contain himself. "We have good news, Mrs. Thompson. A friend has found summer work for us at the Grand Union Hotel in Saratoga Springs. I'll be cutting meat; Erika will do laundry."

"Congratulations. Is your friend a meat cutter or in the laundry?"

"Neither," Erika replied, smiling. "He's a bellboy at the hotel."

"Jason Dunn," added Karl. "He used to work with me in Crake's meatpacking plants on Fourteenth Street. During the strike he got a job in a restaurant and then in a hotel. He's been at the Grand Union for a year. We've kept in touch."

Pamela congratulated them, wished them well, then turned to Karl. "A client of mine needs information about Crake's plants. Can you help?"

He frowned at Crake's name, but he finished his coffee and

said, "I'll try." He told her that the plants operated at full capacity from dawn to dusk six days a week. At night, they shut down, and a small shift of workers cleaned and repaired machinery and tools, and did other maintenance. The main entrance was locked. Workers and deliveries used a service entrance in the rear. Since the strike and the union's collapse, only a few guards were needed to protect the plants.

"How shall I get inside?" asked Pamela.

"Contact the head manager, Mr. Jeffrey Porter." Metzger warmed to his topic. "Porter's a heartless bastard, but smart and efficient. Pretend you're an important person. He will guide you himself and tell you that the noise, stench, and offal are the signs of profit and progress. The Italians will smile and look happy at their work. You may see enough to judge for yourself."

Monday morning, Pamela and Harry took a cab to the pork-processing building, a large, brick, three-story, boxlike structure. Passageways connected it to several other buildings belonging to Crake's company, but it was the one closest and most convenient to his secret room. Disguised with a beard, Harry posed as a philanthropic businessman and Pamela's escort.

In a letter to Porter she claimed to be a social worker and needed to see where her clients worked or might find work. She assured him that she wasn't squeamish and knew the difference between a packing plant and a music hall. Mrs. Helen Fisk, an influential patron of St. Barnabas Mission, supported her request for a tour.

Porter's office was in a corner of the building's ground floor and consisted of a suite of rooms, all of them clean, well-lit and well ventilated, and fully insulated from the noises, sights, and smells of the adjacent factory floor. A female clerk in a spotless white frock showed them into Porter's private office. He wore a dark gray suit and tie, his hair slicked back and parted in the middle, and he sat at a gleaming gray writing table. Neat stacks of business paper lay before him. A white telephone was off to one side. Uniform rows of gray file boxes stood on white shelves covering the gray walls behind him. There were no colorful flowers or bright pictures in the room, only unrelieved grays and whites, in striking contrast to the gore throughout the rest of the building.

For a moment, Porter scrutinized his visitors with steel gray eyes, then greeted and seated them in simple upholstered chairs. He gave them a brief description of the company, the largest and most modern meatpackers in the New York area.

Pamela made a sweeping gesture over the room. "Does the strikingly efficient appearance of your office make a statement about your industry?"

"Yes, indeed, Mrs. Thompson." He pursed his lips and waved a hand toward the files. "This office expresses the rational spirit that governs the modern meatpacking process. We are among the leaders. Efficiency in the service of profit, that's our motto. I'm proud of our packing plants and happy to show you through one of them. You will see the most productive meat processing east of Chicago."

Porter took them to the stockyard adjacent to the main plant. More than 500 hogs had come in by train overnight. As Pamela and Harry arrived with their guide, men were forcing the hogs up a chute into the third floor at the western end of the plant. The visitors watched from a gallery as hogs entered the building and were hoisted by their rear legs onto a moving overhead trolley. Amid ear-splitting squeals and shrieks, swarthy men in blood-soaked aprons slit the animals' throats as they passed by. Blood flowed in rivulets to drains in the floor. Other men dropped the still-twisting and turning animals into a large vat of boiling water.

Pamela tore her eyes away from the carnage and exchanged glances with Harry. His face was pale. Through gritted teeth, he murmured, "This is like war. The hogs are losing." Nearby, Porter gazed at the scene, detached and calm, his mind apparently fixed on the process.

A machine scooped the hogs from the vat and sent them through a scraping machine to remove their bristles. They were hooked up to yet another trolley and passed rapidly between two lines of men.

With a hint of awe in his voice, Porter said, "The proprietor, Captain Jed Crake, a remarkable man, has personally put on an apron and performed most of the tasks that you are observing. Watch closely. This is a crucial moment in the process. Each man has a specific task in the second or two as the carcass goes by him: One severs the head, and it falls through a hole in the floor; another slits the body; a third widens the opening; and a fourth pulls out the entrails, which fall through a hole in the floor; and so it goes on until the carcass is completely stripped of its 'waste' parts. It's then cleaned and sent on to the chilling room, where it hangs for twenty-four hours."

He led them to the floor below. In one room, men were scraping and cleaning the entrails for sausage casings; in another, they were boiling and pumping away grease from scraps to make soap; in a third, a stamping machine was pulverizing bones for fertilizer; and so on.

The stench was unbearable. Pamela held a perfumed kerchief to her nose, but to no avail. Her stomach was roiling dangerously. Harry stiffened. Even Porter began to wilt. He quickly moved his visitors on to the cutting room, where giant men with huge cleavers neatly dismembered the carcasses into hams, forequarters, and sides of pork.

The smells, the noise, the violence of the scene excited Pamela. She recalled Jed Crake's powerful body and imagined him wielding a cleaver and splitting a carcass with a single blow.

The butchered pieces slid down chutes to the ground floor for pickling, smoking, boxing, wrapping in oilcloths, or packing in barrels. Porter explained, "The finished products will be trucked out the doors into refrigerated boxcars and carried away to meat shops throughout the Northeast."

At the end of the tour, Pamela and Harry stood for a minute in the doorway gulping breaths of fresh air. Porter seemed unfazed.

He turned to them. "In the process you witnessed, I challenge you to find a single unnecessary movement by man or machine or a wasted second. Every bit of the hogs we buy is turned into money for the company. To borrow the tired saying: We use everything but the squeal. We apply a similar process to cattle, sheep, and chickens in adjacent buildings."

Pamela asked, "How can the workers sustain the fast pace that you set?"

Porter seemed to relish the opportunity to reply to her question. "To reduce fatigue and inattention, we calculate the capacity of workers for different tasks and rotate them accordingly. To avoid accidents, the workspace is kept clean and well lighted, and tools in good condition. The discipline here exceeds, by far, that of an elite regiment in Napoleon's army. If a man faints, the men around him pick up his work until a replacement is brought in."

Pamela and Harry thanked Porter quite sincerely for an instructive tour, then retired to a nearby coffee shop. They ordered only strong tea. It would be hours before their stomachs could take food.

While waiting, they sat still and reflective, then Pamela said, "We've just witnessed a preview of how American industry will develop in the near future toward division of labor and the mechanization of production. But that aside, have we come any closer to figuring out how Crake disposed of Ruth's body—assuming that we rightly suspect that he killed her?"

Harry stroked his beard, then nodded. "Crake knew personally that the packing process could destroy a human body as thoroughly as an animal's. But he also realized that the process was tightly controlled and he couldn't easily slip a cadaver into it."

"Could he nonetheless have bribed or persuaded Porter to help him try?"

Harry shook his head. "Such a vulgar, irrational idea would repel Porter."

"Then perhaps Crake found an opportunity in the night shift when the plant would be largely dark and empty."

"That's possible. We must contact the night manager at the time of Ruth Colt's disappearance."

Through Mr. Porter, Pamela and Harry arranged to meet Mr. Emil Schmidt at seven that same evening at the service entrance for a glimpse of the night shift. He brought them into his small, cluttered office, brought out glasses, and offered them schnapps. "Against the cold," he said. Harry accepted; Pamela took a cup of hot tea instead.

Schmidt was a thin man in his mid-fifties with a wary look in his eyes. There was also alcohol on his breath, but he was sober enough to ask, "Why would you come here on a cold winter night to watch men clean a packing plant?"

Pamela explained her interest in the conditions of the working poor. "With this experience I'll better understand them and can be of more help."

The wariness in his eyes disappeared. "I've had a taste of poverty. Good luck."

"Tell me about yourself," she asked in a kindly voice, suspecting that he drank to banish loneliness.

"I came from Germany as a young man and worked as a mason. During the war, I served under Captain Crake in Sherman's army. Afterward, we kept in touch at meetings of the

G.A.R. A dozen years ago, I went to work for Crake and became night manager here."

"Would you show us what goes on here at night?"

"Follow me," he said. "We'll visit the hog building you saw this morning."

From the gallery on each level they watched crews mopping the floors, mechanics greasing gears and repairing the trolleys, and cutlers cleaning and sharpening the knives and other tools. A mason and his assistant were fitting new bricks into a worn section of the floor. About a hundred men appeared to be at work under the insistent gaze and prodding of several foremen.

"How long is this shift?" she asked Schmidt.

"The men will finish here about midnight and work in the other buildings until five in the morning."

"When the buildings are empty at night, do watchmen patrol them?"

"Yes, they look out for fires and for thieves who would steal the knives and other moveable equipment. I'm here as well. There is also a pair of guards at the service entrance as long as it's unlocked."

"Who handles special deliveries during the night shift?" asked Harry.

The question seemed to surprise and annoy Schmidt. "Why, I do," he replied, testily, "and I take them to their proper destination."

"Are there many?"

"A few."

Harry seemed to be fishing for an indication that Crake brought Ruth Colt's body here, concealed as a special delivery, in the early-morning hours after the cleaning crew had left and the building was empty.

Schmidt might have suspected the drift of Harry's questions. He looked increasingly uncomfortable, his replies short.

At a wink from Harry, Pamela declared their visit at an end.

She thanked Schmidt and remarked how she wished that other workplaces in the city were as clean and well organized as Captain Crake's.

Schmidt mumbled a thank you and a good-bye.

Suspicions had also grown in Pamela's mind. "Mr. Schmidt knew more than he was willing to admit." She and Harry walked in the dark toward their carriage on Fourteenth Street. A bitter cold wind gusted from the west. She shivered.

"He owes loyalty to Crake, who keeps him on the job. I sensed that the foremen didn't respect him. They smirked and rolled their eyes when his back was turned. He probably tipples through the night."

Pamela added, "I can imagine Crake arriving in disguise with Ruth's body. He forces Schmidt to help him. They wait until the watchmen have settled down with a bottle of whiskey. Then he and Crake find a place to hide the body. Crake warns him never to tell anyone what happened."

"That's a plausible scenario. I'll take you home, get a little sleep, then return here at five with one of my spies. When Schmidt leaves the plant, I'll point him out and the spy will keep track of him. I fear he will go to Crake and they'll talk about us. He'll become alarmed and react."

"That's unfortunate, Harry. Our investigation of Crake was supposed to be secret. Nonetheless, we must confront Mr. Schmidt."

# CHAPTER 5

## *Counterattack*

*Tuesday, February 20*

As his train pulled into Grand Central Station, Captain Crake was out of sorts. The warm baths and the Georgia sun had made him feel good. But the long, bumpy, jerky train ride exhausted him and triggered blinding arthritic pains. He also worried about what his enemies, known and unknown, were doing while he was away and no longer in control.

At home, he secluded himself in his room and rested. The pains got worse. He summoned the Swedish maid, Birgitta Mattsson, to draw a bath for him and afterward give him a massage.

Within hours he was feeling better and looked ahead to a summer of baths, massages, and mineral water in Saratoga Springs—with high-stakes gambling thrown in for good measure. He would leave his business in the capable hands of Mr. Porter.

That evening, he dressed and sat down to supper with his young, pretty wife, Rachel. The atmosphere at the table was strained. His spies had reported to him in Georgia that Rachel seemed intimate with their mutual friend, Robert Shaw, during long sojourns in the countryside together.

Now, over the soup course, he asked, "Rachel, do you think it wise to be seen frequently alone with Robert? People are talking."

"Oh, Jed," she replied. "They will always find some reason to gossip. Pay no attention to them. Robert is just a good friend who escorted me to gambling casinos and dances while you were away. I would otherwise have died of boredom." She gazed at him with guileless concern. "Did you miss me, Jed?"

"Not really, dear. Birgitta looked after me."

"You're fortunate to have her, Jed." Rachel raised her wineglass and took a sip.

Her expression was largely hidden, but he detected a line of concern on her brow.

After supper, Jed went to his study and called in Mrs. Kelly, the housekeeper, one of the few persons in his life who had his interests at heart.

"Anything worthy of note happen while I was gone?" he asked in a friendly way.

"Here in the house we had no problems, but . . ." She hesitated.

"What happened, Mrs. Kelly?" His interest was piqued.

"I was attacked in Central Park on a bright Sunday afternoon."

"Really?" Crake started, then relaxed. His housekeeper had a taste for the dramatic. "Tell me about it."

She related the purse-snatching incident in the park and how a nice lady, named Pamela, recovered her purse and befriended her. "We had tea together in my apartment and then I showed her your trophies in the War Room. She seemed impressed. Was that all right?"

"I trust your judgment, Mrs. Kelly. Still, in New York, as you know, we must always be cautious with strangers."

Later that night as he prepared for bed, Mrs. Kelly's incident came back to his mind, and he pondered the friendly stranger who showed interest in the War Room. "What harm could come of it?" he asked himself. "None," he replied. "Forget it." But the question continued to itch until he fell asleep.

The next morning, he felt well enough to return to work in his office at the pork-packing plant. He called Mr. Porter into his office. Their conversation reassured him that all was well. In particular, the workers were content despite the increased tempo of production that Porter had introduced. Though the country's economy was in deep depression with banks failing and railroads going bankrupt, Crake's meat business was thriving.

Then, as Porter was about to leave, he mentioned the distinguished couple who toured the main plant, the day before yesterday.

"They left with a good impression of conditions here. That's important. Our open door to discerning visitors costs nothing, builds good will, and counteracts the carping criticism of reformers."

"Did you get their names?" Crake put a hint of disapproval into his voice.

"Mrs. Pamela Thompson and Mr. Harry Miller. I checked on their references. The detective at Macy's said she's fair-minded and trustworthy. Mrs. Fisk said she's genuinely helpful to poor families, especially the children. I felt reassured. We have nothing to hide, do we?"

Crake ignored the question. With a perfunctory, "Thank you, Porter," and a wave of his hand, Crake sent the manager back to his office. Then he leaned forward in his chair, stroked his chin, and asked himself, "Why did this Pamela visit my study and tour my pork-packing plant? Should I be concerned?" Perhaps not, he thought. She might simply admire his military exploits or his success in business and want to know more about him. No harm could come of it.

The rest of the morning Crake walked through his buildings, observing the packing process with a practiced eye, satisfying himself that it was working as well as Porter claimed. In his heart, Crake didn't fully trust his manager. His obsessive focus on the efficiency of the packing process might ultimately prove wrongheaded. Crake couldn't say why; he just felt uneasy.

After lunch with several plant supervisors, Crake returned to his office to discover that Inspector Williams had come for an unexpected visit and was waiting in the outer office. Crake held out his hand and gave the officer a cordial greeting.

The two men had a business relationship of mutual convenience. It had been tested two years ago during the meatpackers' strike. Crake paid Williams a large bribe. In return, Williams arrested the union's leaders for conspiring to endanger public safety and to damage Crake's property. Williams also allowed Crake's thugs to beat up union organizers and vandalize the union's office. Recently, Williams had arranged the dismissal of a female clerk's accusation of assault against Crake.

Why was Williams here today? Again, Crake felt uneasy. The inspector appeared only when there was trouble or he needed money.

Williams began with a concerned expression. "Jed, I thought you should know that a pair of Jeremiah Prescott's private investigators have searched your private room on Fourteenth Street, unlocked your cabinet, and found clothes and weapons that could implicate you in the disappearance of Ruth Colt several weeks ago."

Crake felt his heart begin to race. His brow broke out in a cold sweat. "How dare they!" he exclaimed weakly. He struggled to regain control of himself. "Did they have permission?"

"Unfortunately, the owner's son was present and agreed." Williams raised a calming hand. "Prescott must know that even this evidence is circumstantial. Without the girl's body he doesn't have a case that would stand up in court. His investigators will continue searching, so be alert." He smiled sympathetically, then rose to leave. "Let me know if I can be of any further assistance."

"You've been helpful, sir, beyond the call of duty," said Crake. "My clerk will send you something for your expenses."

As soon as Williams was out of the building, Crake called in his clerk. "Find Emil Schmidt. Don't wait until the night shift. I want him here immediately."

An hour later, Schmidt was ushered into Crake's office, a bewildered look on his face.

Crake asked levelly, "Did you show a Mrs. Thompson and Mr. Miller through the packing plant two nights ago?"

Schmidt's eyes widened in apprehension. "Why, yes, Mr. Porter referred them to me. Is something wrong?"

"Indeed!" he replied through clenched teeth. "They intend to ruin us. Do you perceive my meaning? Keep them out."

Schmidt stammered, "Yes, sir." Then he hurried from the room.

Now thoroughly alarmed, Crake called in his clerk again. "Tell Jimmy Gilpin I need to speak to him urgently. I'll go to him at seven this evening." Gilpin could be relied on to put an end to Prescott's private investigation and, if necessary, his investigators.

Crake dressed for the occasion in a plain brown business suit and took a cab to the pool hall on Twenty-third Street. Gilpin was standing under a bright electric light in a haze of cigar smoke, watching a game of pool. He had a childlike smile on his smooth, round face. When he saw Crake, he gestured toward the door to his office.

There was a slimy, reptilian quality about the man that made Crake squirm. But occasionally he had to rely on his services. Behind the façade of a busy pool hall, Gilpin ran a ruthless and very profitable protection racket among the area's brothels and gambling dens. His services to Crake's meatpacking company included severely beating union leaders during the recent strike. He spread terror among the union's rank and file by threatening to harm their families and selectively assaulting a few to show that he was serious.

"Have a cigar, Jed." Gilpin reached into a gilded humidor on his writing table.

Crake waved it away. "No, thanks, Jimmy. Doctor's orders."

"Then what can I do for you, Jed?" Gilpin leaned forward in his leather chair, his brow furrowed slightly in feigned sympathetic concern.

"Private investigators, named Mrs. Thompson and Mr. Miller, are poking around my packing plants." He gave Gilpin a brief account of Prescott's investigation. "I want it stopped. Do whatever it takes."

Gilpin pursed his lips. "Jed, that's a tall order. Prescott is clever and tough. To take him on, I'll have to hire smart, expensive operatives."

"I know," said Crake impatiently. He hated to bargain with this savage. "I'll meet your price. Here's an advance." He shoved a thick envelope across the table.

Gilpin palmed the envelope into a drawer and smiled. "The project looks interesting, Jed. I'll begin with the Thompson woman."

Over the weekend, Pamela and Harry tried to visit with men from the night shift. Metzger had given some names. However, none would speak to them, nor would Emil Schmidt. The management clearly had warned the men to avoid contact with private investigators or be fired. Harry and his spy followed Schmidt secretly, hoping to catch him drinking and trick him into a confession, but without success.

On Monday afternoon, Pamela left her office and set off for home to meet Francesca, who needed help with schoolwork. At the door, the concierge gave Pamela an envelope and said, "An errand boy left this for you."

Pamela detected a note of apprehension in her voice.

"He was a nasty little ruffian," the concierge added.

Pamela put the envelope into her purse, started up the stairs, then asked, "Has Miss Ricci come home from school yet?"

"No, she hasn't. Is something wrong?"

"I hope not."

Once inside the apartment, Pamela tore open the envelope and gasped. A bloody fingerprint prefaced the single-page note.

> Unless you agree to stop investigating a certain
> decorated war hero within twenty-four hours, you
> will never see your Francesca alive. Post your
> answer in your front window. If you later renege
> on your promise, we will kill her and you for good
> measure.

Pamela immediately rushed over to Prescott's office.

"Is something wrong?" he exclaimed as she burst into the room.

"I'm distraught. Crake's thugs have kidnapped my Francesca and threatened to kill her." She handed him the bloody note.

"I see the hand of Jimmy Gilpin. His lawyer has composed the note, the lawyer's clerk has typed it, but it's Jimmy's idea to take a hostage. He orchestrated similar violence that broke the meat cutters' union."

"What shall we do?"

"Whatever he asks. We dare not risk Francesca's life. Gilpin would surely kill her and drop her body on your doorstep. We'll suspend the investigation for the time being. You may inform Virgil Crawford. He and I will settle the business details later."

Crawford met Pamela at the door to his office, a look of surprise on his face. He beckoned her in and asked what had happened.

"Gilpin has kidnapped Francesca and demands that we stop our Crake investigation. Mr. Prescott says suspend it."

"I'm sorry to hear this, Mrs. Thompson, but I agree we shouldn't risk Miss Ricci's life."

They moved to his writing table. He sat upright, arms resting on the table, and listened attentively to Pamela's detailed report on her investigation.

"My colleagues and I are morally certain," she concluded, "that Captain Crake killed Ruth Colt and perhaps other young women. But our evidence is circumstantial and wouldn't prevail in a court of law where the burden of proof in a capital case is high, and even higher than usual where a wealthy, powerful man is concerned. I regret that we could not find the victim's body. Crake must have found a way to hide or destroy it in his packing plant, or bury it in the river."

Virgil lowered his eyes for at least a minute, as if to study the desk's polished surface. His lips pressed tightly together. He seemed to be fighting back tears. Then he drew a long, slow breath and looked up at her.

"Dear Mrs. Thompson," he began, "I'm not surprised that Crake cannot be convicted and properly punished for his crimes. You and your colleagues did all that is humanly possible. The fault lies in a corrupt judicial system where justice is for sale. It's sad and outrageous that Crake is free to prey upon poor, young, naïve women."

"If it's any consolation, sir, his housekeeper says that he has returned from the Georgia spa with less rather than more strength. Perhaps his predatory instincts have also weakened."

"What is his condition?" Crawford seemed curious.

"His kidneys are failing; his arthritis has worsened. He plans to spend the entire summer season in Saratoga Springs, desperately hoping that the baths and the mineral springs will cure him."

Crawford appeared to thoughtfully reflect. "I'm disappointed, Mrs. Thompson, but I'm also patient and hopeful. Your investigation hasn't been in vain. There will be other opportunities to bring Crake to justice, of that I'm sure."

"I'll tuck the case into the back of my mind," she told him. "And I'll be ready when the time comes."

Crawford's expression became inscrutable. Something had come into his head that claimed his full attention. He smiled and brought their meeting to a rapid close. "I'll settle with Mr. Prescott for your expenses and stipend. Thank you, Mrs. Thompson. I'll be happy to use your services on another occasion."

As she stepped out onto the street, Pamela sensed strongly that she had been used in a complicated chess game between the Crawfords and Crake. It was far from over.

Pamela put a sign in her window facing Union Square, saying in large letters that she accepted Gilpin's terms. From behind the curtains she watched people passing by. Many glanced at the sign. It was impossible to detect who were the kidnappers. Finally, she gave up and waited anxiously. In her mind she saw Francesca, bound and gagged in a dark, windowless room. Pamela tried to banish the thought. Finally, she distracted herself with vigorous housecleaning.

At about ten o'clock in the evening, the bell rang and Francesca appeared in the doorway, looking a little bewildered, but otherwise none the worse for her experience in New York's underworld. Relieved, Pamela embraced her. They sat down at a table and Francesca began her story.

"On my way home from school two men pulled me off the

sidewalk and into a coach. They tied me up and blindfolded me, drove to a foul-smelling place, and carried me downstairs into a room."

"Did they harm you?" asked Pamela anxiously.

"No, they only pricked my finger. A woman came into the room and asked how I was. I said I was hungry. She fed me bread and cheese, and took me to the bathroom."

"Could you hear any conversation or any sounds at all?"

Her brow creased with the effort to recall. "No, only a faint clanging of a streetcar bell. I don't know how much time passed. Then the same two men picked me up and drove me away. Finally, one of them untied me and removed the blindfold. We were parked on a side street near Union Square. The other man held a knife to my throat and said, 'Go home. If you call out for help, we'll kill you in the street.' It was dark. I walked as fast as I could and am glad to be home."

She gazed at Pamela with a confused expression on her face. "Why did the men kidnap me?"

Pamela briefly explained the search for Ruth Colt. "We think she was murdered. Her killer feared we might discover him and hired someone to take you as a hostage. He ordered us to end the investigation or you would be killed. We couldn't risk your life, so we did as he said. Then he released you. We're relieved to have you back safely."

While Pamela served hot chocolate and buttered bread, Francesca asked, "Couldn't the police have arrested the killer?"

Pamela hesitated to reply. She usually shielded Francesca from the seamy side of life—the girl already knew that only too well. Their conversations focused on schoolwork, music, and art.

"In a word, Francesca, the police work for him. That's how business is sometimes done in New York these days. There's talk of reform. I'm hopeful that things will get better, but not just yet."

"What am I to do?" she complained, stirring the chocolate. "Hide out here in the apartment all day and night?"

"No, you will go to school as usual. As a precaution, I'll arrange for a companion to walk with you. Frankly, I think your kidnapper will keep his side of the bargain. He's basically a businessman of sorts and needs to appear reliable."

Francesca seemed satisfied and drank her chocolate with relish. When they were clearing the table, she asked Pamela, "What shall I do during the summer? I really want to get away from New York."

"I've been thinking about that, Francesca. How would you like to work in Saratoga Springs at the Grand Union Hotel? You would be among rich, fashionable people and hear music all day long. My clients at St. Barnabas Mission, the Metzgers, recently got summer jobs there. The hotel is expecting a busy season, despite the country's depression. Would you care to be a chambermaid?"

Francesca's eyes widened at the thought. "I'd love to."

"Then I'll write to the management."

# CHAPTER 6

## *An Old Soldier*

*Saratoga Springs, New York*
*Friday, July 6, 1894*

Francesca Ricci, now a chambermaid with a month's experience at the Grand Union Hotel, knocked on the captain's door. No response. She cautiously stepped into an entrance hall. "Anyone here?" she called out. Late in the afternoon, most guests would be in the dining room. It was a good time to empty wastebaskets and ashtrays, and air out the rooms before the guests returned. "Is that you, Francesca?" came a man's deep voice from the bedroom.

"Yes," she timidly replied. A frisson of fear shook her. She really wasn't comfortable with Captain Crake. Some days he was a proper gentleman, other times he behaved more like the devil himself. Francesca was inclined to give him the benefit of the doubt. He was a sick old man with arthritis and other ailments, and obviously in pain.

His beautiful young wife was more of an aggravation than a help to him. No wonder that he sought comfort with chambermaids. Most tried to avoid him. It fell to Francesca, the most recent among them, to clean his rooms. Early on, he had heard her sing. Francesca had made it clear that she would sing for him only if he'd keep his hands off her. As a pretty girl from Mulberry Bend in the slums of New York, she had learned how to protect herself. Crake seemed to respect her.

"I was taking a nap," Crake shouted through the door. "Do your work. I'll come out when you're ready to sing me a song."

Francesca loved popular American songs, as well as her native Italian. She dreamed that one day she'd sing in concert halls and become rich and famous. Her friends on Mulberry Bend used to say that wouldn't happen, but Francesca believed in miracles. One might happen to her. A rich gentleman like Captain Crake might like her songs enough to promote her.

She finished her chores and called out, "Cleaning's done, Captain. It's time for a song."

He came out of his room, dressed in fine clothes for the evening. He was a tall, broad-shouldered, big-chested man and rough in his ways. They said he was a hero in the war and a successful businessman afterward. Now he was rich but couldn't enjoy life. She sometimes felt sorry for him.

"What do you have to offer tonight?" he asked, settling into a chair. "Cheer me up."

"Then I'll sing 'Funiculì, Funiculà,' a popular song from Naples about the cable cars that go up and down Mount Vesuvius, filled with sightseers in a holiday spirit." She cleared her throat and launched into a verse of the Italian original, waving her arms and dancing to the lively rhythm. Without missing a beat she switched to the English version, then closed with the refrain:

> "Listen, listen, music sounds a-far!
> Listen, listen, music sounds a-far!
> Funiculì, funiculà, funiculì, funiculà!"

Crake chuckled. "I like your spirit, girl. You sound like Italians in my meatpacking plants. They sing a lot. I hire them right off the boat. They work hard, don't complain about the low pay or hard conditions in the plants."

She resented his attitude toward her people, but she didn't complain. She sang a couple of his favorite sentimental songs, then bowed. She could sense when it was time for her to leave. Music seemed to soften his hard heart. He would soon want a woman's comfort.

He thanked her, then pulled from his pocket a simple gold bracelet and handed it to her.

"Here, this is for pleasing an old man. A month ago, I gave the bracelet to my wife, but she doesn't enjoy wearing it—says it looks cheap. She wants fancy jewelry."

"Thank you so much, but I couldn't accept it. I sing simply to please you."

His voice filled with menace. "But I insist."

Fear welled up in her. She couldn't bring herself to say no. She took the bracelet, murmured her gratitude, and hurried from the room.

Crake rose from his chair, took a deep breath, and shuffled to the liquor cabinet. Alcohol was bad for his kidneys, said his doctor. Crake nonetheless poured a shot of whiskey and drank it in one gulp. That girl left just in time, he said to himself. In another minute, I'd have been on top of her.

He put away the bottle. He was getting hungry. His wife would linger in the dining room with friends. Meanwhile he would go to the barroom for roast beef on rye with horseradish and a pint of beer. That would put him in a good mood for the dance tonight. Virtually a cripple, he would have to sit for hours and watch his wife turn her charm on lusty young men. A dozen or more would line up to dance with her. Brazen whore!

\* \* \*

Tonight's dance was held in the hotel ballroom and was called a "hop," from the typical step of the popular German schottische. The dress code was simpler than for the more formal balls. Crake entered the ballroom in a tan summer suit with a brown tie. Rachel was at his side in a light blue silk gown, a string of pearls around her neck, and a small diamond tiara on her blond head. She looked like a queen—a spoiled one, he thought.

They walked about the room, nodding to familiar faces and chatting with acquaintances. As the musicians mounted the podium and prepared their instruments, Crake took a seat among the spectators, most of them elderly and decrepit like him. At the far end of the room, one of the largest in the country, an enormous painting, *The Genius of America*, covered the wall. Crake couldn't judge its artistic merits, or even make out most of its details. Someone told him that George Washington was in the picture along with naked black people being lifted up out of slavery. Crake recalled that he had done some of that lifting in the South during the war—mostly wasted effort. Blacks down there were little better off now than before.

The music director announced the first dance: a schottische. Robert Shaw approached and asked Rachel for the dance. She turned to Crake and got his grudging approval. She and her partner joined the dancers and began hopping about, light on their feet and synchronized with the caller.

Crake looked on, sourly, and reflected on Shaw's appeal to women. To give the devil his due, he was a handsome, engaging British gentleman in his forties, who gave fencing lessons in athletic clubs and earned a living in gambling dens. "He knew Rachel before I did," muttered Crake to himself, "and still charms her."

A waltz followed the schottische. Rachel's new partner was a callow Harvard student who had tippled to bolster his self-confidence. After the waltz came another change of partners and another schottische. And so it went throughout the evening with occasional pauses for refreshment.

At the halfway point, brimming with vitality, Rachel rejoined Crake. Wracked with pain and bored, he told her, "We'll go back to our rooms now. I'm tired and in pain."

"No, please!" She pouted. "There are more dances to come, and afterward I was hoping to go to Canfield's Casino. But I'll need an escort to get in, as well as to gamble. Won't you go with me?"

"You know I love to gamble, especially at the casino where my credit is good and the stakes are high, but I just can't do it tonight. The arthritis is getting worse. In less than an hour I won't be able to bear the pain."

"Would it be all right, then, if Rob were my escort?"

Crake thought, if he refused, she would pout all night or probably sneak out with the rascal anyway. "I don't mind," he muttered. She kissed him on the cheek and skipped back to the dance floor and Robert Shaw.

Crake followed her with narrowed eyes. Before he left the ballroom, he hired a spy to keep an eye on her. She would soon get a big surprise.

# CHAPTER 7

## *The Last Day*

*Saturday, July 7*

An hour after sunrise, Crake awoke, stiff and sore, keenly mindful of his sixty-plus years. Getting up was painful. He sat on the edge of the bed, pulled up a small table, and rang the bell. The smell of coffee had already wafted into the room.

"Just a minute, I'm coming." The voice from the kitchen had a pleasing accent.

It was Swedish. He knew that much about Birgitta. She also had strong fingers that worked miracles on his aging body, at least for a few hours. That was better than nothing.

As promised, she entered the room with a tray of coffee, buttered toast, and strawberry preserves. Her thick blond hair hung braided down to her waist. Her eyes were light blue, her gaze steady and direct, and her smile friendly. He couldn't play games with her as he did with other maids, though she was comely enough. She kept him at a proper distance. And that was just fine as long as she made him feel better.

There was an extra cup on the tray. "Join me, Birgitta," he said. "We'll talk about my schedule for the day."

She pulled up a chair, poured coffee for herself, and they toasted each other.

"Has my wife come back?" he asked, keeping his voice level. He glanced at a framed wedding photo on the wall. He was already a gray haired man looking uncomfortable in a black frock coat, stiff collar, and white tie. She was petite, much younger, and enjoying herself in a white satin gown.

"Not yet," Birgitta replied, her voice as level as his.

Last night, Rachel had not returned from Canfield's Casino. So, where was she? Perhaps still at the casino. Canfield allowed high-stakes gambling through the night. Shaw had little money or credit, but he could play on her behalf with her husband's credit. The spy would soon come with a report.

"To hell with her," said Crake with feeling. "Give me the morning massage. Then we'll go to the spring in Congress Park for the water."

He finished the coffee, and she took away the tray. While she was in the kitchen, he removed his nightclothes, wrapped a towel around his loins, and lay facedown on the bed. She soon returned, sleeves rolled up to her elbows, and began to rub his body. Her strokes began lightly, tingling the skin. She gradually went deeper, relaxing the cramped muscles, loosening the stiff joints. She was soon working in rhythms that seemed to reach into his soul.

He let his distressing cares ebb away: first to go was his unfaithful wife, and second, Robert Shaw, her paramour. And he let loose the ungrateful, troublesome workers at his New York meatpacking plants, and the backbiters and competitors envious of his power and wealth. Then went the horrid memories of the war in the South, especially the gruesome, painful deaths of his comrades. The last to leave were the bitter years he had endured as a youth under the fist of his harsh, abusive father on their hardscrabble Pennsylvania farm. An image of his mother came up as well, cowering in the kitchen while his father raged against her, beat her, or showered her with contempt.

The hour passed swiftly. "You should feel better now," she said. "You may wash and shave and dress for the morning. Call if you need help with your shoes."

At first, it had seemed strange to have a female valet. Yet, he'd come to like it. In a leap of fantasy, he dared to think he'd have been better off if he had married her rather than Rachel. He scolded himself. "I must be growing soft in the head."

In the pavilion at the spring, Birgitta found a table, and a trim, young black boy brought glasses of water. Crake sniffed. For years he'd started the day with a shot of whiskey and a beer. This spring water tasted of sulfur, but his doctor said it was good for his failing kidneys. His eyesight was also weak. He sighed softly. He was only a few years past sixty and he was falling apart. To come here, Birgitta had to help him over rough patches in the road and up and down stairs.

Nonetheless, he was enjoying the cool morning breezes and the low murmur of conversation around him. Birgitta had brought along a New York newspaper and read interesting bits to him. Suddenly, she stopped.

Crake asked, "What's going on?"

"Your wife and Mr. Shaw have just arrived. They're coming toward us."

A surge of anger raced through Crake's body. Before coming to the spring, he heard from his spy that Rachel and Shaw had left the casino at midnight and spent the early-morning hours in a notorious boardinghouse in the town.

As the villains drew near, Crake gripped his cane as if about to strike. Birgitta laid a calming hand on his arm. "Jed," she whispered urgently, "let them be. Confront them in private."

He relaxed his grip on the cane and snarled under his breath, "Right. I'll deal with them later."

"Well!" exclaimed Rachel, the word slurred from fatigue or alcohol, or both. "Look who's here, the old soldier and his faithful nurse. Rob and I have good news. We beat the house last night and walked away with over twenty thousand dollars. Like a good sport, Canfield congratulated us."

Shaw added, "We played poker past dawn."

"You must be exhausted and famished," said Crake dryly.

"A little tired," said Rachel with a pout. "But we've had a champagne breakfast at the Phila Street Café along with other gay night birds. It was really quite festive there."

"We can speak more about your triumph later. Are you going back to the hotel?"

"Yes, I want Birgitta to give me a massage and rub the evening's fatigue away. Then I'll take a nap." She cast a coy glance at the maid. "I see she's been keeping you company, Jed. Aren't you fortunate to have her?"

Crake replied with a curt nod. He felt a powerful urge to strike out with his fist and smash her lying teeth into her empty skull. He turned to Birgitta. "Let's go."

In the hotel's foyer, Crake said to the maid, "Go to the cottage and take care of Mrs. Crake. I'll distract myself elsewhere." The short fuse to his temper was burning dangerously low.

To cool down, he went to the hotel's barroom for beer and dim-witted conversation with its patrons, some of them drink-befuddled even before noon. Their only topic these days was baseball and the prowess of the New York Giants. In a few weeks they would chatter on about the Saratoga track, the thoroughbred horses, and which one would win the Travers Cup.

The beer worked its magic. Feeling better, he moved from the bar to the billiards room. It was quiet and mostly deserted this time of day. While idly knocking the cue ball around the table, he reflected again on his wife, Rachel. When he married her four years ago, he could hardly have expected her to become virtuous. After all, he had picked her up in a brothel. She was a beautiful, lively creature. Until recently, she had added spice and joy to his life.

Then Shaw appeared. At first, she called him a dear friend. For months they carried on like brother and sister. He now realized that, while he was in Georgia, they became lovers. Their affair would soon reach the scandalmongers and make him look foolish, a cuckolded husband. "That must stop," he muttered through clenched teeth. He hit the cue ball with a powerful blow. It flew over the edge of the table, bounced across the marble floor the length of the room, and crashed into the opposite wall. The other players turned and stared at him. He called out, "Sorry," laid down the cue stick, and left the room.

He needed to do something to occupy his mind. An old business acquaintance from New York had recently become the hotel's food manager. It could be useful to renew ties with him. Crake's company sold tons of meat to the Grand Union Hotel.

The new manager welcomed Crake into his office and a business conversation ensued. Finally, he said to Crake, "I'd be happy to show you the new equipment in our meat room." They took the elevator to the basement, where meat cutters were busy with their knives.

"We've installed the latest improvements in electric lighting," said the manager. "The cutting room used to be a dark place. Now it's as bright as day. At the same time, we've also bought the highest quality of steel knives. Since then, we've had far fewer accidents."

The manager pointed to one of the meat cutters at work on a side of beef. "The blade of his new boning knife takes the sharpest edge in the business. He'll show it to you."

The meat cutter turned around, the bloody knife in his hand, and locked eyes with Crake. They both started. Crake took a step back. The meat cutter was Karl Metzger, the burly, scowling German who once worked in Crake's meatpacking plants. They exchanged hostile looks. For a brief moment, a tense silence fell over the men. Then Metzger slowly lowered the knife, as if reluctantly, and returned to his work.

As they left the basement, Crake said to the manager, "That German, Metzger, is a major troublemaker. He led the union in a strike that nearly ruined my business. You must get rid of him immediately."

"I'm grateful for your advice," said the manager, suddenly concerned. "Up to now, I've had no problems with Metzger. He's a skillful meat cutter and well-liked by the others. But I'll consider carefully what you've said before going to Mr. Wooley, the proprietor."

Still searching for a way to pass the time and shaken by his encounter with the German meat cutter, Crake wandered out of the hotel onto Broadway. At midafternoon, the July sun made a promenade uncomfortable even under the street's arcade of tall elm trees. When Crake saw the sign for Mitchell's Saloon, he also realized he was thirsty again. At the long mahogany bar, he drank a couple of glasses of beer, then beckoned the barman.

"Any games going on in there?" Crake eyed a door at the rear of the room.

The barman studied Crake. "You don't look like one of those 'reformers' who want to close us down."

"I take that as a compliment," said Crake. "I'm a gambling man. The mayor approves of me." Crake was thinking of Mr. Caleb Mitchell, popular mayor of Saratoga Springs, who owned the saloon and the profitable gambling den in the back room.

The barman smiled broadly. "His excellency is hard at work in there. Why don't you see what he has to offer?"

When Crake walked into the den, Mitchell was observing a crowd of men at a roulette wheel. His eyes immediately caught Crake in a penetrating glance and mouthed a welcome. Crake was soon betting at the wheel. He lost a few dollars and was about to try his luck at poker when Robert Shaw walked in with a beer and sat by himself.

For a moment they stared at each other. Shaw smirked. Crake's anger flared up. He approached Shaw and in a quiet, measured voice said, "Last night, you slept with my wife." He leaned forward and hissed, "I'll make you pay. You'll be a dead man before the end of summer."

Shaw sipped from his glass and gazed at Crake with contempt.

As Crake stalked out of the room, he muttered "insolent bastard" and made a mental note to hire Jimmy Gilpin for the job.

For an hour, he paced back and forth in the hotel garden, mulling over his marriage to Rachel. Then his knees began to pain him. By the time he returned to their cottage, he was in a cold fury, his mind made up. He burst into her room. Dressed for dinner in a shimmering red silk gown, she was standing before the mirror and inspecting her coiffure. Birgitta was at her side looking on. She glanced at Crake, shook her head, and mouthed, "No!"

For a few moments he mastered his temper and said levelly, "Miss Mattsson, please wait in the parlor. I'll speak to you later. Now I have something to say to my wife."

The maid averted her eyes and walked quickly from the room. Crake closed the door and strode up to his wife. She stood glued to the floor, eyes wide with fear. She flashed a nervous, childlike smile at him.

"Whore!" he shouted and slapped her so hard that she fell back against the mirror and sent it swinging wildly. "For appearance's sake, we shall dine together and attend this evening's concert. After a few more days of pretending marital bliss, we'll return to New York and consider what to do with our marriage. At the least, I'll remove you from among the beneficiaries of my will."

Crake was swaying and breathing heavily. Gradually, his anger subsided. He muttered, "I apologize for losing my temper and striking you." He left the room and found the maid in the parlor, tight lipped and pale. As he approached, she seemed to tremble. She had heard everything.

Crake said, "I acted like a brute. Go to Mrs. Crake and repair the damage. At five, we'll leave for dinner. You will then be free for the rest of the day. Meanwhile, I'll collect my wits and finish some legal business." Crake fixed her in a taut gaze. "I trust you'll say nothing about this incident."

Early that evening, as the orchestra was settling into its chairs, Crake and his wife entered the hotel's garden. At dinner, his violent outburst in the cottage was put behind them, if not forgotten. He walked slowly with a cane, looking stolidly ahead, lines of pain etched on his face. She forced a sweet smile, fanned her face briskly, and nodded to acquaintances left and right.

The musicians tuned their instruments. This evening's conductor, the cellist Victor Herbert, stepped up onto the podium and a hush came over the crowd.

"Ladies and gentlemen," he began, "we have a special request for the popular song 'Marching Through Georgia.' This is the thirtieth year since General Sherman's glorious campaign during the late war. With us tonight is one of its brave veterans, Captain Jed Crake."

The crowd turned toward the captain and applauded.

He waved his hand, but he didn't smile. This attention was unexpected and unwelcome. After the war, he had polished his reputation for heroism and had never been challenged. But recently, a former comrade and he had a falling out. Since then, the comrade had grown embittered and had insinuated that Crake's military record had a dark side. Crake now preferred less limelight.

Rachel glared at him behind her fan and whispered, "Jed, you should look pleased. People are curious about your experience in Georgia. It must have been exciting and terribly important. After all, you and your comrades brought the war to an end and saved the Union."

"Nothing glorious about it," he snarled. "Dirty business. Sherman said it was hell."

As the orchestra launched into the tune and the crowd joined in, Captain Crake fell into uneasy thinking. Who had given his name to the conductor and had requested the song? Rachel seemed as surprised as he.

This wasn't the first worrisome allusion this summer to his past life. An hour ago, heads turned when he walked into the dining room. At dinner, perfect strangers inquired politely about his private life in New York City, doubt lurking in their voices. Enemies had brought tales about him from the city and were stoking curiosity. His spies in the city had earlier warned him that private detectives were asking questions that linked him to the mysterious disappearance of prostitutes. He'd put a stop to the snooping, but rumors persisted.

He suffered through the song; but when it finished, he leaned toward his wife. "My arthritis is killing me. I'm going to our rooms for my medicine. I'll come back as soon as I feel better." She frowned, then shrugged; but he shuffled away.

For the summer, he had rented a suite of rooms on the ground floor of one of the hotel's so-called cottages. At the door he fumbled with the key. His eyesight had failed to the point that he had to feel for the lock. Finally, he got the key in and turned it. "Damn!" he exclaimed. His wife had left the door unlocked. Silly, careless woman! She kept valuable jewelry in her bedside cabinet. Anyone could walk in and steal it.

He let himself in and went directly to the washroom. The laudanum wasn't where he had left it. His wife was constantly moving things around and he had to hunt for them. Eventually, he found the drug, prepared a dose, and drank it down. While he waited for its soothing effect, he stretched out on a divan and fell into a fitful sleep.

Memories from the war came back again to haunt him. Body parts—human and animal—melded into grotesque monsters. Lurid flames leaped from burning buildings. Screams of women and men pierced his ears. A beautiful woman's defiant face, battered and bruised, loomed up before his eyes. He tried to drive these images away but couldn't.

Then he woke up, soaked in sweat. He had no idea how long he slept. The room was dark except for a thin shaft of gaslight slanting through the transom window. Music played in the distance. A floorboard creaked. For a moment he lay still and listened. Someone was in the room.

He called out, "Anyone there?"

A board creaked again, this time closer. A dim light from a lantern shone on him. Groggy from the drug, Crake struggled in vain to rise. A shadowy figure approached him, and a spark of light glinted off metal. A searing pain ripped through his chest. Life ebbed from his body.

# CHAPTER 8

## Troubling News

*New York City*
*Monday, July 9*

Two days later at midmorning, a pale and agitated aide rushed up to Pamela Thompson. "One of our girls is in trouble."

On vacation for two weeks, Pamela was working at St. Barnabas Mission. The first thought to leap to her mind was an unwanted pregnancy. "Who is it?"

"Francesca Ricci," the aide replied. "But it's not what you're thinking. In Saratoga Springs they say she was trying to steal something and killed a rich man. She's in jail." The aide handed Pamela a telegraphed message from Helen Fisk, her friend and patron of St. Barnabas.

DEAR PAMELA,
MR. JED CRAKE WAS STABBED TO
DEATH SATURDAY EVENING IN HIS
ROOMS AT THE GRAND UNION
HOTEL. THE POLICE SAY HE
CONFRONTED MISS RICCI STEALING
HIS WIFE'S JEWELRY. SHE STABBED HIM

AND FLED. STOLEN JEWELRY WAS
FOUND IN HER ROOM. THE POLICE
ARE HOLDING HER IN THE TOWN
JAIL. I VISITED HER THIS SUNDAY
AFTERNOON. SHE ASKED FOR YOU.
HELEN

Pamela stared at the message, shocked and incredulous. Her knees began to buckle. She lowered herself into a chair and breathed deeply. Francesca was her ward and a friend, and had lived with her up to a month or so ago.

There couldn't be two Jed Crakes. The murdered man had to be the Captain Crake whom Pamela investigated a few months ago. When she last heard of him, he was ill but still alive in New York City. That he should die violently at Francesca's hand must be a mistake.

"Would you speak to her mother? Mrs. Fisk sent a copy of the message to her."

"Of course." Still shaken by the news, Pamela followed the aide into a parlor where Signora Ricci was sitting. A slender, careworn widow and too ill to care for Francesca, she had given up the girl to the mission.

"My daughter, Francesca, wouldn't murder anyone," she exclaimed in heavily accented English. "Can you help her?"

"I'll try." She calmed and comforted the anxious mother, then asked if Francesca had reported having any problems in Saratoga Springs. Her occasional notes to Pamela were brief and cheerful.

"Oh no, she has written that she was pleased with her work and the people were kind to her."

Pamela thought that's what a daughter would write to keep her mother from worrying. "I'll see what I can do. At the least I can arrange for legal counsel."

An exploratory trip to Saratoga Springs was feasible. Prescott, her boss, was at his cabin in the Berkshires near his son, Edward. She didn't know when he would return to the city, but he wouldn't mind what she did on her own time.

A single woman in Saratoga, even a forty-year-old widow like herself, would feel awkward by herself as a private investigator. At least at the start, she would need a companion. Fortunately, Harry Miller, her fellow investigator in Prescott's firm, also had vacation time and might be willing to join her.

Miller's home was a room in a boardinghouse on Irving Place near the Prescott office. With a compliant smile, his landlady showed her into a small parlor and left to call him. She knew that Pamela and Miller worked together solving crimes, a legal but disreputable business.

He entered the parlor in rumpled clothes and glassy eyes.

"Harry! Have you been studying?" Pamela put a teasing reproach in her voice. He devoted nearly every free hour to his law books and new investigative techniques.

"I confess to the crime. What brings you here?"

She explained Francesca Ricci's predicament, then showed a sketch of the girl. "Would you help me investigate her situation in Saratoga Springs? I apologize for this short notice."

He stared at the portrait. "She's a beautiful young woman. When did you learn to sketch?"

"In school," she replied. "I sketched scenes when I traveled abroad and also portraits for friends. I stopped when Jack died and my life fell apart. Recently, Francesca encouraged me to take it up again. She wanted a portrait of herself to give to her mother."

"That speaks well of her. She sounds like a good daughter and might be unjustly accused."

He hesitated, apparently torn between his precious hours of study and this opportunity to save a person from a fate he himself had once suffered. His years in Sing Sing left raw wounds in his spirit.

Finally, he said, "We'll take the first train tomorrow to Saratoga Springs, speak to Francesca, and assess her situation. Charged with murdering a rich man, you say? Clearing her won't be easy."

In the coach to Grand Central Station the next day, Harry asked, "Is your ward Francesca Ricci a likely murderer?"

"I doubt it. She's sixteen, poor, and foolish at times, but she's not violent. Her father died in an accident at a construction site shortly after her birth. Poverty and illness overwhelmed his widow, and she couldn't give Francesca a proper upbringing. Still, she grew up to be a bright, musical, and beautiful girl."

"Any criminal inclinations?"

"A few. She often skipped school to sing for pennies on the street and to indulge in petty shoplifting. Several months ago, Macy's detective caught her stealing a bracelet and handed her over to the police. I managed to save her from prison, but the arrest went into her record. A court placed her in my custody with the warning that if she failed to reform, she would be sent to a house of detention."

"Does she take that warning seriously?"

"I believe she does. Some of her friends have gone to prison, so she knows what it's like. She has told me that she detests the police for their roughness and disrespect toward her and other Italians."

Harry grimaced. "So, what's new?"

"I must admit she might have provoked them. Since she moved into my apartment, her behavior has improved, especially her attendance at school and her grade reports. I tutor her. We sing Italian songs together and she sings in church. So, when she had an opportunity to work at the Grand Union Hotel for the summer, I recommended her to the management."

A skeptic through training and experience, Harry shook his head. "Nonetheless, we can't declare that she's innocent of this crime. Before living with you, she seemed vain and undisciplined, even willful. True, you've straightened her out. But, in Saratoga, she might have fallen back into her old ways and robbed Crake, then impulsively killed him to escape going to prison."

Pamela inwardly shuddered. Harry could be right. Under certain circumstances, anyone could fall from grace. Nonetheless, she would trust her own reading of Francesca's character and rely on the law's presumption of innocence.

As they boarded the train for Saratoga Springs, Pamela remarked to Harry, "I'm anxious about this trip. We'll have to contact Francesca promptly. She's virtually alone in that bustling town—the journalist Nellie Bly calls it Sin City."

"What's worse," Harry added, "the hotel will want a quick, simple resolution of the case. The police will hold her previous poverty and delinquency against her, and will pressure the girl to confess. She might soon face the prospect of years in a state prison—or worse."

Before getting involved in Francesca's predicament, Pamela would have liked to speak to Prescott, her boss. Unfortunately, she could reach him at his Berkshire cabin only in an emergency.

As the train pulled out of the station, Pamela asked Harry, "What would Prescott think of our trip?"

Harry reflected thoughtfully for a moment. "He'd approve of our good intentions but warn us to be realistic. Francesca's arrest in Saratoga Springs wouldn't greatly surprise him. At the time of her arrest at Macy's he doubted that she would change her bad habits."

Pamela shook her head. "He might also fault my judgment in taking on responsibility for the girl. This investigation will have to win his approval and support."

During the ride north along the Hudson River, Pamela glanced sideways at her companion. He had fallen silent and looked sad, more than usual.

"What's the matter, Harry?" she asked gently.

"My son William will be confirmed at church on Sunday. I'm not invited." His lips seemed to quiver.

She encouraged him with a sympathetic smile.

"My ex-wife poisons the boy's mind against me. He calls me a jailbird. That's hard to take." Miller stared out the window.

Pamela was aware that the NYPD had dismissed Harry for protesting against the police cover-up of a murder involving Tammany Hall, the city's Democratic organization. Harry was then falsely charged with trying to extort money from the organization. Wrongly convicted, he served four years in Sing Sing. His wife left him, taking their two children with her.

Pamela reassured him. "As your son grows older, Harry, he'll think for himself. Then he'll learn the truth and be proud of your integrity and achievements. Prescott says you're the best detective in the city."

Harry smiled wryly, leaned back, and closed his eyes. The train rumbled on.

At noon, they arrived in Saratoga Springs' busy D&H railroad station. Pamela and Harry engaged a carriage for a short ride to the Grand Union Hotel. At the last minute, Prescott's clerk had reserved adjoining rooms for them, though it was near the height of the tourist season and the hotel claimed to be fully booked.

From the sidewalk on Broadway, his eyes wide and arms akimbo, Harry looked up at the giant, six-story brick building. A three-story porch girded it, offering a shaded stage for hundreds of guests sitting in rocking chairs or walking about. A huge American flag flew over the central tower.

"Have you been here before?" he asked Pamela.

"Several years ago my husband and I stayed for a month on three occasions. He maintained it was the largest, finest hotel in the world. More big business deals were struck in the porch's rocking chairs than in many Wall Street offices. While he smoked a cigar and talked finance on the porch, I listened to the Boston Symphony Orchestra in the garden, or watched the women's fashion parade on Broadway, or walked with my daughter, Julia, in Congress Park. I feel nostalgic already."

After claiming their rooms, they hastened to the town jail to speak to Francesca Ricci. The officer on duty studied their credentials, glanced skeptically at Pamela, and looked up at a clock on the wall. "I'm short-handed and can't leave the desk. Come back in an hour. The bitch will still be here."

Pamela sensed that Francesca wasn't a model prisoner. Nonetheless, the officer was obnoxious. "We'll wait."

He sighed impatiently, but after a few minutes he called a guard and told the visitors curtly, "Follow him."

Francesca was locked in a cell with three females awaiting arraignment. "Prostitutes," the guard said. He moved Francesca to a small, bare, grimy room with a battered table and a few wooden chairs.

Pamela sat at the table facing a sullen Francesca in handcuffs. Harry stood off to one side. The guard lounged against the wall near the door and picked his teeth. Francesca glared at him and banged the cuffs on the table. He tried to appear indifferent to her taunting, but his eyes smoldered with contempt and irritation.

"Are you well treated?" asked Pamela.

Francesca shrugged. "They don't beat me."

"Did you steal jewelry from Mrs. Crake or kill her husband?"

"No."

Pamela realized that the girl would not speak freely while the guard was listening. So she asked him, "Could you let us talk privately?"

He frowned, but he left the room. The girl made a gesture to his departing back that Pamela suspected was a nasty Italian insult.

"Tell me, Francesca, what happened that night?"

"When Mr. and Mrs. Crake went to the concert, I aired their rooms as usual. Then I returned to my room. Late that night, as I was reading in bed, a big, fat police detective and Mr. Winn, the hotel detective, came to my door. The officer questioned me, searched the room, and found Mrs. Crake's bracelet in my mattress. He said she had reported it missing. I said it was a gift from Captain Crake. The officer said I was lying and took me to jail."

"Why would Crake give you his wife's bracelet? That sounds farfetched."

Francesca reflected for a moment, the effort creasing her brow. "It's strange, but it's true. I often sang for him. That afternoon, he handed me the bracelet. I told him I couldn't take it. He looked angry and insisted. I was afraid he would hurt me. He was old and sick but still a big, strong man. I was confused. I couldn't sell it in a pawnshop. Even a dishonest dealer might turn me over to the police. So I hid the bracelet until I could figure out what to do with it."

"Isn't it odd that he'd give away his wife's bracelet without asking her?"

"That's what I thought," Francesca replied. "Frankly, I think he was angry at her. They say he gave her the bracelet a month ago to make up after a quarrel. It's engraved *RC*. There's talk among the maids that Mrs. Crake is carrying on an affair with Mr. Shaw. If I'd given the bracelet back to her against his wishes, I might have found myself in the middle of a family fight."

Harry turned to Pamela. "By taking the bracelet away without asking his wife, Crake might have intended to punish her infidelity. Giving the bracelet to a chambermaid added insult to the injury."

Pamela added, "If Crake's wife found out about the bracelet and later killed him, she could use it to implicate Francesca, a convenient scapegoat."

"That's plausible," Harry agreed. "Or, the police detective could have suspected Francesca simply because she was Crake's chambermaid. By chance he might have found the bracelet in a routine search of her room. Crake's killer could also share the detective's preconception of chambermaids. He or she might know Francesca and found a way to steer the investigation toward her."

Pamela asked Francesca, "Does anyone seem to show special interest in you?"

The maid struggled to recall. "Men sometimes stare at me with lust in their eyes, but there's a bellboy whose eyes are especially intense. I shudder when he stares at me." She described him as a slim, quick, clever man, maybe thirty years old, with curly blond hair, light complexion, and deep-set brown eyes. "He tries to talk to me; but I don't like him, and I tell him to leave me alone."

Pamela made a mental note to search for the man. "Tomorrow, Francesca, you will be taken to the county courthouse in Ballston Spa, a few miles to the south of town, to hear the charges against you. You will have a lawyer. Plead innocent. The judge will set a date for your trial." She smiled and spoke gently to the girl. "For your own sake, be polite to the police and to the magistrate. We will be there and try to keep you out of prison. Then we'll find out what really happened. Unfortunately, the police seem to have made up their minds. We doubt that they will be helpful."

# CHAPTER 9

## Initial Impressions

*Saratoga Springs*
*Tuesday, July 10*

From the jail, Pamela and Harry went to the empty Crake cottage facing the hotel's garden. A police officer blocked the entrance. Harry showed him their identification papers. Eyes squinting, he read them slowly.

"Mr. Tom Winn, the hotel detective, is inside," said the officer finally. "I'll see if he can be disturbed."

"Have you met Winn?" Harry asked Pamela.

"Yes, on previous visits to the hotel," she replied. "He's an approachable, decent man, well-known and liked in the town. For most of the year he runs a carriage and sign painting business. House detective is his summer job."

"Then he's poorly qualified for a homicide investigation," said Harry, frowning. "For Francesca's sake, I hope he's aware of his limitations."

"I've heard that he was a local part-time cop or watchman before going to work for the Grand Union."

"That doesn't make me feel better."

At that moment, the officer returned with Winn, who beckoned them into the cottage. A stocky man about forty, he bowed to Pamela, appearing to recognize her.

"Pamela Thompson, a friend of Helen Fisk," she reminded him. An older widow, Helen was a tall, imposing figure and a rich, prominent patron of the hotel.

"I recall your face. You were here together with your daughter, Julia, a lively, beautiful girl. How is she?"

The question nearly brought Pamela to tears. Would she ever get over the loss? For a moment she struggled, then replied evenly, "Julia died of influenza in 1890, shortly after our last visit to Saratoga. My life turned upside down for a few years."

"I'm truly sorry." He gazed at her, then remarked softly, "For a parent to lose a child in the bloom of youth is the worst thing I can imagine."

"Thank you, I'm back on track and working as a private investigator."

"I'm acquainted with your Jeremiah Prescott, a clever lawyer. If he takes on the maid's defense, he'll have an uphill struggle. Granted, she hasn't confessed, and the evidence against her is circumstantial, but it's convincing. The hotel management wants the case to be prosecuted with the least possible disturbance to the guests. The local authorities are of the same mind."

"If Prescott takes the case, he'll mount a vigorous defense," said Pamela. "That's what Miss Ricci is entitled to."

"I agree," remarked Winn. "Follow me to the crime scene."

As they entered the ground-floor parlor, the detective pointed to a sofa. "Mrs. Crake found him lying there."

"Any sign of struggle?" Harry asked.

"No, Crake had taken a drug and was probably semiconscious at best. In his wife's bedroom, her jewelry case was open and a bracelet missing. It was hidden in the maid's room."

"What led you to suspect her?"

"She was the last person to see Crake alive, though she claims to have left the cottage *before* he returned from the concert. A bellboy contradicts her. He saw her leave *after* Crake had returned. She doesn't have an alibi and claims Crake gave the bracelet to her. Mrs. Crake insists that's a lie."

Pamela asked for the bellboy's name.

"Jason Dunn. I questioned him. In the evening Dunn often ran errands in the garden."

"When did Mrs. Crake discover the body?"

"Near midnight. She had been playing cards at Canfield's Casino. When she returned to the cottage, she found the room dark and her husband dead. I was called immediately. After confirming the crime, I summoned the police."

"Do you have any questions about this case?" Harry asked.

Winn hesitated before replying. "I wish I knew precisely when the murder took place. From the time Crake left the concert until his wife discovered his body is about four hours. We found no bloodstains in the maid's room or on her clothes. She had enough time to clean up."

"You just mentioned Crake's body. Could we see it?"

Winn glanced at Pamela. "Are you really prepared for this?"

"I've seen murdered men's bodies before. I won't faint."

Winn flashed her a thin smile. "It's in the basement ice room now and will go to the morgue later this afternoon. Follow me."

They descended to the basement. Winn unlocked the ice room. Crake's body was laid out on a wooden table and covered with a cloth. Winn pulled back the cloth from the torso, revealing a single knife wound to the heart. "He bled copiously. I mopped up most of the blood to make the body appear less horrific to his wife. She fainted anyway."

Miller asked, "Where's the knife?"

"The police haven't found it," replied Winn. "They think it was an eight-inch boning knife from the meat-cutting room in the basement. Miss Ricci could have picked up one while visiting Italian women next door in the laundry and returned it afterward."

Miller bent over the body and inspected the wound. "The blade was thin and single-edged like a boning knife, but narrower. The weapon could have been a dagger." He stepped back and stared at the corpse. "As I imagine the scene in that dark cottage, the killer's single blow hit the heart with incredible luck or an expert's skill. Even with light, a nervous sixteen-year-old girl would have stabbed Crake wildly and have missed the heart."

"Are you insinuating that this crime might be an assassin's work?"

"That's how it looks to me."

"The thought crossed my mind," Winn admitted. "But, who hired the assassin? I can't think of anyone."

"Have you looked?" Harry asked evenly.

"That's a job for the police detective." Winn glared at Harry for a moment, then explained that the medical examiner would finish his work the next day. The body would be sent to the military cemetery in Erie, Pennsylvania, where Crake wanted to be buried. He came from the area and had relatives there.

Pamela asked, "Wouldn't his widow have a funeral for him in New York and bury him in a local military cemetery like Cypress Hills in Brooklyn?"

Winn replied dryly, "She's really not a grieving widow, just a clever courtesan intent on his money. She couldn't care less about the burial of his body. Now, I must be going."

Harry thanked the detective and signaled Pamela that they, too, should leave. When they were alone in the garden, he asked, "What's next?"

She reflected. "Well, tomorrow we must visit Francesca again. Thanks to Tom Winn, I have some questions for her. In the meantime, let's try to find that witness, Jason Dunn."

Late in the afternoon, Jason was standing near the reception desk, just as Francesca described him—a slim, handsome man, his eyes deep-set, golden brown, and intense. Pamela started toward him, but the desk clerk gave him an errand and he was off in a flash.

Harry beckoned her and patted his stomach. They hadn't eaten since breakfast. Nonetheless, she signed for him to wait. She asked the clerk, "When could I speak to the bellboy Jason Dunn?"

"I'll send him to your room after dinner."

Pamela joined Harry at the entrance to the dining hall. A crowd had gathered, waiting for the master waiter to seat them.

"Gossip must flourish like weeds here," Harry observed. "We might pick up useful news."

They eavesdropped and gathered public opinion on the recent murder. Predictably, most visitors were relieved that the police had taken the maid into custody. No one doubted she was guilty. Conversations quickly turned to afternoon events, the forthcoming food, and the evening music.

In due course, the master waiter opened the door, causing a stir in the crowd. "Don't worry, ladies and gentlemen. Our hall can accommodate a thousand diners."

A small army of black waiters in black coats and stiff white shirts stood at attention by the tables. Each table was covered with white linen, decorated with cut flowers, and set with silverware for four persons. As he seated Pamela and Harry, the master waiter said with pride, "You will find that our menu compares favorably with the best restaurants in New York City."

A middle-aged couple, Mr. and Mrs. Wood, arrived late, when most seats were occupied or reserved. The master waiter seated them with Harry and Pamela. The Woods proved to be affable and well-educated people. They had come to the hotel already in June and had a trove of local gossip. The first course, clam chowder, diverted everyone's attention to the food.

After the chowder, Pamela brought up the topic of Crake's murder. Mrs. Wood was impressed that the local police had solved the case so quickly. She and her husband held the general opinion that the maid was guilty.

There was a break for the next course, broiled pompano, a fish from Florida, with potatoes julienne. The Woods had ordered a bottle of white wine and now offered some to Pamela and Harry. Out of politeness, they agreed to a glass each.

Pretending ignorance, Pamela asked, "What sort of man was the victim, Captain Crake?"

"Actually," Mrs. Wood replied, "he's rather well-known. During the past three or four summers he has come here for his health—severe arthritis, I believe—and frequented the springs and the baths. He gambled a great deal and usually won. We occasionally dined with him and his wife. His speech and manners were rough on the edges, if you know what I mean. She's a lively, cultivated, attractive young woman who loves to shine and amuse herself."

"And spend his money," Mr. Wood added. "Crake was a ruthless, successful businessman and made a fortune in meat-packing and railroads."

"I've noticed," said Harry, feigning ignorance, "that Crake is referred to as a captain. Was he involved in the war?"

"Yes," replied Mr. Wood. "He distinguished himself in Georgia late in sixty-four. A captain of cavalry, he routed a company of rebels, single-handedly, or so the story goes. The army gave him a Medal of Honor. After the war, he touted his exploits at reunions of the Grand Army of the Republic."

His wife waved a hand. "A rumor is making the rounds that his military service wasn't as glorious as he loudly claimed. While in Sherman's army, he did skirmish with Confederate cavalry. But mostly he chased after the Georgia militia of untrained young boys and feeble old men, and he slaughtered rebel cattle, burned rebel barns, and terrorized rebel women and children."

Months ago, Pamela had already formed an unflattering impression of the victim: a ruthless businessman suspected of assaulting young women. Now she added the image of a cuckolded husband and false hero. "I wouldn't be surprised," Pamela began, "if the Crake you described might have made enemies along the way. Could one of them have done him in and shifted the blame to the maid?"

Mr. Wood shrugged. "How is that possible? Before the police arrested her, they must have thought of other suspects." His voice now seemed uncertain.

Pamela persisted. "No one saw her kill Crake, and she has denied doing it. True, the circumstantial evidence seems compelling, but it should be tested. For example, the maid claims Captain Crake *gave* Mrs. Crake's bracelet to her. It could be true. We should take care. If the maid didn't kill Crake, then the killer is still among us."

"That's a sobering thought," remarked Mrs. Wood. "But here comes a meat course, spring lamb with mint sauce. Let's leave Crake's murder for another day."

After dinner, Pamela called Harry to her room to meet the bellboy Jason Dunn. She had already learned that this was his second season at the Grand Union. According to the hotel's manager, Jason came with sterling recommendations from hotels in New York City. Raised in South Carolina, he had moved to New York as a young man looking for work. He was trustworthy, resourceful, and well mannered.

There was a knock on the door. Pamela opened and found a handsome man in a smartly pressed bellboy's uniform.

"Jason Dunn, at your service, ma'am."

For a fraction of a second, she was speechless, struck by his golden brown eyes. Then she invited him in and gestured to a chair. He looked puzzled. She explained who they were and added, "We have a few questions."

He immediately became wary. "Mr. Winn and the police detective have already questioned me. What more can I say?" His English had retained a Southern accent.

"That was then," Pamela replied. "Tell the story again. Perhaps you'll think of a new detail or two. That's how the mind works."

He reflected for a moment, then began in a tentative voice. At dusk in the evening of the seventh of July, the front desk sent him to the hotel garden to deliver a message. When he arrived, the orchestra was playing. So he stood behind the crowd, off to one side, looking for the person to whom the message was addressed. His gaze drifted to the nearby hotel cottages. Captain Crake was entering his. That was close to 7:00. Near the end of the concert, about 9:00, Jason was back in the garden and saw a young woman hurry from the Crake cottage toward the service stairway.

"That woman was Miss Ricci in a chambermaid's apron and bonnet." His tone was now firm.

"Are you sure, Jason?" Pamela asked. "By that time, it was dark. The garden lanterns throw a weak light and only a short distance. Could you see her face?"

He wavered. "In that light her features weren't distinct. But I knew she served those cottages in the evening. And the person I saw had Miss Ricci's size and shape, and her way of walking. No maid is quite as beautiful."

Pamela turned to Harry. "Any questions?"

He shook his head. "Thank you, Jason. You may go. We'll speak to you later."

After he left, Harry said, "Jason's attitude toward Francesca appears suspect to me. He probably has made advances to her and she rebuffed him. Now he's punishing her. His description of her is vague. A clever killer could dress and act as a chambermaid. We need to know more about him to challenge his testimony in court."

"True," said Pamela. "Still, he might have recognized her. Perhaps Francesca hasn't told us the whole truth. She could have entered Crake's cottage later than she said and found him dead. Tomorrow, we shall have to confront her."

# CHAPTER 10

## Crucial Decision

*Wednesday, July 11*

After breakfast, Pamela and Harry returned to the town jail. Francesca's anxiety had worsened. Tears stained her cheeks, and her eyelids were heavy. She probably hadn't slept for fear of the arraignment looming before her in Ballston Spa.

Pamela offered her a pastry from the hotel's breakfast table. She sniffed. "I'm not hungry. This afternoon they're going to send me to prison. I'll be there forever."

"Perhaps for only a week or two, until we find Captain Crake's killer. We're prepared to defend you if you tell us the truth. The bellboy said you left the cottage later than you told us. Is that true?"

"No, he's mistaken or lying. He's angry because I don't like him. I was in my room. I didn't stab Captain Crake." Her eyes began to tear.

Pamela took her hand. "Trust us, Francesca. Mr. Miller and I shall leave now. But this afternoon, we'll go to the courthouse for your arraignment and speak on your behalf. We'll also ask Mr. Prescott what more could be done."

\* \* \*

Late in the morning, Pamela and Harry rented horses in the livery stable behind the hotel and rode to Ballston Spa, ten miles south of Saratoga Springs. They arrived in time for a short visit with Francesca. She was sullen and had little to say, though she appeared well treated.

The county seat was a charming village, bustling with summer visitors there for the mineral waters. Prescott's office had contacted Mr. Barnes, a local attorney with a good reputation. Pamela and Harry met him for lunch at the Whistling Kettle and discussed Francesca's situation. He seemed competent and genuinely concerned, so they engaged him to represent her before Judge Houghton that afternoon.

The arraignment took place informally in the judge's chambers in the courthouse. Mr. John Person, the prosecutor, briefly presented the state's case against Francesca, stressing her background in petty crime, her lack of an alibi, and her possession of Mrs. Crake's bracelet. The judge then called on Francesca. "Young lady, did you kill Mr. Crake?"

She rose to speak, bowed politely to the judge, and said clearly, "No, your honor." Barnes's coaching had almost entirely removed the Italian inflection from her speech.

Barnes then argued that the prosecutor's evidence implicating Miss Ricci in Crake's death was merely circumstantial, and no one witnessed the crime.

"My client insists that Mr. Crake gave her the bracelet."

"But Mrs. Crake says he didn't," retorted Houghton, then called on Pamela, "Mrs. Thompson, as the girl's guardian, what do you have to say on Miss Ricci's behalf? I understand that she has a criminal record."

Pamela acknowledged Francesca's truancy and her arrest at Macy's. "But, sir, she has never committed a violent act, and her behavior has improved since coming into my care. Her attendance at school and her grades are now excellent."

Judge Houghton appeared to reflect thoughtfully for a few moments, then ruled that the evidence justified holding Francesca for trial in the autumn. "Issues involving the bracelet will be discussed then."

That timetable pleased Pamela, at least as it lessened the danger of the trial becoming a circus. With the end of the tourist season, journalists would pay less attention. She also would have time for what might be a lengthy, complicated investigation.

However, the judge denied Francesca bail, claiming, "She might sneak back to New York City and disappear."

Pamela argued, "I'll be personally responsible for Francesca. She's not violent and threatens no one. It's cruel to put such a young person in jail with hardened criminals."

Her protest appeared to nudge the judge's conscience. He addressed Sheriff Worden, "I want Miss Ricci's detention to be consistent with her tender age and sex. House her apart from adult inmates, and allow Mrs. Thompson to provide her with books, clothing, and such additional care as she may need."

Outside the courtroom, Pamela visited briefly with Francesca, both of them sobbing. It was as distressing a good-bye as any Pamela could remember. At that moment, she felt helplessly responsible for this emotional shock to a young person in her charge. She also had grown fond of Francesca and hopeful for her prospects in life.

Her distress gave way to anger at the injustice of putting a young woman in prison on flimsy grounds, though still innocent in the eyes of the law, while Crake's killer walked free through the streets of Saratoga Springs.

Pamela took Francesca's manacled hands. "I'll not rest until I get you out of here." Then the sheriff led Francesca away. Pamela urged Mr. Barnes to look after Francesca while she investigated Crake's murder. Finding his killer was the surest way to free the girl.

From a nearby hotel, Pamela immediately telegraphed Prescott:

> MISS RICCI'S CASE COULD REQUIRE A
> COSTLY AND TIME-CONSUMING INVES-
> TIGATION. WOULD YOU COME HERE
> AND HELP US DECIDE WHAT TO DO?

Pamela and Harry returned to the Grand Union. He immediately began to investigate the bellboy Jason Dunn. How credible was his testimony concerning Francesca? What were his secrets? Meanwhile, Pamela waited anxiously for Prescott's reply.

It arrived that evening.

> I'LL LEAVE THE BERKSHIRES FROM
> LENOX TOMORROW FOR SARATOGA
> SPRINGS, ARRIVING IN THE
> AFTERNOON. RESERVE A ROOM FOR
> ME AT THE HOTEL. I'LL STUDY THE
> CASE AND DETERMINE WHETHER TO
> TAKE ON FRANCESCA'S DEFENSE.

She sighed. The terse message didn't indicate how he was leaning. She would have to wait and hope.

Concealed in the shadows, Harry observed Jason enter Mickey's Tavern on Washington Street, west of the D&H tracks. For a few minutes, Harry waited outside, recognizing many hotel workers. Then he went inside and sat at a small table with a view of Jason and two male companions drinking beer. One of the men produced a pair of dice, and they started playing for pennies.

Harry signaled a waiter and asked confidentially, "Who are the two men with Mr. Dunn?"

"The big German is Karl Metzger, a butcher at the hotel. The slim, handsome gambler in charge of the dice is Rob Shaw, a Britisher."

In less than an hour, Harry had gathered the impressions he needed. As he left, he reflected thoughtfully. Crake's bitter enemy Metzger had access to boning knives; Dunn had been close to the scene of Crake's murder; Shaw was bedding Crake's wife. What might they talk about, quietly, while they tossed the dice? The death of Captain Crake? Harry asked himself, "Could the three of them have been in it together?"

The next day, Pamela met Prescott at the station. As he climbed down from the train, he greeted her with a wan smile. Something wasn't right, but she sensed he didn't want to talk about it.

As they walked the short distance to the Grand Union Hotel, he studied the building and remarked, "It seemed huge when I was here a few years ago on legal business, but it has since grown even larger along Congress Street."

"From that visit, you might also be familiar with the county court in Ballston Spa. Miss Ricci is in the jail."

"Yes, I had legal business there. Fortunately for her, if I may say so, the old courthouse and jail were torn down five years ago. Still, even the new jail must be a dreadful place for a young woman. We'll visit her tomorrow and make sure she has decent accommodations."

That evening in Prescott's room, Pamela and Harry brought him up to date on the Crake case. He mostly listened and asked questions concerning Metzger's conflict with Crake, Shaw's romance with Crake's wife, and Dunn's obscure motivation. Part of Prescott's mind seemed elsewhere.

Pamela suspected that contentious issues with his separated wife, Gloria, were distracting him. When Harry left, Pamela was tempted to ask what had happened in Lenox. But by this time, Prescott looked so tired and distressed that she decided to wait until he was ready.

On Friday morning, while Harry followed Robert Shaw around Saratoga, Pamela and Prescott visited the county jail in Ballston Spa and found Francesca in a small interior cell with two rough-looking older women.

Prescott complained to the jailor, Mr. Wilbur Smith. "Sir, the judge gave explicit instructions to place Miss Ricci separate from adult inmates."

The jailor glowered. "It doesn't cost him anything. We have a tight budget."

"I'll pay the difference," said Prescott. He arranged to move Francesca to a private room with a window, barred, to be sure, where she could sing without disturbing anyone. Pamela also brought her fresh undergarments, a book of her favorite music, and toiletries.

Though their visit seemed to please her, she remained listless and sad. Prescott pressed her to speak about the "stolen" bracelet.

"Had you seen it before Captain Crake gave it to you?"

"Mrs. Crake wore it often during the day. When she dressed for dinner, she'd toss it aside and put on a fancier bracelet for the evening. She'd pull up her sleeve and wave her arm around so everyone could admire it."

He turned to Pamela. "Where is the 'stolen' bracelet now?"

"Here in the courthouse, probably in the sheriff's office. It was presented as evidence during Francesca's arraignment but not examined. I've looked at it and saw problems I'd like to point out to you."

"Let's talk to the sheriff."

* * *

That afternoon, Prescott and Pamela met Sheriff Worden in his office and asked to examine the bracelet. He had earlier said he was too busy, so they made this appointment.

With a sigh, he opened his safe. "The town police brought the bracelet here together with other evidence for the court." He laid it on a table. On the wide gold band was a lightly etched floral pattern. On the underside, opposite the jeweler's mark, was inscribed *RC*.

"I was stunned when I noticed the initials," remarked Pamela. "I also recognized the design and the jeweler's mark, Tiffany on Union Square. The bracelet looks like Ruth Colt's."

"The company probably made dozens of them," said Prescott dismissively.

Irritated, Pamela lightly rubbed the *RC* initials. "They must be Ruth Colt's."

"And, of course, Rachel Crake's initials as well," Prescott countered. "Still, an extraordinary coincidence."

This discussion confused the sheriff. Pamela gave him a brief summary of the Ruth Colt investigation. "There's a strong possibility that Crake killed her and possibly other young women."

She explained that Crake must have removed the bracelet from the murdered girl's wrist. Later, after a quarrel with his wife, Rachel, he gave her the bracelet in a false gesture of reconciliation. On July 6, still angry with his wife, he offered it to Miss Ricci.

The sheriff's lips parted in astonishment. He shook his head. "I see that the issue of the bracelet is complicated. The girl's story begins to look plausible. But, for the time being, I'll reserve judgment on Crake. It's hard to believe that one of our decorated heroes committed such crimes. Did you report your findings to the NYPD?"

"Ours was a private investigation," Prescott replied. "We reported confidentially to our client, who must remain nameless.

Had we found the victim's body with signs of homicide, we would have gone with our evidence to the police."

"Unfortunately," added Pamela, "the body is still missing."

When they returned to Saratoga Springs, Pamela proposed tea and sandwiches at the Phila Street Café. Prescott looked pale and drawn. He hadn't eaten since breakfast and probably hadn't slept well recently.

After they placed an order, she asked, "Is something the matter, Jeremiah?"

Her use of his Christian name seemed to startle him. Then he smiled. "You've read my mind, Pamela. Yes, I should bring you up to date." The waiter arrived with the food, interrupting him.

Prescott and Gloria's only child, nineteen-year-old Edward, who had just completed his second year at Williams College in Williamstown, was the chief bone of contention between his parents. Pamela was a discreet outside observer, but her heart went out to the young man.

When the waiter left, Prescott continued. "This summer, Edward is gardening in Lenox at Ventfort, the great Morgan cottage that the financier J. P. Morgan's sister built last year near my cabin. Edward wanted to work in fresh air with clean dirt, beautiful flowers, and the like. So I placed him at Ventfort and apprenticed him to Mr. Huss, a master gardener from Switzerland."

"I'm happy for Edward," said Pamela. "That garden is the finest in the Berkshires. Last year, however, he wanted to become a lawyer. Has he chosen a new direction in life and intends to become a master gardener like Huss?"

"It's too early to say, but that's what my wife, Gloria, fears. She hotly objects and accuses me of encouraging the young man to follow his fancy. He should become a gentleman lawyer like her father and earn lots of money and social prestige."

"Has she gone beyond complaining?"

"I'm afraid so. Through her banker friend George Fisher she has arranged an extended visit to Ventfort as guests of the Morgans."

At the mention of Fisher, Pamela must have unwittingly frowned.

Prescott remarked, "Yes, you are thinking of *the* Fisher, president of your late husband Jack's savings and loan bank on Union Square."

"Fisher's not one of my favorite people. He called me a thief, an accomplice in Jack's embezzlement of the bank's funds. How close is his relationship to Gloria?"

"They claim to be merely good friends, but they travel together. He's a widower; she's legally separated from me. I haven't heard of any scandal. Society appears to be showing tolerance."

"Nonetheless, their visit to the Morgans seems remarkable."

"You may not know that Fisher and Morgan are friends and play billiards together. I fear Gloria will try to put Edward back on the right track, as she sees it, and turn his summer and mine into a nightmare. She and Fisher will arrive shortly. Edward is already upset."

There was little that Pamela could do but sympathize with Prescott. He looked so dispirited. His best remedy was to distract himself in the Crake case and the fate of Francesca Ricci. His family problems could be put on hold.

That evening, Tom Winn lent Prescott a key, and he and Pamela visited Crake's cottage again. Still unoccupied, it would soon be emptied and thoroughly cleaned. They stood together silently in the middle of the parlor, Prescott studying the scene of the crime. Its emptiness was eerie. As Pamela's gaze fixed on the sofa, an overpowering sense of what had happened there made her light-headed.

"Are you all right?" he asked.

"Yes, let's take a closer look at this place."

Cleaned and pressed for the next veterans' reunion, Crake's uniform still hung in the armoire. His other belongings were packed neatly in drawers and cabinets. A large, mostly empty trunk stood in a closet.

"What's that?" A fancy framed document above the mantel had caught Prescott's eye.

"It's the certificate accompanying his Medal of Honor," Pamela replied. "I saw it in the War Room of his Fifth Avenue mansion. Congress honored him for conspicuous bravery near Savannah, Georgia, in December 1864. And here is the medal itself." She opened the green velvet–covered case resting on the mantel.

Prescott studied the medal and shook his head. "Even after thirty years and on vacation, the old soldier carried with him this memento of the greatest moment of his life."

As they left the cottage, Pamela asked Prescott, "What's your thinking on the case thus far?" She was growing anxious, but she understood his situation and prodded him reluctantly.

"The bracelet now seems less damaging to Francesca's case than I thought. Crake might indeed have given it to her. Whether a jury would agree is another matter. Because she's poor and foreign and has a petty criminal record, they might doubt her story. I will have to find a more plausible suspect than her. The hotel and the police won't help and most likely will get in the way. The search could be complicated, drawn out, and expensive."

"You aren't going to give up now, are you?"

Her question appeared to sting. "Not yet, Pamela. With help from you and Harry, I'll devote the weekend to observing the three known suspects—Metzger, Dunn, and Shaw; there could be more. Then I'll decide."

She couldn't hide her disappointment.

He noticed. "I'm sorry, Pamela. My resources are limited.

Requests for pro bono work pour into my office almost daily. I must choose those I can handle best."

On Saturday morning, Prescott toured the hotel's basement to see Karl Metzger cutting meat and to examine his knives. During the rest of the day and on Sunday, he watched Jason Dunn running errands and spoke to him on the hotel porch. He also talked to Tom Winn, to other hotel employees and guests, and to the police for a sense of the obstruction that a private investigation could expect. In the evening, he observed Robert Shaw, gambling at Canfield's Casino.

By Sunday evening, Prescott seemed to have gathered enough impressions and information, and he called Pamela and Harry to his room. His expression remained inscrutable while he summarized the facts of the case and listed the pros and cons of a possible investigation.

Meanwhile, Pamela's anxiety had grown unbearable. If he said no to this case, what would she do? Take leave from the firm and carry on the investigation alone? Impossible. She lacked the money and the skill. Her heart sank. She would have to abandon Francesca to an uncertain fate.

When he finished speaking, he leaned back, stroking his chin. Through long minutes of suspense, his mind seemed to work toward a conclusion. Then his poker face began to relax into an enthusiastic smile.

"This case has moral weight and intrigues me," he said. "I'm impressed by Harry's argument that Crake's killer is expert in the use of a knife. Miss Ricci is not. Therefore, she appears wrongly charged with murder. The local police are distracted and will not help her or us. There are many suspects who could and would have killed Crake. So, I'll commit the resources of my firm to solving Crake's murder and freeing Miss Ricci."

Pamela breathed a deep sigh of relief. "How shall we proceed?" she managed to ask.

"You will remain in Saratoga Springs and search among the suspects for Crake's killer. Harry will help you here and in New York City, where I also have other work for him."

"And will you take part in this investigation?"

"I see myself exploring Crake's military service. In four years of war, Crake must have had hundreds of opportunities to make deadly enemies. Did he assault women in the South during the war, as he did recently in New York City? If so, he may have left behind angry men and women, still eager to settle scores with him if they could. Tomorrow morning I'll return to New York City and speak to Clarence Buel, an acquaintance who knows more about the war than any man alive. He's surely acquainted with Crake, a decorated hero. I hope Buel will point me to the right path."

After Harry retired to his room, Prescott asked Pamela to join him for a walk in the hotel garden. The air was pleasantly warm and fresh. From the garden fountain came the soothing sound of splashing water. They spoke about friends and acquaintances he had just met in the Berkshires.

She turned the conversation to what was pressing on her mind. "At lunch on Friday, you mentioned that Gloria and her banker, George Fisher, would be together at Ventfort. How are they getting along?"

"They appear to suit each other. Both hope to shine in high society. He lacks manners, but he's rich. She has manners but lacks money. According to gossip, they are discussing marriage."

"How shall they overcome the legal obstacle?"

"She must divorce me, most likely in Connecticut. She established a legal residence there three years ago, obviously to meet the law's requirement. She'll probably charge me with 'intolerable cruelty,' a common legal device. I won't contest the divorce—our marriage ended essentially years ago. And I shall ignore her accusations. Everyone knows they are legal fictions. My lawyer will represent me before the judge. It could be done soon."

They had come to a poorly lighted part of the garden and were alone. "Then would you be free?"

"Yes, finally." He took her hand. She drew near to him. For a long moment, they gazed at each other in the dark. Then they walked arm in arm back to the hotel.

# CHAPTER 11

## *Grieving Widow*

*Monday, July 16*

In the morning, Pamela went with Prescott to the railroad station. As she waved good-bye, she felt a catch in her throat. He would be away only a few days, but she would miss him. When the train rolled out of sight, she stared into the distance, reflecting on last night's conversation in the garden. They had emotionally come another step closer together, but marriage remained far removed. Something could come up to prevent it. With a shake of her head, she turned her mind to today's task: to determine what role, if any, Rachel Crake played in her husband's death.

At midmorning, as Pamela was walking in the hotel garden, Rachel emerged from the cottage in a simple black silk gown and bonnet but without a veil. Her face was pale and drawn. Accompanied by Birgitta, she walked to the nearby Bethesda Episcopal Church.

Pamela followed them into the church, where a small congregation had gathered for Morning Prayer. The two women settled down apart from the others and didn't appear to attend to the service. Usually outgoing and lively, Rachel sat quietly, perhaps calculating the next step in her gradual return to normal social life. Her visit to the church seemed meant to tell the world that her period of deep mourning was over. That was sufficient respect for the man who had paid her bills but gave her little genuine affection.

After leaving the church, the two women walked in the hotel garden and heard a small orchestra playing popular tunes. Pamela sat nearby with her sketchbook and roughly drew Rachel's features. The sketch would be finished later. She had a hunch it could prove useful.

As Rachel came out of seclusion, the need to investigate her grew more urgent. A major suspect, she might leave Saratoga Springs with her secrets and disappear forever. To keep track of her, Pamela sought help from her friend Helen Fisk. As a patron of St. Barnabas Mission, she would be sympathetic to Francesca Ricci and willing to help clear her name.

Every summer, Helen rented one of the cottages at the Grand Union Hotel and entertained lavishly. In her leisure hours she studied the remarkable variety of people on Broadway, and on the hotel's spacious porches and at its brilliant balls. A network of gossips kept her informed of the gambling dens, horse races, and regattas. In Saratoga Springs she knew everybody worth knowing, including the Crakes. She disliked both of them but found them intriguing.

That afternoon, Pamela went to the Congress Spring to meet Helen. Young black waiters scurried about bringing trays of glasses to customers in summer dress. Helen arrived with her dog, a French poodle called Yvette. Serious conversation wasn't possible in this bustling, noisy setting. Pamela and Helen drank their water, walked out into the park, and sat on a lonely shaded bench overlooking a pond. Yvette sat at Helen's feet, observing a duck swimming among pink water lilies.

Pamela described Francesca's situation and added, "To free her, we must find Captain Crake's killer."

"What can I do, my dear Pamela?"

"As a start, could you tell me about Rachel Crake? I need to know her better."

"Gladly," Helen replied, her eyes brightening at the opportunity. "She was born, in fact, a Crake, the captain's distant niece. Raised in genteel poverty, she was educated in a young women's finishing school. Since her divorced parents largely ignored her, she settled down in a luxurious New York City brothel."

Pamela remarked, "I have learned that Rachel and the captain met there, married shortly afterward in a private ceremony, and lived together for four years."

"That's correct. But she tired of Crake, a much older man, crippled by arthritis and absorbed in business. She kept up an appearance of marital fidelity until she met Robert Shaw and then gradually put aside the pretense."

"What can you tell me about Shaw?"

"There's a whiff of scandal on him. The youngest son of a prominent Scottish family, he enlisted in the British army and took part in colonial wars in South Africa. His gambling and sexual adventures got him into trouble, and he apparently killed a man. He fled to New York, where he swindled money from wealthy women with promises of marriage. The New York police charged him with fraud, but the women refused to testify. Most recently, he worked for the police as an informant in brothels and gambling dens."

"Had the Saratoga police known his story of seduction and fraud," Pamela remarked, "they might have taken a closer look at him before hastily arresting my Francesca."

Pamela idly tossed a crumb from her pocket to a waiting sparrow. In seconds a flock of sparrows had gathered at her feet. Suddenly alert, Yvette stared at the birds for a few moments, then ignored them. Pamela emptied the rest of the crumbs from her pocket and met Helen's eye.

"If Rachel wanted to rid herself of her husband, she found

the right accomplice in Robert Shaw. Did she have a sufficient motive for the captain's murder?"

"That depends," Helen replied. "If Rachel was a beneficiary of his will or life insurance, she and Shaw might have conspired to kill him for the money."

"That's hardly a novel idea," Pamela remarked.

Helen smiled wryly. "I'll ask a clever lawyer friend in New York for Crake's beneficiary. Meanwhile, approach Rachel with caution. Her flighty appearance masks a cunning intelligence and a ruthless pursuit of money and prominence. I suggest starting with her servant, a Swedish woman."

"I've heard of her, Birgitta Mattsson. Why would she be helpful?"

"Since Crake's death, Rachel pays her poorly and treats her dismissively. When she thinks no one is watching, she looks unhappy. But she doesn't dare betray her mistress or she would lose her livelihood, poor as it is. You might find a way to bribe her, or she might unwittingly give you clues to Rachel's possible role in her husband's death."

"Miss Mattsson is understandably skittish. I'll find a discreet way to approach her," Pamela said.

"Meanwhile, I suggest that this evening we visit Canfield's Casino, Rachel's favorite haunt in Saratoga. She was there, together with Shaw, on the night of the captain's murder. Could you bring along a male escort? Canfield requires female guests to have one."

"Will Mr. Miller be satisfactory?"

"Yes, he will do, but you must dress him up. Canfield measures guests by their money, their clothes, and their manners, in that order. Character doesn't matter. Meet me in the hotel foyer at nine." She rose from the bench and set off, Yvette at her heel.

Pamela and Harry were waiting in the foyer five minutes early. He looked distinguished in a gentleman's formal evening costume. His chin was up, his back was straight, his expression was confident. Gone was the hangdog look, the disguise he sometimes put on when he didn't want to be noticed. Before leaving New York, she had persuaded him to bring the costume along.

"I'll have to rent it," he had complained.

"Charge it to Prescott's account, Harry. You may need it to mingle in Saratoga society."

She walked across the foyer and back, and stood in front of a mirror. "Harry, how do I look?" She was wearing a blue silk evening gown to match the color of her eyes. Her black hair was in a chignon.

He shot her a shy, brotherly smile. "You look great."

In a few minutes, Helen Fisk arrived, gave an approving glance to both of them, and called for a cab, though the casino was only a leisurely five-minute walk away.

In the casino's entrance hall, they entered their names into a register lying open on a high desk while a burly clerk scrutinized them. Harry paid a membership fee and explained that the two women were his guests.

Pamela glanced to the right to catch a glimpse of the barroom, reserved for men. A blue haze of cigar smoke drifted from the room together with bursts of raucous male laughter. A waiter led her and her companions into the reading room on the left, where women could be served.

It was elegantly furnished with highly polished mahogany tables, upholstered chairs and sofas, a giant Oriental rug, and crystal chandeliers. Fine lace curtains covered the windows. The most recent New York and local newspapers hung on a rack near long shelves of books. Pamela and Helen sat at a table and ordered tea. Miller sauntered into the barroom and a few minutes later returned with a glass of whiskey.

He toasted his companions, took a sip, and smacked his lips. "The finest whiskey I've ever tasted. And I paid a small fortune for it."

"The proprietor, Mr. Richard Canfield, will be pleased," Helen remarked. "He bought the casino late last year and has refurnished it at great expense. He also hired Monsieur Jean Columbin, a renowned French chef, to offer a menu that some say is superior to Delmonico's in New York. You won't find a more elegant casino anywhere in the country."

"How does Canfield pay for it?" asked Pamela.

"He extracts what he needs, and more, from the casino's patrons. Every summer, many of the wealthiest men in the country enjoy its elegant ambiance and outstanding amenities. Canfield extends easy credit to them and pays out their winnings in cash. In the end, the house wins, of course, but its guests leave pleased and return again and again. It's said that Canfield will gain back his purchase money in two months."

Their waiter arrived with the tea and a tray of French pastries. Pamela puzzled over his strong accent. In French she asked for a Savarin. With a smile, he said in French, "You speak my language well, madame." With a flourish, he put the pastry on her plate.

Helen noticed the exchange and remarked, "On a recent trip to France, Canfield hired fifty professional waiters and a master waiter for this place. By the way, he also collects art. His taste is remarkably good for a self-taught man."

In the next moment, Helen gave a little gasp. Rachel Crake entered the room in a simple black silk gown. A brilliant diamond-studded broach hung on a gold chain around her neck. Her companion was a clean-shaven, slender man in a formal black suit. All heads turned toward the couple. "Rachel and her friend, Robert Shaw," whispered Helen.

This was Pamela's first opportunity to study Robert Shaw in the flesh. His features were delicate, his lips sensual, his complexion clear and pale, his hair the color of wheat. A few years older than Rachel, he looked much more presentable than her murdered husband.

Pamela took out her sketchbook and began committing Shaw's features to paper as well as to her memory. She would need a few more sittings, especially for his eyes. They were dark and hooded, concealing his thoughts and feelings.

The newcomers approached a table where three fashionably dressed women sat. Shaw hurried off toward the gambling parlor.

Harry leaned toward Pamela. "I'll keep an eye on him while I play a few games to pay for this evening's expenses. I've been shadowing him for a week. I hope he doesn't recognize me."

The women at Rachel's table welcomed her with a mixture of familiarity and solicitude. They ordered punch and a deck of cards, and were soon playing poker for pennies. Rachel appeared subdued, though hardly crushed or despondent.

"Do you know her companions?" Pamela asked Helen.

"Regular summer visitors from New York City." Helen lowered her voice. "In fact, they're prostitutes of the better sort, here on vacation but willing to practice their profession slyly on the side."

"Really? Here?"

"Only at certain luxurious private residences in the town. Certainly not at all in the casino, nor in the main hotels. At the Grand Union, Tom Winn would watch them like a hawk. And Canfield doesn't allow even a hint of sexual impropriety—bad for the casino's reputation. He argues that gambling and playing on the stock market are honorable professions, but prostitution is not."

Eventually, Rachel and her companions seemed to tire of playing for pennies and beckoned the waiter. He hurried up to them, heard their request, then led them from the room.

Helen explained, "He's taking them to an intimate upstairs parlor where they'll buy drinks at inflated prices and play for high stakes for a couple of hours."

"It's said, Helen, that the company a person keeps reveals her character. What have we just learned about Rachel Crake?"

"She hasn't burned her bridges. Years ago, in that New York brothel, Crake won her with an offer of money and social position she couldn't refuse. Nonetheless, she didn't fully trust him. So, she remained friends with these women, her path back to the brothel."

"I wonder," Pamela began, "about her alibi for the night of Crake's murder. She said that she was here playing cards with them, and they vouched for her. Her name and Shaw's are in the guest book together with theirs. Could she have slipped out with their connivance?"

"I think you need to speak to Mr. Canfield," replied Helen. "He would know better than I. Tonight he's too busy and distracted. Make an appointment to see him in the morning."

Harry followed Shaw to a roulette wheel and watched him play. His mental concentration was intense, almost inhuman. Within minutes, he won a few hundred dollars; then he lost it all in a turn of the wheel. His expression scarcely changed. He studied the wheel. If it had even a slight tilt, it might favor certain numbers. Then he moved more money into play.

Harry sat down at an adjacent poker game and won a few dollars. As he left the game, he noticed a familiar face at a table: Mr. Wood, the gentleman whom he and Pamela had dined with on the day of their arrival.

"May I join you?" Harry asked.

The man brightened. "Of course, this drink is on me." He beckoned a waiter. "Two whiskeys, please."

Harry could see that this wasn't Mr. Wood's first drink and soon got him talking about Shaw. "He comes every night," said Wood.

"Including Saturday, the seventh?" Harry asked.

"Yes, of course, I wasn't watching him every minute. You can imagine that the casino was packed with people coming and going."

So, Harry wondered, could Shaw have slipped out of the casino and stabbed Crake? Or, might he have hired someone else to do it?

Harry finished his drink, thanked Mr. Wood, and returned to the poker table. With sidelong glances he drew a picture of Shaw in his mind. Well mannered, his movements quick, his speech cultivated, he appeared the model of a gentleman gambler.

After winning enough to pay for the evening, Harry rejoined Helen and Pamela in the reading room.

He announced, "Mr. Wood just told me that Shaw was here at the gaming tables on the night of July seventh, as Rachel alleged to the police. However, the casino was crowded and busy. Could she have covered for him while he slipped away for an hour and killed her husband?"

Pamela replied, "We may find out when we meet Mr. Canfield tomorrow morning. I've made an appointment. At first he said he was too busy and had already told the police all that he knew. I pointed out that the police investigation had been hasty and was threatening a young woman's life. Our investigation might unearth critical information that the police overlooked. Finally, he said, 'Come to the casino for breakfast at eight and we'll talk.' "

"You must have charmed him," Harry remarked. "Canfield's reluctance is understandable. What would happen to his reputation if we proved that Rachel and Shaw used the casino as cover for their murder of Crake? Reformers already call the casino a den of iniquity. They would demand that the police shutter the place."

"You're right. I'll lower my expectations for tomorrow."

# CHAPTER 12

# The Investigation Widens

*Tuesday, July 17*

The next morning at eight o'clock, Canfield led his visitors to an upstairs apartment for a conversation over breakfast. A table was tastefully set with fine china, silverware, and fresh-cut flowers. He had just come from his barber and was wearing a light silk maroon morning robe. A waiter appeared. Canfield ordered a fruit crepe with whipped cream. Pamela and Harry asked only for coffee and toast.

Harry brought the conversation around to Crake's murder on the evening of July 7.

Canfield grimaced at the allusion to violence. "What do you need to know?"

Pamela asked about Rachel's movements on July 7. "When she and her companions were in the private room upstairs, was a casino waiter present?"

"Not every minute," Canfield replied. "He usually anticipated their requests for poker chips or drinks and so forth, then left them in peace. If they needed anything, they could ring a bell to call him."

"Can a casino employee verify Rachel's story that she was in the casino until midnight?"

Canfield sprinkled sugar on his crepe. "The police asked that question. I passed it on to my employees. None of them saw her leave the casino until shortly before closing at midnight." A sardonic smile flashed on his face. "At any time in the evening, of course, she could have lowered herself on a rope from an upstairs window and later climbed back up. We might not have noticed."

Harry brushed the taunt aside with a slight wave of his hand. "Do you know if Robert Shaw was away from the casino for an hour or two on that night?"

"We are as vigilant as possible without annoying the patrons. Shaw could have stepped outside for an interval and come back. The doorman might have been briefly distracted and didn't notice him. On Saturday nights the casino is very busy."

On the way back to the hotel, Pamela turned to Harry. "Canfield and his staff haven't given Shaw a convincing alibi. On a busy Saturday night, he could have slipped away from the casino without being noticed. Unfortunately, the police didn't challenge him. They had already fixed the blame on Francesca."

While Harry went off to investigate Shaw, Pamela set out to make the acquaintance of Rachel Crake's Swedish maid, Birgitta Mattsson. At midmorning, she observed her enter Congress Park, carrying a small basket. Pamela followed her on a winding, shaded path to an ornamental pool, circled by benches. In the center was a lovely decorative fountain. The maid chose a bench under a tall elm tree, set the basket beside her, closed her eyes, and breathed an audible sigh of relief.

After a few minutes listening to a concert of bird songs and trickling water, Birgitta opened her eyes, uncovered the basket, and pulled out a newspaper, a bottle wrapped in a cloth, a cup, and a sweet pastry. Pamela walked past the maid, engaged her with a casual smile, and got a smile in return. She was fair haired, blue eyed, and comely.

Pamela sat on a bench next to the maid's, smiled again, and said, "I couldn't help but notice your newspaper—it's printed in a foreign language."

"It's Swedish," said Birgitta, "and comes from New York. It keeps me in touch with the old country." She hesitated to say more. Her shoulders sagged a little.

Pamela encouraged her with a sympathetic expression. "I know how hard it is to be lonely in a foreign country. Where do you come from in Sweden?"

"Stockholm, a beautiful city, the country's capital."

Pamela urged the maid on with questions. An educated woman, she knew English before she came to this country four years ago.

"They say Captain Crake used to sing your praises. Your massages made him feel well at least for a while. How did you learn to do it?"

"My father was a medical doctor in Stockholm and used massage in his practice. Some of his female patients preferred that a woman massage them, so he taught me the technique and put me to work. When he died, I wanted to continue. I was good at it, if I may say so. But I wanted to be paid and earn a decent living. That didn't seem possible in Sweden. So I moved to New York and began to massage Captain Crake—and his wife as well."

Pamela gestured to the basket. "I'm sorry to keep you from your picnic. I'll be on my way."

"Please stay. I brought along an extra cup. Would you share the coffee and the pastry with me?"

"Delighted! I enjoy picnics in the park."

They introduced each other, laid out a red-and-white-checkered cloth between them on the bench, and poured the coffee. Conversation was easy. The maid seemed starved for congenial company.

Eventually, Pamela ventured to ask, "Since the captain's death, how has it been to serve his wife?"

"Difficult," the maid replied. "I feel trapped. Since Captain Crake died, his wife and Mr. Shaw watch me closely, as if I'm likely to steal clothes, or jewelry, or the silverware and try to sell them in the village. She has also cut my wages, since I no longer nurse the captain. I've offered to resign, but she says she needs me for a while until she recovers from her husband's death. She insists she's too stressed to break in a new maid. If I were to leave, she wouldn't give me a satisfactory recommendation and would spread malicious gossip about me. I'd be unable to find a suitable position, especially with so many men and women out of work." Her lips began to quiver.

Pamela nodded sympathetically and shifted her inquiry in a less emotional direction. "Rachel seems scarcely touched by her husband's death. Was she really his wife?"

"Not at first." The maid glanced over her shoulder and lowered her voice. "She was his little tart. Then they made it legal." The maid appeared to grow nervous and took a drink of her coffee.

"Don't fret," counseled Pamela. "Everyone knows her. She's called 'the merry widow.' Still, you have to be careful. If you ever wanted to change jobs, I might be able to help you."

"And what do you do for a living?" asked the maid, showing reasonable curiosity.

"I work for a lawyer who helps people find answers to difficult questions."

"Can you give me an example?" Birgitta cocked her head in amused skepticism.

"Right now I'm helping Mr. Tom Winn at the Grand Union Hotel figure out who killed Captain Crake. Was it the chambermaid, Francesca Ricci, or someone else?"

Birgitta frowned. "Everyone thinks she's guilty. Did the police make a mistake?"

"She's not been tried yet, so we don't know. Others could have done it."

"Really? Do you suspect Rachel Crake?"

"No, she has a strong alibi. But I wonder about her friend Robert Shaw."

Birgitta fell silent. "I think we should drop the subject for now, lest I get into serious trouble. I'll think on these matters. For the time being, we shouldn't be seen together."

Pamela detected a frisson of fear in her companion's voice.

Early in the afternoon, Pamela and Harry met Tom Winn in his office to arrange for their private investigation of certain hotel staff and a few guests.

"I'm a cautious man," Winn said. "You'll have to persuade me that it's a sound idea. The hotel management insists above all else that I safeguard the hotel's reputation and ensure a restful stay for our guests. What have you learned thus far?"

Harry described the affair between Rachel and Shaw, and added, "It's common knowledge in the hotel. Witnesses saw Crake threatening Shaw in Mitchell's gambling den. He might have decided to kill Crake to protect himself. The casino hasn't given him a sufficient alibi. We've checked."

"And I should point out," said Pamela, "that Karl Metzger, the German butcher, also hated Crake. We need to check his alibi. Moreover, we haven't precisely identified or found the murder weapon. It could be a dagger rather than the butcher's boning knife. Finally, I'll mention again that Francesca has neither the skill nor the temperament to have inflicted Crake's wound."

"Granted," said Harry, "we're far from accusing anyone, and it isn't yet time to go to the police. Still, a killer might still be at large, possibly in the hotel."

Winn frowned. "I admit to reservations concerning Miss Ricci's guilt. There probably should be a wider investigation."

Harry asked, "Then wouldn't it be better that private professionals do it? The police would be much more disruptive."

"You're right," Winn admitted. "Go ahead—discreetly."

Pamela started out to resolve the issue of the murder weapon. If it was a boning knife, how could Crake's killer have gotten hold of one? Clearly marked as hotel property, they were expensive and nearly new. When not in use, they were locked away in the meat cutters' room in the basement. It wasn't easy to steal one. A thief's most convenient access to the room was through the laundry nearby.

Late in the afternoon, Pamela went down to the laundry to test the attitude there toward Crake. She spoke to an older woman who appeared to be in charge and learned that one of the new laundresses, Erika Metzger, openly expressed hostility to Crake. In an unguarded moment she had said, "May his soul rot in hell!"

Pamela wasn't surprised. Back in February, Pamela had spoken to Erika and her husband, Karl, and was aware of their bitter feelings toward Crake. Now she wondered if the Metzgers could have conspired against him. Could their friend Jason the bellboy also be involved?

Late that evening, while walking in the hotel garden, Pamela shared her impressions of the Metzger family with Harry. She asked, "Was the old hostility between Karl Metzger and Crake still strong at the time of his death?"

"Apparently it was," Harry replied. "Earlier this evening in Mickey's, the hotel butchers told me about a recent confrontation. On the morning of the day he died, Crake was touring the hotel basement and, unawares, approached Metzger cutting meat. For a moment it looked like the German might lunge at

Crake. Afterward, Crake denounced Metzger to the food manager as a radical troublemaker and demanded that the hotel fire him. The management is still discussing the matter with Mr. Wooley."

Pamela recalled her conversation with Metzger, a German immigrant, back in February. His bitterness toward Crake was palpable. He had crushed the meat cutters' strike at his Fourteenth Street plants and forced Metzger out of the business.

"I sympathize with Metzger," Pamela said. "But we must consider him a suspect. He had a powerful motive for revenge and the boning knife to carry it out." She reflected for a moment. "I have two questions for the Metzgers. First, do they have solid alibis for the evening of Crake's murder? And second, if they did kill Crake, why did they shift the blame onto Francesca Ricci?"

Harry agreed. "Let's question them separately and then compare notes."

*Wednesday, July 18*

Late in the morning, Pamela found Erika Metzger at lunch, sad-eyed and alone at one end of a long table. Black women sat at the opposite end. In the middle, Italian women formed a cluster speaking their language, while a few local white women sat together, chatting in English. Metzger was the only German and spoke halting English. She understood the language well enough.

Pamela sat next to her but not too close, leaned toward her, and asked softly in rusty German, *"Guten Tag, Frau Metzger. Darf ich mit Ihnen sprechen?"* ("Good day. May I speak with you?")

Metzger looked up, startled, then pleased. *"Das würde mich sehr erfreuen, Frau Thompson. Es ist mir peinlich dass niemand hier spricht Deutsch."* ("That would please me very much. It pains me that nobody speaks German here.")

Continuing in mixed German and English, they renewed their acquaintance. Erika complained that Crake's conflict with her husband left the family destitute and homeless. Her eyes began to tear. "Karl feels humiliated. All his life he has worked hard, succeeded in whatever job he has taken, and earned the respect of his peers. He's now moody and discouraged.

"When I try to cheer him up, he says, 'I'm now an old man with a bad reputation. Who would hire me?' "

"How does he feel toward Captain Crake?" asked Pamela.

"He's very angry." Erika hurried to add, "But he didn't kill him. The Italian girl did it."

Pamela expressed surprise. "Why should she?"

"He caught her stealing. Her people are thieves and have no morals. They stole my husband's job. We shouldn't let them into the country." She was growing upset and distrustful. "I have nothing more to say about Mr. Crake and, anyway, I don't have time to talk."

"Mrs. Metzger," Pamela spoke gently, "I'm gathering information for Mr. Winn, the hotel's detective. I don't work for the police. Just tell me what your family was doing the evening of July seventh."

The woman hesitated, chewing on her lower lip. "After work, we ate supper together in our room as usual—soup, bread, and fruit. Afterward, I went to St. Peter's Church hall and played cards. My husband went to his favorite saloon to drink beer with other Germans. The next morning, we heard about Mr. Crake. Good riddance. They'll probably hang the girl. They should give her a medal instead."

Early in the evening, Harry found Karl Metzger at Mickey's Tavern, sitting with the bellboy Jason Dunn and a couple of butchers. They were laughing and joking while they scraped pennies from the table. Robert Shaw was also there, picking up a pair of dice. It looked like the end of a friendly game of chance.

In a few minutes Metzger was sitting alone, staring into an empty beer glass. Family groups occupied the other tables.

"Mind if I join you?" Harry took care not to sound too friendly. He ordered a pitcher of beer. When it arrived, he offered some to Metzger.

He shrugged, then managed a thin smile and extended his glass. "Thanks. Warm weather builds up a man's thirst." He spoke English with a heavy German accent.

The beer opened a conversation. Harry's own troubled past, including years of wrongful imprisonment, prepared him to empathize with Metzger. He soon had the man telling his story. When it came to his union's conflict with Crake, the German's eyes narrowed, his jaw grew rigid. "Crake was Satan's apprentice." He clenched his glass. "The world's a better place with him dead. But that won't improve my lot. He ruined my reputation."

"Where were you on the night he was killed?"

"Why do you want to know?" In an instant, Metzger's mood turned ugly.

"Tom Winn, the hotel detective, is gathering information from men and women working here. There are hundreds of them, many more than he could handle alone. I'm helping him."

"Well, you can tell Mr. Winn to mind his own business. But if he must know, I was here till ten, then at home." He got up to leave. "Thanks again for the beer."

Late that evening, Pamela met Harry in the hotel parlor and exchanged impressions of the Metzger family, strengthening their belief that the family had the motive and the means to kill

Crake on July 7. Their alibis weren't perfect. For much of the evening they were alone together.

Harry seemed dissatisfied. "If Karl Metzger were to kill Crake, would he call attention to himself by using his own boning knife?"

Pamela replied, "A reasonable, calculating butcher, or his wife, would probably use a hammer or a club instead. Still, Karl Metzger could have acted under the influence of his anger and used the tool of the trade from which Crake had banished him."

Harry looked skeptical. "Good guess, Pamela."

# CHAPTER 13

## *The Forager*

*New York City*
*Monday, July 16*

While Pamela and Harry were investigating potential suspects in Saratoga Springs, Prescott had returned to his office. He would examine the murdered man's military experience to find out if Crake had shown a dark side of his character under the cover of war. Perhaps he betrayed a comrade, provoking him to revenge. The man who might know, Clarence Clough Buel, worked just a few blocks away in an office of the *Century Magazine* on Union Square. Prescott arranged a meeting with him for the next day.

Buel had produced the enormously popular *Battles and Leaders of the Civil War,* some 230 articles by veterans from general to private, Union and Confederate. While preparing the project, he had approached Prescott for a story from his four years in the Union army. But memories of the carnage still haunted Prescott and he turned down the invitation. Nonetheless, his interest in the project continued from a distance.

Buel would be familiar with a soldier as well-known as Crake, and he might have picked up scandal about him that couldn't be used in the *Battles and Leaders,* or shared for public consumption. Since Crake's death, Buel might feel free to speak to Prescott privately or at least direct him to someone who would.

Over lunch at the University Athletic Club, Prescott described to Buel his investigation into Crake's death. "I believe that the resolution of the case may lie in Jed Crake's secret life. Do you know if anything he did during the war would motivate someone to murder him?"

Buel reflected for a moment. "It's well-known that he excelled in killing the enemy and destroying their resources for waging war. Countless rebels would have loved to kill him in battle. But with the return of peace, they no longer hated or feared him, or had a personal reason for revenge. There's nothing in his public record but praise. His superiors singled him out for promotion and a Medal of Honor. You appear to be looking for hidden criminal or dishonorable acts that would move someone to private vengeance."

Prescott nodded and took a bite of veal.

Buel continued, "Crake was never indicted. However, I strongly suspect him of at least two serious crimes. His victims have not received justice." The enormity of the crimes caused Buel's voice to catch.

Prescott put down his knife and fork, and cocked his ear.

"In December of 1864, Captain Crake led a small foraging detachment of the Ninth Pennsylvania Volunteer Cavalry to the prosperous Crawford plantation some thirty miles south of Savannah. Such expeditions were typical of General Sherman's march through Georgia. His army lived off the land. The Crawford plantation was a prime target. Its wealthy owner, Mr. Horace Crawford, an executive of the Savannah Shipping Company, was a prominent supporter of the rebel cause. Crake's men took whatever provisions the army needed, slaughtered the remaining livestock, destroyed crops, and burned the barns and other outbuildings.

"Meanwhile, Captain Crake, Sergeant Samuel Tower, and Private Higgins ransacked the main house of its valuable silverware and jewelry. Crake believed that a treasure in gold and silver was also hidden there. He conspired with Tower and the private to divide the entire loot among themselves—he taking the largest portion."

"He's already violating military law," Prescott remarked. "The plunder belonged to the army."

"Correct," Buel agreed, then continued. "To force Mr. Crawford to reveal the treasure's location, Crake threatened to rape his wife and daughter. Crawford then led Crake and the private to the basement, where he drew a pair of hidden pistols and shot the private dead. His second pistol misfired. Crake ran him through with his saber. Enraged now, he rushed upstairs and beat and raped Crawford's wife and daughter, and shot his young son. Then he and Tower set fire to the house and left with the valuables they had found. But the main treasure was, in fact, safely hidden in a Savannah bank."

"Why didn't the army court-martial Crake for the attempted theft and the rape of the two women?"

"Samuel Tower was the only military witness and he remained silent, perhaps because he was implicated in the crime. I can only conjecture that the Crawford women didn't complain because they believed that the rapes would shame them. They also didn't trust the Union army to give them justice."

"How did you find this out?"

"Many years later, Tower learned of my *Battles and Leaders* project and asked to be included. His cryptic reference to Crake and foraging in Georgia intrigued me. I asked him for a ten-page article for consideration. A few months later, he sent me a detailed manuscript of the Crawford incident and a similar atrocity involving Crake in Columbia, South Carolina.

"Unfortunately, his comments on Crake couldn't be verified and would have attracted a lawsuit for slander. Tower also demanded too much money for the manuscript and insisted on anonymity. I returned the manuscript but kept a copy."

Buel showed Prescott a recent letter from Tower, now living in the Pennsylvania Soldiers and Sailors Home in Erie, still accusing Crake of rape.

"I didn't reply. He's a crank and shouldn't be encouraged. Since then, the Crawford incident has bubbled up in my mind. From time to time I've studied the Ninth Pennsylvania Cavalry, particularly its foraging in the Savannah area, as well as its notorious behavior in South Carolina. I've also glanced at the Crawfords. Mrs. Crawford died shortly after the incident, but her daughter, Edith, and son, James, recovered and then prospered in commerce after the war. Several years ago, they moved to New York. I asked James Crawford for an interview, but he declined. Still, through these inquiries, Tower's tale gained credibility in my mind."

When Buel finished, Prescott remained silent for a long moment, shaken too much to speak. Crake's raw violence had appalled him. He wasn't entirely surprised. Crake had shown similar brutality toward Ruth Colt. But Prescott's attempt to sort out rationally what he had heard soon failed. A riot of vile images stirred in his imagination, calling up some of his old demons from the war. In the warm and stuffy dining room he began to feel faint, then dizzy and nauseous.

Buel immediately recognized the symptoms. "We'll take a walk, Prescott, and clear your head." He helped him up from the table and led him to the club's inner courtyard.

Exercise, a change of scenery, and Buel's compassionate understanding of a soldier's malady helped Prescott to recover quickly. He thanked Buel, then asked him, "Since Crake is now dead, would you lend me Tower's manuscript. It may be relevant to my client's case." He explained Francesca Ricci's predicament. "To clear her, I must pursue all possible leads to Crake's killer. The surviving Crawfords could be suspected in his death. Their home in New York is a convenient train ride to Saratoga Springs. Further investigation may clear them. In any case, justice must be served."

Buel reflected thoughtfully, then said, "I'm now willing to lend you the manuscript for your personal use, but without permission to publish it." He also gave Prescott the address of Sergeant Tower in Erie at the Pennsylvania Soldiers and Sailors Home and the Crawford business address in New York City.

After Buel left for his office, Prescott lingered at the club, nursing a brandy. He could reach Erie by an overnight New York Central train. Tower would be wary: He could be thrown out of his home for malingering. It was only his word against Crake's heroic reputation. But perhaps now that Crake was dead, Tower might give out his information for Francesca Ricci's sake.

Tower's witness would damage Crake's reputation. But, more important, it would bring the Crawfords within the scope of the investigation. A desire for revenge probably lay behind Virgil Crawford's insistence that Crake be investigated in Ruth Colt's suspicious disappearance. Crake had to be punished one way or another for what he did to the family.

The overnight train to Erie arrived early in the morning of July 18. Prescott waited until a decent hour and went to the Pennsylvania Soldiers and Sailors Home. After introducing himself to the director, he explained that he was doing research on the war.

"May I speak to old Samuel Tower? He might have heard that his former captain Jed Crake was murdered a week ago in Saratoga Springs. I can bring Tower up to date on the details."

The director agreed and led Prescott into a parlor. "I'll fetch the sergeant, as he likes to be called."

Tower shuffled into the room on a cane. Bald, deeply bent, and toothless, he looked ancient and decrepit. But his bright, beady, little black eyes revealed an alert mind.

He saluted Prescott. "Thanks for stopping, Captain. Tell me about Crake. He was murdered, you say? How did I miss that?" A servant arrived with a tray of lemonade and sweet biscuits.

Prescott gave a brief account of the crime and its investigation. "The police have arrested a chambermaid, but she may be innocent. The evidence against her is circumstantial. One of Crake's enemies might have killed him."

"That wouldn't surprise me," said Tower. "He rode roughshod over anyone in his way. Do you have someone particular in mind?" Then he chuckled, aiming his cane at an invisible enemy. "I didn't kill him. I might have done it years ago, but not anymore. I'm anchored here."

"During the war, you and Crake were close friends. What happened?"

"After the war, he became rich in meatpacking and railroads. I wasn't so lucky and lost everything in gold and silver mines out west. When I asked him for help, he replied that lending to me was like throwing money down a rat hole. I felt betrayed and could have killed him then. I had done him many favors. Now it doesn't matter. The doctor tells me I'm not long for this world." He tapped his chest and added, "A bad heart. And my kidneys are failing."

The room fell silent for a few moments. Then Prescott remarked, "I had in mind the Crawford incident in December sixty-four near Savannah."

"You've been in touch with Clarence Buel at *Century Magazine,* I see."

"I know the bare facts. Could you tell me why Crake was so brutal toward Crawford's wife and children? His behavior deserved a court-martial."

"It did, indeed. He was a proud, passionate man of common stock and allowed no man or woman to hold him in contempt. Mrs. Lavinia Crawford was an outspoken rebel, embittered by the loss of her eldest son, a Confederate officer, at Gettysburg in sixty-three. From the outset, she defied Crake to do his worst. She fancied herself an aristocrat and treated his blue uniform, his captain's rank, and his own person with open disrespect. She called him a vile thief, a vicious brute, and other names I can't remember. He grew red in the face. She mocked him and egged him on, said he was common as dirt. Still, he kept his temper under control. Then, when Mr. Crawford shot Private Higgins in the basement, Crake exploded. He charged into the library like a maniac, waving his bloody sword.

"She screamed at him, 'You filthy beast, you killed my husband.'

"He struck her hard on the mouth and continued to beat her with his fists. The daughter and son screamed for help. I called out to him to stop and took a step toward him. He drew his pistol and aimed at me. His eyes were dark and wild. He breathed heavily. 'Get out of the room or I'll kill you,' he said.

"I saw that he was out of his mind. He really would kill me, or anyone else who tried to stop him. So, I left the room. He bolted the door behind me. Through a window in the door, I could see what followed. He ripped off the woman's clothes, beat her savagely, and violated her. Through it all, she didn't even whimper. That seemed to madden him even more, and he attacked her daughter in the same way. Then he shot all three of them and set the drapes on fire."

Tower paused, eyes cast down, and drank his lemonade. The atrocity seemed to overcome him. After a few moments, he put down his glass, drew a shallow, wheezy breath, and resumed his story.

"Finally, Crake came out of the room, the rage draining out

of his body. He nearly fainted in my arms. I had to help him outside to his horse and into the saddle."

"Was there *no way* you could have stopped him?" asked Prescott.

For a moment, Tower's eyes flashed brightly. He resented the question. "At the time, part of me felt that she and the rest of the family deserved to be severely punished. They and their kind had torn the country apart, caused a bloody conflict, and didn't feel one bit sorry. So, I might not have tried to stop Crake as much as I should have. He became their jury, judge, and executioner."

"What happened afterward?"

"Soon after leaving the plantation, our detachment ran into the local Georgia militia. That occupied our minds for a few hours. In the fighting, Crake was his old self, rallying his men, charging the enemy. Afterward, as we approached our camp outside Savannah, Crake sidled up to me and asked if I was going to report him. I replied that I wasn't responsible for writing a report; he was. However, if our commanding officer or the provost marshal were to question me, I would give them truthful answers, no more, no less."

"How did Crake react?"

"He stared at me and didn't say a word. Then he spurred his horse and rode away. He was angry. I worried. He could cause me serious trouble. But no charges were brought against our detachment, and none against Crake in particular. I figured that Crake's victims had perished in the fire, so there were no witnesses to bring forward a complaint. Much later I learned that the daughter and the son had survived; but for whatever reason, they remained silent."

"Did the Crawford incident later affect your relationship with Crake?"

"We carried on as if nothing had happened. Soon Savannah surrendered; the Ninth Pennsylvania Cavalry advanced with

Sherman's army into South Carolina. For Crake and me, it was business as usual, mostly skirmishes with rebel cavalry. We occupied the state capital, Columbia, without a fight. Then came another incident involving Crake. Our men uncovered a warehouse of whiskey. That night, I wasn't with Crake, but I later heard rumors that he was involved in an orgy of drunken rape. This time the victims were black women. Again, he wasn't cited, and I didn't feel obliged to report him.

"The war soon ended. As civilians, we occasionally met afterward and carried on as if nothing untoward had happened. Meanwhile, he prospered. I didn't. Several years ago, I asked him for a loan. He refused. Since then, we've been out of touch." He stopped as if uncertain what to say. Finally, he remarked, "Crake was a brave soldier but a wicked man. If the Crawfords killed him, I would say rough justice was done."

The next day, back in his New York office, Prescott reflected on what he had learned about the Crawfords. Was their experience at Crake's hands so dreadful that they would still seek revenge thirty years later? To judge from Virgil Crawford's pursuit of Crake in the Colt case, Prescott had to say yes. But *could* they have done it?

Late in the afternoon, Peter Yates arrived at the office. He had investigated the Crawfords' whereabouts on July 7, when Crake was killed. "Their business address is at Pier 35 on the Hudson River in the general offices of the Ocean Steamship Line. James Crawford is the chief financial officer of the company. I was told that he was out of the office. A porter said that James and his sister, Edith, lived ten minutes away in a town house on Washington Square. When I came, the building was shuttered. A caretaker came to the door and said the Crawfords were not at home. 'When did they leave?' I asked.

"The man didn't know when and where they went. The neighbor next door saw them leave with a couple of trunks on

July first and overheard them tell the cab driver, 'Grand Central Station.' Finally, at the local post office I got their forwarding address from a helpful clerk."

Yates paused expectantly.

"Yes, what is it?"

"The Grand Union Hotel on Broadway in Saratoga Springs. To judge from the trunks, they'll stay for the season. Now, isn't that a coincidence?"

"I agree! It's beginning to look like we may have found a pair of possible suspects in the death of Captain Crake. I'll let Mrs. Thompson know."

At dinner the following day, Pamela sat with Harry in the dining room. They were expecting the main course when Jason Dunn approached and handed Pamela a telegram. "It's from Prescott," she said, then read it aloud:

> MISS EDITH CRAWFORD AND BROTHER
> JAMES CRAWFORD ARE REGISTERED IN
> GRAND UNION HOTEL. POSSIBLE
> SUSPECTS IN CRAKE'S MURDER.
> INVESTIGATE THEM. I RETURN TO S.S.
> WITH DETAILS. MEET ME AT THE
> AFTERNOON TRAIN.
> PRESCOTT

"Well!" murmured Harry. "That's intriguing news. We've been here ten days and haven't heard of those people. They apparently don't call attention to themselves."

At that moment, Jason Dunn walked by. Harry beckoned him. "Could you tell us, Mr. Dunn, who are the Crawfords, and are they here this evening?"

Without turning his head or looking up, Jason said softly, "They are arriving as we speak."

The master waiter was leading a middle-aged couple down the main aisle of the room. She was silver haired and erect, her features delicately chiseled and her manner graceful. As she passed by Pamela's table, she spoke with a lovely Southern accent to the master waiter. Her brother, his features refined and handsome, was in a wheelchair pushed by Virgil Crawford.

For a brief moment Pamela gaped with surprise. When she last saw Virgil in February in his private office, he looked severe, clear-eyed, and confident, fully up to the challenge of investigating Jed Crake's recent crimes against women. Now, he seemed tentative and solicitous as he wheeled his crippled cousin through a crowd of waiters and diners.

Virgil glanced at Pamela, recognizing her. But he didn't wink or smile. The Crawford pursuit of Crake should remain secret even beyond his death.

The master waiter placed them at a table across the aisle in plain view of Pamela and Harry. The main course arrived, a lamb stew. During the meal, Virgil acted like one of the family without a trace of servility, adding to the conversation while deferring to his cousins.

In the hotel garden after the meal, Pamela said to Harry, "We must visit Helen Fisk immediately and learn all we can about the Crawfords. They've apparently had a shocking experience at the hands of Captain Crake."

"Yes," said Harry, "I can hardly wait for the details."

# CHAPTER 14

## Southern Suspects

*Saratoga Springs*
*Friday, July 20*

When Prescott's train arrived at the station late in the afternoon, Pamela and Harry were there to greet him and brought him through crowded streets to the hotel. He registered at the reception desk for a room next to Harry's. Both rooms were being cleaned, so they retreated to a quiet corner in one of the public parlors.

When they had settled down, Pamela asked, "Could you tell us what you learned from Sergeant Tower?"

"I'll start at the beginning." He described the ailing, resentful Tower, then related his account of the incident in December '64 at the Crawford plantation in all its horrendous detail.

The ferocity of Crake's assault on the Crawford family shocked Pamela, while Mrs. Crawford's fanatic heroics baffled her. She felt pity for Edith and James, hapless victims.

"What an appalling story!" she exclaimed at the end. "Just imagine what they witnessed! Besides the injuries to themselves, how could they ever forget what Crake did to their mother? If I were them, I'd never forget or forgive."

"Even after thirty years?" Harry asked.

"That's what we have to determine," replied Prescott. "Time heals many wounds, and the Crawfords' success in business might have drawn their minds away from their wartime tragedy. Perhaps they wouldn't risk their wealth and reputation in an attempt to get even with Crake." He glanced from one assistant to the other. "What have you learned about the Crawfords while I was gone?"

Pamela replied, "Last night, my friend Helen Fisk told me that for several years they've spent July and August at the Grand Union Hotel, lodging in a suite on the ground floor. They avoid the limelight. Edith brought along a two-year-old thoroughbred filly named Savannah and has entered her in the Travers Race, the high point of the thoroughbred racing season. Brother James believes that Saratoga's waters, its cool, clean air, its music, and congenial atmosphere ease his pain. The ground-floor location is also convenient for him. He never talks about his crippled condition or the war. Some say, as a young man, he was injured in an accident."

"We know now," added Harry, "that it wasn't an accident. Crake's shot or his kicks must have paralyzed James from the waist down. Being crippled for almost thirty years and nonetheless successful in business testifies to great strength of character. Still, he isn't ever likely to forgive Crake."

While they were involved in this discussion, the Crawfords entered the parlor, their cousin, Virgil, again pushing the wheelchair. They recognized Pamela and Harry, and seemed to hesitate for a moment. Edith said a word to James. He replied and they came forward, smiling politely.

James began, "We've heard about you and your assistants, Mr. Prescott, and would like to become better acquainted. Social conventions are relaxed here. We needn't wait for someone to bring us together." He extended a hand to Prescott and introduced himself and his sister. He waved toward Virgil, who had deferentially stepped back. "And that's our cousin, Virgil Crawford. We're from New York and spending the season here."

Edith Crawford addressed Prescott. "Through the director of the soldiers' home in Erie we've learned that you spoke to Sergeant Tower. He's not a trustworthy source of information in matters that concern us. We would like to invite you to our rooms for tea and a mutually beneficial conversation. Shall we say in an hour?"

"At your service, ma'am. My assistants will come with me. They are deeply involved in these matters and should hear what we say."

The Crawfords glanced at each other. James gave the number of the ground-floor suite and added, "Then we'll meet in an hour." He beckoned Virgil, who turned the wheelchair around, and they left the room.

Prescott turned to Harry and Pamela. "What do you make of that?"

"The Crawfords keep themselves well informed," Harry replied. "They must have engaged the director of the home in Erie to report on Tower's activities. The old sergeant is threatening them."

Pamela added, "I see Virgil's hand in this chance meeting with us. As the family's secret agent, he found out that we were investigating Captain Crake's murder and were in this parlor. He may wonder how close we've come to them."

An hour later, with Pamela and Harry standing behind him, Prescott knocked on the door. Virgil, now playing the butler, led them down a hall and ushered them into a tastefully furnished sitting room. To the right and left were doors presumably to the brother's and sister's bedrooms. Virgil's would be near the entrance.

Edith rose from her chair and showed the visitors to places

at the tea table. A silver tea service was there, together with a tray of sandwiches. Virgil poured and withdrew.

Pamela's eye followed the servant until he disappeared. He would be listening on the other side of the door.

Edith noticed her. "Virgil's been with us since he was a boy."

James explained, "He's kin, part of the family. After the attack on our plantation, when he was free to leave, he chose to live with us."

Edith added, "He serves as a versatile valet for James and is implicitly loyal. Years ago, when we spent a year in France, we brought him along to learn French cuisine. He became an excellent cook and fluent in the language."

Prescott opened the conversation with a question about Edith's horse, Savannah.

She replied, "I rode her this morning. She's in perfect condition. We expect her to win the Travers Cup in a few weeks. I could sing her praises all day, but that's not why we're here."

Her brother came to the point. "We want you to know that Sergeant Tower is trying to extort money from us by threatening to publicize certain embarrassing details of an incident that occurred in the late War Between the States. May I assume that he has shared his story with you?"

"He did, but he swore me to secrecy and declared he would deny having spoken to me. He didn't indicate that he was trying to extort money from you."

Edith leaned forward anxiously. "What use will you make of what he told you?"

Prescott replied, "I'm a detective, not a journalist. I've no interest in digging up dirt to embarrass you or to make money. I only want to find out whether an incident thirty years ago near Savannah is related to the death of Captain Crake almost two weeks ago in this hotel. In other words, did the appalling violence that you and your family suffered at Crake's hands move you to kill him?"

The room fell silent. Edith Crawford blanched, her gaze bent inward to that distant horror. Her brother clenched the armrests of his wheelchair.

He replied evenly, "We didn't kill him." He went on, "I believe you should hear what really happened rather than Tower's version." He went on to tell basically the same story as Tower with a few significantly different details.

"When Sherman's army reached the Savannah area, we knew they would find us, sooner or later, and loot the plantation in order to replenish their supplies. So my father hid our most valuable possessions, personal records, and the like, in Savannah. The war was almost over. The Confederate army lacked the strength to defend the city and would soon withdraw. Therefore, Sherman had no reason to pillage or destroy it.

"Crake's foraging detachment descended on our plantation like a host of locusts devouring or destroying everything within reach. Father and Mother should have stood aside and allowed the looting to proceed. Unfortunately, the death of our older brother at Gettysburg in sixty-three and the collapse of the Confederacy deeply upset them—I dare say, unhinged their minds. Crake's blue uniform, and worse, his rude, arrogant demeanor triggered in them a fit of anger. My mother spit on Crake. My father sent a messenger for the local militia, then pulled out his pistol and shot one of the soldiers. Crake, in turn, shot us. Father and Mother died; Edith and I survived."

"Should Crake have been punished?" Pamela asked.

James shrugged. "When I recovered, I thought of prosecuting him. But it was impossible. In fact, his actions were loosely consistent with Sherman's instructions to use lethal force in case of resistance. We had resisted—futilely and with disastrous consequences. On a much larger stage, isn't that what happened to the Southern states during the war?"

"I take your point," replied Prescott. "You must know that Tower places all the blame for the violence on Crake and claims

Crake forced him out of the room at gunpoint. He observed your torture through a window in the library door."

James sniffed. "There was no window in the door. Tower was in the room with us, tied us up, slapped and insulted us."

Pamela intervened. "Tower made another statement that must be tested, though it raises a painful matter. Still, it establishes a powerful motive for Crake's murder. I'll have to address you, Edith." Pamela filled her voice with all the compassion she could muster. "Sergeant Tower asserts that Crake violated you and your mother. Is that true?"

Edith gasped. James seemed dumbstruck. Even Prescott and Harry flinched.

"If he had," Edith sputtered, "I wouldn't be here today. At the earliest opportunity, I would have killed myself for shame."

James added, "And as soon as I could have held a pistol, I would have found Crake and killed him, regardless of the consequences."

Pamela wasn't convinced, but she didn't press the point.

Harry asked, "How has Tower tried to extort money from you?"

James replied, "He has insinuated that demand in messages to us. Thus far we have called his bluff with the threat of legal action that would force him in disgrace from the soldiers' home."

"Extortion and slander are crimes. Why haven't you gone to the police?"

"We much prefer to keep this matter private. To bring Tower to court would be risky, costly, time and energy consuming. In any case, we are told that he hasn't long to live. We are patient."

Prescott said, "We needed to go over these painful memories. Now may I ask what were you doing the night of July seventh, when Crake was killed?"

Edith replied, "We attended Victor Herbert's concert in the hotel garden. From a distance we saw Crake and his wife. Afterward, we returned to our rooms. James was tired. We read for an hour and went to bed."

"Did you ever make yourselves known to Crake or his wife?" Pamela asked.

"If you mean, did we ever confront them, especially the captain; no, we didn't. In such a large hotel, it's possible to avoid personal contact with villainous people. Still, we noticed them. Neither his appearance nor his manner has changed much in thirty years. She advertises herself at every opportunity and must be noticed."

Prescott indicated that it was time to go, though the tea and the sandwiches had hardly been touched. This exposure of the family's wartime crucifixion appeared to have drained the brother and sister. Nonetheless, they managed to keep up appearances and expressed no resentment toward their interrogators.

As Pamela walked past the fireplace, a fine miniature portrait on the mantel caught her eye and she stopped to gaze at it. "It's the work of a master," she exclaimed.

"My older brother, Arthur, an officer in his uniform of the Ninth Georgia Infantry," remarked Edith. "He died at Gettysburg."

"I'm truly sorry," said Pamela. "He must have been a remarkable man." The artist had captured the young man's wavy, golden hair and physical beauty, and the hint of an extraordinary spirit. His deep-set, luminous brown eyes witnessed to his intelligence and his open, generous nature. She had the odd feeling that she had seen him recently, or someone who looked like him.

Prescott came up beside her and stared intently at the portrait. Slowly, his lips parted and a strange expression came over his face.

"This can't be true," he murmured. Then he turned to Edith. "I wish I had had the honor of meeting your brother." He shook James's hand. "We shall have to meet again. Good evening."

Pamela and Prescott walked silently together in the hotel park. Harry had gone off in search of Robert Shaw. At the far end of the park, they stopped to rest and Pamela finally asked Prescott, "What was it that struck you so strongly about that portrait of Arthur Crawford? And what did you mean that it couldn't be true?"

"Do you remember seeing the military sword on my office wall over a year ago?"

"It's still imprinted on my mind." She also recalled nearly every word of the conversation that followed. At Gettysburg, Prescott had seen a Confederate officer fall. He was dead by the time Prescott reached him, but he took the man's sword. Afterward, he tried in vain to discover his family and return the sword to them. So he hung it on the office wall as a reminder of the madness of war.

Prescott continued, "For a moment there by the mantel I thought the man in the portrait, Arthur Crawford, was that fallen Confederate officer of the Ninth Georgia Infantry. His sword is now on my office wall."

"Could you be mistaken? His features in the portrait must differ greatly from those of the corpse you saw on the battle-field."

"I agree. Still, the resemblance is remarkable. This isn't the time to discuss the matter with the Crawfords—perhaps later, when the Crake case is resolved."

Pamela remarked, "The portrait made me think that I've recently seen someone who resembles Arthur Crawford."

A waiter walked through the park ringing a bell for supper. Prescott asked, "Shall we have a drink before eating? Let's find Harry and go to my room."

\* \* \*

When they settled into chairs, Prescott offered them a shot of his whiskey. Harry accepted, Pamela declined.

Prescott toasted them, then asked Harry, "Did the Crawfords kill Crake? What do you say?"

"We can't arrest and convict them on the evidence we have now. But they remain possible suspects. Tower might have lied to you about his part in that foraging incident in Georgia. In fact, he may also have fabricated the sexual violence in order to extort money from the Crawfords. But their own account of the incident is sufficiently gruesome to move ordinary men and women to murder. I don't see either the brother or the sister wielding that lethal knife. They would need an assassin, either someone they paid or who shares their hatred of Crake."

Pamela followed Harry's ideas with difficulty. The image of Arthur Crawford on the mantel distracted her mind. Then Harry's remark that the Crawfords would have needed a sympathetic accomplice rang a bell. Pamela recalled the person who resembled the Confederate officer in the portrait.

"I may have found a possible assassin!" she exclaimed.

Prescott and Harry stared at her. "Who?" they asked in unison.

"Jason Dunn." She quickly added, "I see in him a distant, family likeness to Arthur Crawford, especially in the eyes. He also has a Southern accent. I would like to find out if Jason is kin and might share the Crawford hatred of Captain Crake."

Prescott turned to Harry. "What do you think? Is Pamela on to something?"

"To detect a family likeness, I'd have to see Jason and the Crawford portrait side by side. Still, Pamela's suggestion to investigate Jason Dunn is worth pursuing. He was at the Victor Herbert concert that night in the hotel garden and could easily have sneaked into Crake's room. His eagerness to implicate Francesca looks suspicious to me."

Prescott turned to Pamela. "The hotel manager should give you Jason's background. Start there. Harry will help you."

Before going to supper, Pamela sat at her writing table and hurriedly sketched from memory the portrait of Arthur Crawford. Tomorrow, she'd sketch Jason Dunn's features. Then she could put the two portraits side by side. She was sure Harry would see the kinship.

# CHAPTER 15

## Hattie's

*Friday, July 20*

After a brief supper in the dining hall, Pamela returned to her room. A note lay on the floor.

> Mrs. Thompson,
>
> Could we discuss business at Hattie's Café,
> my new Saratoga office?
>
> Virgil Crawford

She wondered what business he might have in mind. He had not been part of their conversation with James and Edith, and might have something of interest to add. The reception desk told her that Hattie's was a decent café on William Street off South Broadway, near the hotel. That seemed safe enough.

After a five-minute walk, Pamela stood before a small, plain building, paint peeling from the brick walls. In this warm summer weather the ground-floor windows were open to the street, and she glanced in. Two black men were playing cards at one table; a white family had gathered for iced tea at another. Helping out at the bar, one of the hotel waiters recognized her and beckoned her in.

For a brief moment, she hesitated. The racial mixture disturbed her. She brushed off this concern. Saratoga didn't have dangerous, hostile neighborhoods like New York's. As she walked in, the customers gave her a momentary glance and went on with their pleasures.

Shortly afterward, Virgil arrived in a tan linen suit and a wide-brimmed straw hat. He wore light fawn gloves and carried a highly polished black walking stick with a pearl handle. She had noticed it before. In the doorway, he stopped and surveyed the room. When his eyes lighted upon Pamela, they brightened with recognition. He smiled politely and greeted her with a slight bow. They moved to a table in a quiet corner.

Pamela glanced at Virgil's walking stick. He was palming the pearl handle. "Is it what I think it is?"

Virgil smiled. "Yes, it's a sword cane from a shop in Paris near the Palais Royal. It has proved useful on New York City's waterfront, where James's shipping company is located. On occasion, I've had to fend off villains who would have robbed him. I doubt that I'll need to draw it in Saratoga Springs. But I keep it handy, just in case." He leaned the cane against the wall.

The hotel waiter came with iced tea. He and Virgil exchanged friendly nods, while Virgil slipped a coin into his hand. In vain, Pamela objected that she would pay her own tab.

"It's my reputation, not yours, that's at stake," he whispered with feigned fear. "They would think I'm cheap."

The other customers watched this encounter with amused side glances.

"Shall we use our Christian names?" Pamela asked.

"Delighted," he replied.

They lifted their glasses and toasted each other. He began,

"You are honest and can be trusted. James and Edith agreed that I should speak with you. We have nothing shameful to hide."

He spoke in beautifully articulated English with a Southern accent. If she were blind, she wouldn't have known that he was black. Even with him before her, she could hardly detect his race. His complexion was fair. The only clues were perhaps his fuller lips, almond-shaped eyes, and tightly curled gray hair.

He went on. "You are wondering whether Edith or James might have killed Captain Crake, since he had given them good reason. Well, they didn't. I felt enough of their pain and humiliation to want to kill him but lacked the courage. Still, I'm glad someone did."

"Would you tell me your place in the family in sixty-four?"

"I was the cook and my wife was a housekeeper in the family's mansion. We were legally slaves and our work could be called servile. But the Crawfords treated us as kin, as far as the slave codes of the South allowed. My father was a visiting Crawford uncle, a handsome gentleman and Confederate officer. He died during the war—from dysentery rather than a Yankee bullet. My mother, a beautiful Crawford domestic slave, gave me all the love I needed."

"And Edith and James?" Pamela asked.

"We were close. Growing up, we had the same tutors and played together."

"How were you a witness to Crake's crime?"

"When he arrived at the mansion's front door and Mrs. Crawford cursed him, I realized that serious trouble was ahead. My wife and I hid in a tiny, secret room behind a bookcase in the library together with the family's most valuable works of art."

Pamela looked askance. "The Union soldiers were supposed to free the slaves. Why wouldn't you and your wife have welcomed them?"

"We didn't trust them. They were said to abuse blacks, especially women."

"Why believe such tales? Confederate sympathizers surely invented them."

Virgil shook his head. "I withheld judgment, until Captain Crake and his men rode into our plantation like a band of vicious thieves. They broke into the slave quarters, as well as into barns and sheds. When they couldn't find what they wanted, they beat black men and women until they revealed hiding places in the woods. I hid because Crake would have beaten me and my wife in the same way."

Pamela wanted to protest that Crake and his foragers were the exception in Sherman's army, but there could have been many more atrocities that she hadn't heard of. "I grant that war can turn even decent men into monsters."

"That's true of all armies," Virgil agreed. "At the time, my cousin James and I often asked ourselves what moved Northern soldiers to fight and die in the South. To put an end to slavery? No, we figured that most of them fought for the thrill of it or for their pay. The few idealists among them wanted to save the Union and keep the country from falling apart. In fact, very few soldiers really cared for black people or respected them. They freed them only to ruin their masters for breaking up the Union and starting the war."

Virgil glared at Pamela, his eyes glowing with passion. "Should blacks be grateful? What could freedom mean to us, penniless and uneducated, with our plantations and our towns in ashes? Northern politicians promised us land and money. Only fools believed them."

Pamela couldn't object. After thirty years, true freedom for most black Americans still seemed a distant hope.

"From your hiding place, how could you see what Crake was doing?"

"We could hear his loud, vicious taunts and vile curses, his heavy blows, and the shots from his pistol. We heard him tell his sergeant to set fire to the house 'and burn the bastards.' When we left our hiding place, the room was in flames.

"The sight on the floor was pitiful. I'll carry it with me to my grave. Mother, son, and daughter were beaten bloody and shot. My wife and I pulled them out of the house and hid them until the soldiers left. The house was ruined. I learned later that Crake had killed Mr. Crawford in the basement."

"What happened to James Crawford that keeps him in a wheelchair?"

"Edith told me that when he was shot and lay on the floor, Crake kicked him several times with his heavy boots and broke his back. Since then, the lower half of his body has been paralyzed."

"He doesn't seem bitter. I'm surprised."

"It was hard at first. He insisted he would walk, have a family, and lead a normal life. After a few years of self-pity, he decided that half a loaf was better than none. He threw himself into the shipping business and prospered. For pleasure, he plays chess with other amateurs and me, sings and listens to music, and reads. His conversation sparkles with wit. He's a joy to be with."

"And Edith? How is she?"

"Crake's blows crippled her spirit rather than her body. She has a sterling character, but nonetheless struggles with anger and resentment."

"Forgive me, but may I touch on a very sensitive issue?" Pamela searched his face for a sign to continue.

His facial expression hardly changed, but his eyes became deeply troubled. "I know what you're thinking. You've heard it from Sergeant Tower. After thirty years, I still cannot bring myself to talk about the matter. You must speak directly to Edith."

"With the plantation in ruins, what did you do?"

"Mrs. Crawford soon died of her injuries. My wife and I brought Edith and James to their town house in Savannah and nursed them there. When they had sufficiently recovered, they asked us to remain with them, no longer as slaves but as servants with good pay and accommodations. It was the best offer we had. We agreed and have never regretted our decision."

"May I ask your wife's name? She's not here. Is she well?"

He shook his head. "Mary died last year. I miss her."

"I'm sorry. It's hard to lose someone who has become part of you. My young daughter died a few years ago and I haven't fully gotten over it."

She finished her tea. "In your note you mentioned discussing business. What did you have in mind?"

"Yes, it's been five months since we suspended our investigation into the disappearance of Ruth Colt. Her body must be found and given a decent burial. We Crawfords also want justice done and Crake's evil deeds exposed."

"I agree," said Pamela. "With Crake dead and his money frozen, his thugs will not threaten my ward, Francesca Ricci. In any case, she is safe in prison, so to speak. On the other hand, the police might obstruct our investigation, fearing that it would expose their links to Crake. Nonetheless, we should resume the search for Ruth. At the moment, I'm engaged at a crucial point in the investigation of Crake's death. I'll speak to Prescott. He can send Harry to New York. He knows the case."

Virgil raised a cautionary hand. "You should remind Mr. Miller to keep the Crawford family out of the public eye."

"I understand. Now, I must go."

He rose from the table and took his cane. "I'll speak with the other customers for a few minutes. I've enjoyed our conversation. If I can be of assistance in catching Crake's killer, please let me know."

Momentarily uncertain, Pamela looked into his eyes. He seemed to mean what he said.

* * *

Upon her return to the hotel, Pamela walked in the garden and reflected on her visit with Virgil Crawford. She hadn't expected him to confess to Crake's death or to implicate Edith in it. But he said enough to suggest that he, or the two of them in collaboration, could have killed the captain. As an experienced chef, Virgil would surely know how to use a knife. The sword in his cane could have served the purpose. Finally, he and Edith shared a strong desire for justice and revenge.

They needed an opportunity. And they had one at Victor Herbert's concert in the hotel garden, the evening of July 7. Virgil could easily have slipped away from the audience, killed Crake, and returned to his place next to James.

Pamela sighed, unhappy with her reasoning. It seemed out of character for the Crawfords to slaughter an old, sick, unarmed man in the dark, even if he were a villain. Could justice be served in that way? Brother James would know of the plan and, as a man of honor, would probably disapprove.

Pamela went to bed, turning her thoughts to Jason Dunn. He might be a Crawford by birth—he looked like one. In any case, he wasn't burdened with a sense of honor and was free from James's control. Jason had the opportunity and the skill with knives to have killed Crake. What was missing was a motive. For that piece of the puzzle, Pamela would have to know the man better.

# CHAPTER 16

## *The Search*

Early the next morning, Pamela went downstairs to the hotel foyer. Before she talked to the manager, she wanted another close look at Jason Dunn.

At the main desk a clerk told her that Mr. Dunn would come on duty at ten. "He wanders the hotel porches with his flute. He's quite good, plays anything you ask, and probably should be in an orchestra, but he's too shy."

A slender, short man, Jason would be hard to see on the busy porches—a mile of them on the front and back sides of the hotel. As Pamela set out, she also listened for the sound of his flute. Threading her way through a maze of rocking chairs and sauntering, chattering guests, she heard all kinds of music from bits of amateur opera to a vulgar "coon song." Musicians seemed to be everywhere, but no flutists. Eventually, she found Jason on the back porch facing the hotel garden. He was playing his flute while he stared across the park at Birgitta, walking toward the kitchen entrance, probably to pick up breakfast for Rachel.

Hidden behind a large box of green plants, Pamela studied the young man and sketched his features. He surely had Crawford blood in his veins. She would finish the sketch later. As she approached him, she cleared her throat. He didn't react, so she called out, "Jason."

He swung around, an angry expression on his face. It quickly disappeared into an embarrassed smile. "Mrs. Thompson, you took me by surprise. What can I do for you?"

"I heard your flute. Would you play a tune for me?"

"I play only to pass the time of day—and to earn a few pennies."

"You play very well. I'd like to hear "The Yellow Rose of Texas.""

By this time a small crowd had gathered. Jason lifted his flute, practiced a few bars of the tune, and then began the first verse. When he reached the refrain, the crowd joined in. At the end, the applause was enthusiastic. A well-dressed man stepped forward, patted Jason on the shoulder, and pressed a dollar bill into his hand.

Someone called out, "Can you play 'Marching Through Georgia'?"

Jason frowned. His eyes momentarily darkened. "I don't know that one." He put away his flute and returned to the rail. The crowd dispersed.

Pamela stood beside him. "That song gets on your nerves, doesn't it? Where do you come from?"

"Charleston, South Carolina, ma'am," he replied. "For the past eight years I've worked in hotels and restaurants in New York City and Saratoga Springs." With Pamela urging him on, he explained that he was a war orphan raised by adoptive parents, Mr. and Mrs. Dunn, who ran a Charleston hotel. At twenty-one, he moved to New York.

"Yesterday," remarked Pamela, "I met an interesting couple from Georgia, the Crawfords. Do you know them?"

He turned to face Pamela, searched her face as if unsure of her intention, and shrugged. "They're rich people, originally from Savannah. I've served them here occasionally and received big tips. Miss Crawford is distant kin to Mrs. Dunn."

Pamela's pulse quickened. "Are the Dunns still living?"

"He died a few years ago. She's seventy but in good health and still owns the hotel. Someone else manages it. She's coming to the Grand Union for the season and should arrive in a few days." He smiled shyly. "Now, excuse me. I must get ready for work."

Pamela remained at the rail for several minutes, wondering how close was the family connection between Jason and Edith Crawford? "I must arrange to meet Mrs. Dunn," she said to herself. "She might know family secrets that could be key to the murder of Captain Crake."

In the meantime, there was more Pamela needed to know about Jason. Tom Winn couldn't help her, but he recommended the clerk in the hotel manager's office. The hotel recruited its staff carefully. Jason's file included interviews and letters of recommendation from everyone who had employed him since his arrival in New York eight years earlier.

The name Crake caught her eye. Jason's first job in the city was in his pork-packing plant. From there he moved to Metzger's meat shop and then to a German restaurant on West Fourteenth Street near the meatpacking district.

Jason's connection to Metzger intrigued Pamela. How much was he involved in Metzger's bitter quarrel with Crake? The answer might lie with Erika Metzger. By this time in the mid-morning she would be having tea—hopefully alone as before. Pamela changed to a simple morning dress to blend in among the servants, and went to the laundry. Erika was at the table, alone and forlorn as before, with a cup of tea in one hand and a plain biscuit in the other.

"May I join you?" asked Pamela in German.

Pleased, Erika gestured to a nearby empty chair. The Italian women paid no attention. The others threw quick glances at Pamela, then ignored her.

Erika continued in German with acid comments on the women in the room, though without looking in their direction. "They pilfer," she said. Pamela asked for her opinion of the rest of the hotel staff. She had good words for Tom Winn: "He's honest and fair. But he's too busy and can't catch all the thieves and whores among the guests."

Pamela brought the conversation around to the bellboy Jason Dunn. "I've noticed that he once worked for your husband. What do you know about him?"

The question seemed to interest Erika, and she gave it some thought. "He does well the work he's hired to do. Back in New York, he eventually tired of cutting meat and became a waiter for cleaner work and better pay. At this hotel, all the waiters are black men. So, Jason is a bellboy. He gets good tips."

Pamela remarked, "But there's something strange about him. He keeps to himself, doesn't seem interested in other people."

Erika corrected her. "Young, pretty women catch his eye. He often stares at them and makes them feel uncomfortable. Occasionally, he makes an awkward advance and is rudely rebuffed. The manager has cautioned him about these matters, so he's more careful now."

"How does he feel toward Captain Crake?"

"He keeps his feelings bottled up inside. But in the fight with Crake at the meatpacking plants, he was as angry as my husband. Jason called Crake a thief, picking the pockets of the poor. Mind you, he said that to me, not to Crake."

"Did he ever criticize Crake here in the hotel?"

"In private he made snide remarks about Crake's attempts to lure young attractive women into his room and bed them. That seemed to upset Jason. I can't say why. Do you think Jason killed him?"

"He seems to have a lot of pent-up anger, much of it aimed

at Crake, but I don't see that he acted on it." The rest period was ending. Erika started back to work. Pamela waved good-bye and left the laundry.

Later in the morning, Pamela met Prescott coming from the barroom. When he saw her, he had to explain, "It's a warm day. I've taken a long walk to the sulky track to watch the horses and needed a beer to quench my thirst."

"Then shall we sit in the shade in Congress Park? You could buy me lemonade. I have something to tell you."

He agreed with a smile and they set out for the park. Once settled on a bench with the drink, Pamela gave him the impressions of Jason Dunn she had just gathered. She added, "Among our potential suspects, Francesca excluded, Jason was the one closest to the scene of Crake's murder. During the concert, Jason was hovering on the edge of the audience. As a bellboy, he could easily have slipped unnoticed into Crake's room and killed him."

"That's plausible," said Prescott. "Through his work in Crake's meatpacking plants, Jason gained experience with boning knives. Crake's killer seems skilled in the use of that instrument. And Metzger's hatred of Crake could also have rubbed off on Jason. We still need to determine if his Southern background and his obscure connection with the Crawfords could also have motivated him to kill Crake."

"Mrs. Dunn will arrive on Monday," said Pamela. "We can ask her."

Prescott shook his head. "She may refuse to cooperate. In any case, we'll add Jason to our list of suspects. Have you heard from your friend Mrs. Fisk about Crake's will?"

"Not yet, but Virgil Crawford and I agreed yesterday that it's time to reopen our investigation of Ruth Colt's disappearance. Could Harry do it? Crake no longer stands in the way."

"I'll think about it and talk to Harry. The Crawfords rightly want closure."

# CHAPTER 17

## Greed Frustrated

*Early morning, Sunday, July 22*

> Come, Pamela. I've received word about Crake's
> last will and testament. Bring your companions to
> my suite after breakfast. Be ready for a surprise.
>
> Helen

The message was lying on Pamela's floor when she returned from the dining hall. Intrigued, she collected Harry and Prescott and hurried to Helen's suite.

A servant ushered them into a spacious, tastefully decorated sitting room. Pamela had seen it before but was still amazed. A large Steinway piano stood in one corner for the celebrated pianists who played at Helen's parties. Small, landscape paintings by old masters from Helen's personal collection hung on the walls. An exquisite blue Turkish rug covered the floor. Even Prescott, a gentleman at home among rich, cultivated people, seemed impressed.

Helen noticed his reaction and remarked, "If I'm to entertain friends in this country village for three months, I must display a few of my treasures to delight them. But you aren't here on a social visit."

When they were seated, and growing eager, she pulled a document from a folder. "This report comes from a clerk in the office of Crake's New York attorney." She cleared her throat and began to read, mimicking a lawyer's measured words and elevated tone.

In the opening paragraph, Crake revoked an earlier will that had assigned the bulk of his estate to his wife, Rachel, then added, "I've become aware of my wife's infidelity with Robert Shaw. She shall not receive a penny from me." Dated July 7, 1894, his new will left most of his estate to the Grand Army of the Republic for the support of needy veterans.

Helen glanced at her visitors for dramatic effect, then continued, "I also assign $10,000 to my good servant Birgitta Mattsson. Her skillful massages have relieved my pain, and her good counsel has often calmed my temper." Helen stared at the document, shaking her head.

A collective gasp of disbelief echoed in the room. Pamela exclaimed, "What welcome news for Birgitta!"

Prescott asked, "Does Crake's wife realize that he has struck her from the will?"

"I don't think so," Helen replied. "But I'm not quite finished. This is a draft that Crake sent to his New York lawyer. He made a few minor changes and returned a final version for Crake's signature. Crake never sent it back."

"But did he sign it?" Prescott wondered aloud.

"Yes," suggested Pamela, "but he probably was killed before he could return it."

"It wasn't in his rooms," Harry remarked. "Tom Winn and the local police would have noticed such an important document when they searched for the missing bracelet. I think Rachel learned of Crake's plan to disinherit her, arranged Crake's murder, and destroyed the new will."

"She might not have found it," objected Pamela. "Crake would have hidden it from her, but he might have confided in Birgitta, his Swedish maid. She's frightened and reluctant to talk. If I bring news of her good fortune, she might open up to me."

At midmorning, Birgitta was sitting as usual by the fountain in Congress Park, drinking coffee, a basket at her side. Her mood appeared somber, her gaze turned inward.

Pamela carefully scanned the area for a spy. A shabbily dressed, elderly woman sat on a distant bench throwing breadcrumbs to a band of lively sparrows. She glanced furtively at Birgitta. Out of sight behind a hedge, Pamela wrote a message:

> That bird woman in the distance is a spy. Meet me
> in the milliner's shop on Broadway. The owner is a
> friend and will show you into a room where we
> can talk unobserved. I have good news for you.

At a moment when the birds seemed to distract the spy, Pamela walked casually past Birgitta and dropped the note into her basket. The maid glanced at the note and mouthed her assent. A few minutes later, she left the park at a leisurely pace and went window-shopping on Broadway. The elderly woman followed her. Pamela hurried ahead of them to the milliner.

At least five minutes passed before Birgitta joined Pamela in a back room used for storage. Cloth and ribbons were piled high on shelves. A rack of brightly colored costumes for a summer Shakespearean production occupied one wall; a large mirror hung from another. The two women sat at a plain wooden table, and for a moment they stared at each other. Then Pamela began, "Did you recognize the old lady who is spying on you?"

"I've often seen her near me and noticed her talking with Robert Shaw. She's apparently working for him. Why is he keeping track of me?"

"I think he wants to control you, partly from fear that you have information damaging to Rachel or him, and partly from carnal desire. How does he treat you?"

Birgitta averted her gaze, then spoke hesitantly. "Shortly after the captain died, Rob—as Rachel calls him—moved into the cottage. He often stares at me with a mocking smile. When Rachel is away and we are alone, he tries to touch me. Lately, while I'm massaging Rachel, he comes into the room to watch. I sense him becoming aroused. Soon, she's excited too. That distracts me, and I lose my concentration."

"Explain what that means," asked Pamela. "I've not given much thought to massage therapy."

"The kind of massage I learned in Sweden is supposed to release tensions, reduce stress, and bring body and soul into harmony, not excite lust. Yesterday, Shaw asked me to massage him. When I said no, he became angry. Rachel scolded me and claimed I was silly. 'Go ahead and massage him. I'd love to watch.'

" 'Not today,' I said, 'I'm too tired.' Afterward, he whispered to me, 'I always get what I want, one way or another. Remember that.' " The maid met Pamela's eye. "I take him at his word. Sooner or later, he'll attack me. What shall I do?"

Pamela was perplexed. Circumstances trapped the maid in the Crake household. "I don't see an easy solution. For the time being, avoid being alone with him. Put off the massage. I'll try to think of a way out. Until then, may I ask a few questions?"

Birgitta replied with a doubtful shrug.

"What do Rachel and Shaw say about Captain Crake when they believe you aren't listening?"

"They're obviously pleased that he's gone. Long ago, she had grown tired of him. When he slapped her that afternoon before he died, she began to hate him. Later, as I was covering the bruise on her face with powder, she stared at me and mur-mured, "He won't do that to me again."

"Did that sound like a threat to you?"

"Sort of," the maid replied. "As Rachel was leaving for din-ner, she told me, 'Don't mind what I said in there. I didn't mean it.' But there was anger in her eyes."

"Did they ever talk about his will?"

"Often. For a while they thought he might soon die of kid-ney failure. He was weak and in great pain. I overheard them discuss how they would move to California and live off his money. But, he disappointed them and recovered. Then in the last days of his life he grew suspicious of Rachel and talked about changing his will."

"How did they react?"

"They worried that he might drop her. Since his death, they don't know whether he changed the will or not. If he cut her out, they will be in deep trouble. They have used his credit ex-travagantly. Recently, Shaw has lost a lot at the casino, laying bets for her. Mr. Canfield has threatened to lend him no more."

"I can tell you this much, Birgitta, that Captain Crake did change his will—I've read it. He cut Rachel out. The bulk of his estate will go to needy veterans." She sought Birgitta's eye. "Ten thousand dollars will go to you."

The maid's eyes widened, her hands flew to her mouth in shock.

Pamela hastened to add, "Don't raise your hopes too high yet. The new will is missing, and we don't know if he signed it. He might have hidden it in a place that Rachel and Shaw wouldn't suspect, either inside or outside the cottage. Can you imagine where that might be?"

For a moment, Birgitta breathed heavily, shaking her head in continuing disbelief. She stammered, "I just don't know. . . ."

Pamela leaned forward solicitously, patiently.

Finally, Birgitta spoke. "Early that morning of July seventh,

after his spy had reported on Rob and Rachel's night out together, the captain took a document from his coat pocket and
began to read it. From the set of his jaw, I realized he was angry
in a frightening way: cold, controlled, and pitiless. When I said
it was time to go to Congress Spring for the water, he folded the
document and stuck it into his coat pocket. On our return, he
said he had business on Broadway and left me. I didn't see him
again until the afternoon when he burst into Rachel's room and
struck her."

Pamela was paying close attention. "Somewhere in the town
he might have signed the will in the presence of a notary public
and the witnesses. He could have left the will for safekeeping
with the notary or in a bank. How shall we find it, lost like a
needle in a haystack?"

Birgitta shook her head. "He must have had the document
in his coat pocket when he returned to the cottage to change for
dinner. Later, as he came out of his room, he patted his pocket,
like men do when they carry something important inside. He
probably still had the document with him when he went to dinner. After dinner he went directly to the concert and from the
concert back to the cottage."

"Right," said Pamela. "Therefore, he might have hidden the
document in the cottage before taking his medicine. If we've
calculated correctly, the will should still be there. Prescott,
Harry, and I must find it."

Birgitta glanced at her watch. "I'm late now and should return to the cottage. Rachel has come back from the casino,
eaten a late breakfast, and will be expecting me to massage her."

"Then leave this shop by the front door. The spy may still be
in the neighborhood and will follow you back to the hotel. She
won't realize that you tricked her and had a secret meeting with
me. In the future, we should meet here again. There's a back entrance if we need it."

As the maid reached for the door, Pamela stopped her. "Say

nothing to Rachel or Shaw about our conversation. This is a delicate moment in our investigation and a dangerous one for you. But, if all goes well, you may benefit handsomely from the captain's largesse."

Pamela was waiting in the hotel's foyer at noon when Harry and Prescott returned from a walk in the country. "You look like you have news," said Prescott. They moved into a parlor for privacy. She reported her conversation with Birgitta. "I'm concerned that Shaw might assault her." Harry shook his head skeptically. "In the two weeks I've studied him, he hasn't been violent. He enjoys the thrill of tricking people, seducing women, and gambling. When challenged, he's likely to run away rather than fight. But he has the strong physique of an athlete or soldier. If cornered, he could be dangerous."

Prescott remarked, "The maid is safe for now. We should focus on Crake's will."

"I agree," said Pamela. "From Birgitta's observations of Crake during his last day, I conclude that he hid the will in his cottage rather than somewhere in the town."

"Then we have no time to lose," said Prescott. "This morning, Tom Winn told me that Crake's cottage would be emptied of all his belongings and thoroughly cleaned later this afternoon. We should search now for the will and any other evidence we might have overlooked. Winn gave me the key. Let's go."

While Harry lifted loose floorboards and tapped for hollow walls or false ceilings, Pamela and Prescott stood in the center of the parlor trying to figure out Crake's mind.

"His estate," Prescott began, "is the most important legacy of his successful business career and a major source of pride. His will is the final, definitive expression of that achievement. I ask you, would he hide it under his mattress, or behind the water closet, or above the kitchen icebox?"

"No," she replied. "He had a strong sense of what was appropriate for him and what was not. Any hint of ridicule of his low birth or lack of cultivated manners enraged him. He was also a braggart and hung the certificate of his Medal of Honor above the mantel in the parlor on the most prominent spot in the most important room."

"So," Prescott concluded, "the will's final version is in this room and on that spot." He pointed to the certificate.

He removed the certificate and together they examined its frame. "The back seems rather thick," observed Pamela.

With a pocketknife, Prescott pried the back loose from the frame and retrieved a document on legal paper. He showed it to Pamela and cried out, "Harry, stop looking. We've found it—Captain Crake's last will and testament."

Harry joined them at a table to study it. On July 7, just hours before his death, Crake had signed the document in the presence of a notary public in the nearby United States Hotel. Two of the notary's clerks had witnessed the signature. Like the early draft of the will, this final version disinherited Rachel and left his estate to the veterans and to Birgitta. Crake's New York lawyer was the executor.

"It looks sound and should survive a challenge." Prescott spoke with an experienced lawyer's assurance in his voice. "I'll notify Tom Winn that we've found it. He'll inform Crake's executor."

"What will become of Rachel and Shaw?" Pamela asked.

Prescott replied, "Even though the will has yet to be probated, the hotel management will surely stop their credit and evict them. The hotel, the casino, and other creditors will have to go to the executor to recover their money."

Harry added with a straight face, "Shaw might find a job in one of the town's low-class gambling dens, and Rachel could go back to her old profession." He turned to Pamela. "What could the Swedish maid do?"

"I've already asked my friend Helen Fisk. One of her maids plans to retire. Birgitta will take her place."

That afternoon, Tom Winn quickly found new, cheap lodgings for Rachel and Shaw, and moved their belongings to a wagon behind the hotel. Pamela looked on as Winn escorted them to a side door. Rachel was teary-eyed, her shoulders slumped. Shaw lifted his chin an inch and swaggered even more than usual, as though this were only a minor bump in the road.

At the door, a police detective handed them a summons to appear the next day in court for a hearing. They would then be ordered to remain in the town until further notice and be available for questioning. As the wagon disappeared, Harry remarked, "If Rachel and Shaw killed Crake for his money, he outfoxed them."

"And they might hang for their trouble," added Prescott.

Every trace of them was gone before dinner. To the management's relief, hardly anyone remarked on their departure.

Pamela helped Birgitta move into a room next to Helen Fisk's. The maid was almost overcome with relief. When she had settled in, Pamela ordered a meal for two in the room. Then she told Birgitta that Crake's will was found and had been signed.

The maid was overjoyed. "He had recently asked about my hopes for the future. I told him I'd like to go to medical school and become a doctor. He may have made that possible."

That evening, Pamela and Harry joined Prescott in his room to discuss the next step in the Crake investigation. They had identified several potential suspects and needed to set priorities.

Prescott turned first to Harry. "Yesterday, Pamela told me that the Crawfords wanted to reopen the investigation into Ruth Colt's disappearance. At first, I was reluctant, since it might distract us from finding Crake's killer and freeing Francesca. But, if we stretch ourselves, we can carry out both investigations. I feel a moral obligation to find Miss Colt's body without delay and confirm Crake's responsibility for her death. This afternoon, Virgil Crawford and I renewed our contract."

"Why now?" asked Harry, his head tilted doubtfully.

"Any delay is risky," Prescott replied. "Emil Schmidt's cooperation at the packing plant is crucial. Without his help, we'll never find the body. Like the rest of us, he could drop dead any day. And the time is right to act. Crake's thugs and allies have had two weeks to realize that Crake can no longer threaten or reward them. They will have little or no reason to shield him from our investigation."

"So, what is our plan?"

"You will return to New York on the early-morning train. Persuade Schmidt to cooperate. If he leads you to the girl's body, the NYPD's detectives will have to agree to a coroner's inquest and the truth will emerge."

Harry glanced quizzically in Pamela's direction.

Prescott took the hint and said to her, "You remain here. I hope to persuade Winn and the Saratoga police detective Michael Brophy to include you meaningfully in the ongoing search for Crake's killer. That's the only way we can establish Francesca's innocence. Both men are busy and not as helpful as we would like. They may also feel uncomfortable working with a private investigator, especially a woman. Should you need help, Harry will be a phone call away in New York." He met her eye. "Do you feel up to the challenge?"

Pamela was indeed uneasy, but she replied in a teasing voice, "I believe I can manage, sir. And, if I may ask, what are your plans?"

"Tomorrow morning, you and I will confer with Winn and Detective Brophy. I hope to persuade them that Francesca Ricci is only one among several potential suspects. They all should be thoroughly investigated."

"And after the meeting, what will you do?"

Prescott smiled thoughtfully. "I'll catch a late train to Lenox and visit Edward at Ventfort. He may need counsel and encouragement. And, as you know, I'm eager to settle certain issues with his mother. You and I will be in touch by telephone and telegraph."

"I'll be thinking of you." She meant it more than she dared to say.

# CHAPTER 18

## Police Detective

*Monday, July 23*

Before breakfast, Pamela and Prescott walked Harry to the station to catch the early train to New York. As they waited for the call to board, they discussed how to pry the secret of Ruth Colt's disappearance from Emil Schmidt. "He'll still be skittish," remarked Harry. "I'll have to charm him." The train arrived and they waved Harry off.

After breakfast, they went to Tom Winn's office. Police detective Michael Brophy frowned when he saw Pamela, then averted his eyes. A tall, heavy man, about forty, with a red face, thick black bristling eyebrows, and a drooping moustache, he chewed on a large, unlit cigar. A black bowler hat perched on his bald head. Pamela wisely suppressed a temptation to snicker. Brophy resembled the popular parody of the uncouth policeman, but the intelligence in his eyes told her that he was nobody's fool.

To appear businesslike, Pamela wore a simple light blue summer dress with a few lace frills on the cuffs and the collar. The detective darted a glance at her but avoided eye contact. After an uncomfortable moment, Winn made the introductions. Brophy tipped his hat to Pamela but didn't remove it and continued to chew on his cigar.

They sat around a conference table cluttered with loose papers and file boxes. With Pamela to his right, adding comments, Prescott briefly identified several potential suspects in the murder of Captain Crake: Jason Dunn, the Crawford brother and sister, Karl and Erika Metzger, and Rachel and her lover, Shaw. Then he examined their motives and suggested how each of them could have killed Crake or hired someone else to do it.

"Francesca Ricci," he concluded, "remains a suspect, but not the only one."

Throughout Prescott's account Detective Brophy sat stony-faced, head tilted at a skeptical angle. Pamela grew anxious that he might be obstinate and uncooperative by nature and resent even the appearance of an attempt to bypass him in this criminal investigation.

Brophy now leaned forward, his thick index finger tapping the table. "Prescott, you've given us clever speculation but little fact. But then you didn't claim to have solved the case, only opened up ways to proceed. My prime suspect is still Miss Ricci, a petty thief of shady background, with the stolen bracelet in her possession. She was observed near the scene of the crime and has no alibi. I've checked all your suspects and they have alibis."

Prescott started to protest.

"Right," Brophy snapped. "A maid is too easily assumed to be larcenous. Who knows, Crake could have given her the bracelet and forgot to tell his wife. No one saw the maid kill him, and she hasn't confessed. Still, Mr. Person, our D.A., thinks he has enough evidence to convict her."

"I'm curious," Prescott asked politely, "who among the other suspects could you imagine might have killed Crake?"

Brophy reflected thoughtfully for a moment. "If one stands out in my mind, it's the German butcher, Metzger. He's an angry rabble-rouser with a grudge against Crake and knows how to use a boning knife."

"That's right. Crake was also threatening his job at the hotel. So, how shall we proceed?"

"For the time being, you may continue to investigate potential suspects." He raised a warning hand. "Don't disturb the hotel's routine or upset its guests. And don't expect money or much help from me. I'm too busy clearing beggars, tramps, and drunks from our streets, chasing petty thieves, and settling domestic conflicts. I'm happy to leave further investigation of Crake's murder to you and your lady associate. It looks like a fool's errand. Prove me wrong." For the first time, he looked directly at Pamela. "By the way, Mrs. Fisk speaks highly of you."

He turned back to Prescott. "Today, I'll meet Mrs. Crake and Robert Shaw, and order them to remain available for further questioning. My spies will keep an eye on them; otherwise, I'm sure they would skip town and never be seen again. I'll give you and Mrs. Thompson all the authority you need to investigate them and the other suspects. Keep me informed. In September, the D.A. will bring Miss Ricci to trial unless you convince us of her innocence. That's the plan." He removed the cigar from his mouth and gave them a crooked smile.

"Walk me to the station, Pamela, and we'll talk on the way. I left my bag there. Did anything in our conversation with Winn and Brophy surprise you?"

"I didn't realize that a police detective would go to Helen Fisk for advice, though I'm grateful for what she gave. The tight limits he put on our investigation were to be expected. His reference to Francesca Ricci's trial insinuates it's a foregone conclusion."

"I fear," said Prescott, "that Brophy takes too much to heart the interests and opinions of wealthy visitors and the great hotels. How would he react if the evidence in Crake's murder pointed to the rich, cultivated Crawfords, rather than to Metzger, the rabble-rousing German butcher, or the poor Italian immigrant girl?"

As the train arrived, the passengers surged toward the tracks. Prescott pressed Pamela's hand. "I'm confident that you will solve the case if anyone can. Be brave and don't let Brophy bully you."

She smiled, pleased with his trust. "I wish you good fortune in Lenox and would like to meet your son, Edward, in the not-too-distant future."

The train gave out a loud, piercing toot. A conductor called all aboard and Prescott jumped into a carriage. As the train pulled out, he waved from a window until the train turned a curve and disappeared. For a moment, Pamela felt a pang of loss. A tear dropped from her eye.

A few hours later, Pamela was back at the station to form a first impression of Mrs. Dunn. As Pamela expected, the Crawfords were waiting in the large, milling crowd. Jason Dunn wasn't in sight. His duties at the hotel might have kept him away. This was the first day of the thoroughbred races in Saratoga, and a surge of new, eager visitors would need his services.

Edith Crawford leaned over the edge of the platform to peer down the track. Lines of concern creased her brow. The train was running late. Her brother, James, sat placidly in his wheelchair by the station house, away from the crowd. Virgil stood behind him, now in a servant's role, as still and elegant as a Greek statue. Did the servant ever speak to his master in public, other than in response to simple questions or commands? And more intriguing, how much did the master confide in the servant behind closed doors?

Finally, the train arrived ten minutes late. It braked to a screeching halt and let off a cloud of steam, while porters rushed to the carriages and passengers hailed them. Most of the passengers had left the train when Edith walked up to an older woman coming out of a parlor car. Over the din, Pamela couldn't hear what they said to each other. Edith's greeting seemed polite but cool. Mrs. Dunn looked sour and worried. Perhaps something was wrong in her relationship with the Crawfords.

Pamela's impression was strengthened when Mrs. Dunn met James Crawford. Mrs. Dunn asked loud enough for Pamela to hear, "Where's Jason?"

James appeared to excuse the delinquent bellboy. Mrs. Dunn huffed, unappeased, then called a porter and set off for the Grand Union. Pamela wondered how Jason had earned her displeasure.

Another person on Pamela's mind was Francesca Ricci. Freeing her was the main reason for being in Saratoga Springs. It was almost two weeks since she had been put in the county jail awaiting trial. Pamela owed her a visit.

The girl's living conditions were far from dire. Mr. Barnes, the local lawyer, generally looked after her welfare. She had a small, clean cell to herself. Her food was plain but nourishing, mostly fresh vegetables and fruit, rice, and occasionally chicken. To keep up her spirits, Antonio Teti, a retired Italian tenor, and his wife, Magdalena, a soprano and versatile musician, visited her twice a week.

Pamela had hired the Tetis through Helen Fisk—they sang at her parties. "Delightful people and accomplished musicians," Helen had said. "They'll cheer up Francesca if anyone can."

Near the courthouse in Ballston Spa, Pamela stopped at the Teti studio. "Our little canary is sad," Antonio reported. "Magdalena plays the concertina, and we sing Italian hymns and songs. Francesca listens. Her eyes fill with tears. She wants to sing with us, but her spirit fails."

Magdalena Teti explained that the jailor and the guards

treated Francesca gently because the judge said they should, but they looked upon her as a convicted killer and disrespected her. In return, she smiled sweetly, while cursing them in Italian. They sensed her contempt and disliked her all the more. "We tell her to be prudent, but she can't."

Today, when Pamela sat down with Francesca, she was sullen. Nothing seemed to please her. The food was tiresome, the same every day. The mattress was lumpy; she couldn't sleep. The guards were ignorant and unfriendly. She couldn't talk to anyone. Even the musical visitors couldn't cheer her up.

"Mrs. Thompson, is this what I should expect for the rest of my life?"

"No, Francesca. I'm sure we'll soon find the person who killed Captain Crake. Then you'll be freed. Our progress seems slow, but we now know a lot more about Crake and the people around him than we knew a couple of weeks ago. A few of them are strong suspects. Be patient."

As Pamela rose to leave, Francesca began to sob. Pamela glanced at the guard. He looked the other way. She hugged Francesca and comforted her. "I love you like a daughter, Francesca. I promise I'll get you out of here or die trying." Pamela handed her a handkerchief.

The girl dabbed the tears from her face. "Thank you, Mrs. Thompson. I appreciate what you're doing. The Tetis are kind and helpful. I'll be all right."

It was dark outside by the time Pamela returned to the Grand Union Hotel. The gaslights turned Broadway into a huge stage. Under the leafy canopy of tall elm trees, men and women of all ages and descriptions strolled up and down the broad sidewalks in fashionable summer dress. In the distance she heard a flute. At first, she couldn't make out the melody. Then it became clear. Jason Dunn was in the hotel cupola playing "Garry Owen," one of the favorite marches of New York's

Sixty-ninth Regiment. On the street a musician with a trumpet picked up the tune and voices joined in.

Pamela sat in a rocking chair on the hotel's front porch to enjoy a cool evening breeze. She glanced at the spectacle on the street below her. A handsome pair caught her eye—Rachel Crake and her lover, Rob Shaw. If Detective Brophy's short leash distressed them, they didn't show it. Rachel still wore a widow's black gown but was as frisky as a young girl without a care in the world. He was all smiles, a cock of the walk.

"Good evening, Pamela." Helen Fisk sat next to her. "I heard that Shaw was incredibly lucky this evening in Caleb Mitchell's gambling den. I suppose he'll bet his winnings at the thoroughbred races tomorrow."

"Thanks for the tip, Helen. I'll find a way to watch him there."

"Any word from Harry Miller in New York?"

Pamela had told Helen about Ruth Colt's disappearance and the investigation that pointed toward Crake as the prime suspect. "Not yet," Pamela replied. "I'm waiting eagerly to hear from Harry."

# CHAPTER 19

## A Change of Heart

*New York City*
*Monday, July 23*

Early in the afternoon, Harry Miller approached a low, brick building on West Twelfth Street, in the city's produce district. Emil Schmidt lived there alone in a rented room above O'Leary's saloon. During the five months while the investigation was suspended, Prescott's clerks had kept track of him. March 1, he had retired from the Crake Meatpacking Company and now worked at odd jobs in the markets. Most of his spare time was spent in the saloon.

"Where can I find him today?" Harry asked the barman, handing him a coin.

He explained that Schmidt was working in the West Washington Market, the vast buildings where fruits and vegetables came by ship on the Hudson River. "He's unloading a ship of the Savannah Line and has promised me a bag of fresh Georgia peaches in exchange for a pint of Ruppert's ale."

Late in the afternoon, when the Savannah ship was empty and the crowd of merchants in the halls had thinned out, Harry found Schmidt stacking boxes of peaches in a wholesaler's stall.

Tired and sweaty from hours of hard labor, he seemed down-cast. When he picked up a bag of peaches and was about to leave, Harry approached him.

"Would you join me for a cool drink, Mr. Schmidt. I'd like a word with you."

Schmidt stared at Harry. "Do I know you? Your face looks familiar."

"We've met. I wore a beard then."

The man's lips parted slightly. A light of recognition slowly appeared in his eyes. "Months ago, you and that smart lady with all the questions toured my night shift." He frowned. "Crake warned me afterward never to talk to you."

"Crake is dead."

"So I've heard." He closed the stall. "I knew you'd get back to me. Where shall we have that cool drink?"

"At Amy's on Twelfth Street," Harry replied.

It was a simple, quiet restaurant a few steps from the market. They sat at a secluded table and ordered beer, bread, and cheese. Harry raised his glass. "Here's to Crake."

"May he be damned for what he did to that girl in January." Schmidt clinked Harry's glass and settled back in his chair. "I've been thinking about her ever since."

"Why did you cover up for him?"

Schmidt took a draught of his beer and smacked his lips. For a long moment he gazed thoughtfully at Harry. "We had served together in Sherman's March to the Sea, and I owed him my job. I thought we were friends, but that changed in January." He hesitated, lowered his eyes, and seemed to struggle with a bad memory.

"What happened then?"

"It's hard to talk about it." Schmidt seemed to choke up, then spoke softly. "Late at night, Crake showed up at the factory door with that girl's body in a cart. I hardly recognized him in shabby clothes and wearing a fake beard. He looked fearful and exhausted, like he'd been through hell. I'd never seen him like that, even in the worst of times in Georgia. Adversity was his natural element. He had such a forceful personality."

"How did you deal with him?"

"I led him and his cart into a storeroom. We were alone. He let me uncover the girl's face. I saw her bulging eyes and the marks of his hands on her throat. I asked him what happened.

"He mumbled something I couldn't understand. Finally, he said, 'I couldn't get it up. She thought that was funny and began to laugh. I warned her. She laughed even more. Called me a silly old man with a burned-out candle. I grabbed her by the throat and shook her and then . . . I choked her.'

"For a minute, Crake and I just stood there, staring at the body. I could sense that he was gaining control of himself. I should have called the police, but I felt paralyzed. Crake began to stare at me. He had figured out what I was thinking. Then he said, 'Schmidt, if you go to the police, my men will chase you to the end of the earth and kill you.' "

Schmidt met Harry's eye. "I knew he'd kill me as easily as one of his hogs. Like a coward, I gave in. For that I can't forgive him."

Harry gave Schmidt a sympathetic nod. "How did you two dispose of the girl's body?"

"Crake left it all up to me. I had to act fast. In less than five hours the plant would open again. I couldn't bear to chop her up, so I tried to think of a burial place in the building. Then I remembered the former cooling system. It was still intact as a backup. Cold air from the ice room used to flow through ducts into the cooling room where we hung the carcasses. The new system used the old ducts. I found an open duct about six feet off the floor. The air inside was freezing cold. I hoisted the body into the duct, then bricked it up and rubbed on a little dirt and soot to match the rest of the wall."

"Did anyone notice the duct was closed?"

He shook his head. "I finished the job maybe thirty minutes before the plant opened, and I let Crake and his cart out the service entrance. Still, I was nervous all day. No one seemed to notice my work or ask about it."

Harry expressed surprise.

Schmidt explained, "The packing process is continuous and dangerous and demands your full attention. Once it begins, no one looks around to see if the old ducts are open or closed."

Harry thought the moment was right. He looked Schmidt in the eye and asked, "Emil, are you ready to give Ruth Colt a proper burial?"

"Yes, I am." His voice was barely audible. He cleared his throat. "Ever since I heard that Crake had died, I've been thinking about that girl. She shouldn't be lying there among slaughtered hogs. It's just not right."

"Good," said Harry. "Then I'll figure out a plan."

On the way to his room on Irving Place, Harry stopped at a telegraph office. Pamela would be eager to know what had happened.

# CHAPTER 20

## At the Track

*Saratoga Springs*
*Tuesday, July 24*

A knock on her door awakened Pamela. She threw on a robe and opened to face Jason Dunn. With a brusque gesture, he handed her a telegram and went quickly on his way. She rushed to the window and read Harry's message in the early-morning light.

> GOOD NEWS. SCHMIDT WILL REVEAL
> RC'S BODY AND TELL ALL. PORTER
> AND POLICE ARE STILL PROBLEMS.
> HARRY

She tried to fill out the message in her mind with what she already knew. Porter would be deathly afraid of scandal and might block Harry's plan. The police might feel embarrassed that a private investigator had done their job. Her hand trembled with excitement as she laid the message on her table and hurried her toilette. She would be anxious until she heard again from Harry of his plan's success.

＊　＊　＊

As Pamela returned to the hotel from a morning walk in Congress Park, the reception desk clerk handed her a personal note from Edith Crawford. She proposed visiting the thoroughbred track on Union Street that afternoon, together with Mrs. Dunn and Virgil, then added, *"James and I have entered our horse, Savannah, in the first race. You would enjoy watching her."*

Pamela moved into a parlor and considered the invitation. This was an opportunity to become better acquainted with Edith, an avid rider, in a place where she felt comfortable rather than under investigation. Rob Shaw could also be observed in his natural element at the track.

They were to meet at the hotel's front door at one o'clock. Edith had arranged for a carriage to the track. Since the races began at two-thirty, they would have a full hour to visit the premises.

Pamela was tempted. Two years ago, Mr. Gottfried Walbaum, the track's new owner, had built a grandstand to accommodate up to 5,000 spectators, as well as a new clubhouse and a betting ring. Saratoga's track now rivaled the best in the country.

She wrote her acceptance and brought it to the clerk. "I'll see that she gets it, ma'am."

Pamela spent the rest of the morning writing at her desk. In a message to Prescott, she forwarded the news that Emil Schmidt was to cooperate in the search for Ruth Colt's body. She also wrote an encouragement to Francesca in prison, promising to report on the fashionable men and women she would see at the racetrack.

Near one o'clock, she went downstairs. At the door, Edith was waiting, her expression a bit sad. "I'm sorry to report that my brother, James, will have to rest in his room this afternoon. He was really hoping to watch Savannah run. The excitement at the track, unfortunately, would be too tiring for him. In his place Virgil will escort us."

Pamela was disappointed, but she would find another occasion to become acquainted with James. Despite his disability, he was clearly the leader of the family and would have had the last word in any measures concerning Crake.

On Broadway, the three ladies and their escort climbed into the carriage and set off for the track. In a few minutes the grandstand came into view with its distinctive row of steeples on the ridgeline of a slate-covered roof. Edith became their guide. "To the right is the clubhouse where we'll lunch while enjoying a view of the track. To the left is the betting pavilion for men. In the grandstand is a place where women may bet."

The clubhouse café was nearly full, but Edith had reserved a table overlooking the track. Wine flowed freely, and a few of the diners were tipsy. Edith's party ordered sandwiches. The women chose lemonade; Virgil had a glass of wine. During lunch, their conversation focused on the two-year-old filly, Savannah. This was her first race at a major track.

"My expectations for Savannah are modest," said Edith. "She's eager and strong, but frisky and needs more training. I hope she doesn't injure herself. She will improve in the coming weeks."

"How much are you involved in Savannah's training?" Pamela had noticed that the horse seemed to fill a deeply rooted desire in Edith to care for a living, sentient being. She also cared for her brother, James, but perhaps with less satisfaction. He seemed to turn largely to Virgil for companionship and service.

"She's my baby," Edith replied. "James and I have hired a professional trainer for her. But while we're in Saratoga, I visit her every day, help with her feeding and grooming, and ride her around the paddock. Being close to her is one of my main reasons for coming here. Back in New York, of course, I can only see her on weekends and holidays at our farm on Long Island."

When conversation drifted to local news of Charleston and New York, Pamela took the opportunity for a closer look at the dining room's interior. It was tastefully furnished with new café tables and bentwood chairs, and embellished with large flower boxes filled with sweet williams, petunias, begonias, and freesias. The clientele was female in the majority and socially mixed. All of them appeared to have money in abundance. Some were fashionably dressed and well-mannered like Edith and Mrs. Dunn; others were heavily painted, their gowns and hats vulgar or bizarre, and their speech and manners coarse. One woman was simply drunk.

After lunch, Edith announced, "It's time to place bets." As Pamela and Mrs. Dunn were unacquainted with this track's procedure, she added, "Follow me to the paddock where the horses are being exercised. You should watch them for a while and then decide which one to bet on."

At the paddock, Edith pointed to a large black horse and whispered to Pamela, "Keep an eye on Polly, the favorite in this race. Her jockey will wear a black silk shirt with a wide yellow diagonal bar across the front and the back. Polly belongs to the track's new owner, Mr. Walbaum from New Jersey, where he has a successful track."

"I've heard of him," Pamela remarked. "His jockeys are accused of bending the rules and winning more than their share of races. Some owners who used to race here aren't coming anymore because of Walbaum's bad reputation."

Edith grimaced. "That's unfortunate for all of us. But there's my Savannah." She pointed to a lively, chestnut brown filly. "Her jockey wears the Crawford colors, a blue silk shirt with a white St. Andrew's cross on the front and on the back." Her youthful eagerness instantly appealed to Pamela and earned her bet.

When everyone was satisfied with their choice, Edith led the way to the women's betting ring. Virgil went off by himself to the main ring for men only. The three women climbed up to a room on the top landing in the rear of the grandstand. Edith remarked, "We could have sent up our bets with a messenger boy, but I thought you'd want to see the bookmakers at work."

"And we needed the exercise," Pamela added with a good-natured smile. Mrs. Dunn muttered a complaint beneath her breath.

Two bookmakers were at a counter at the far end of the room, together with ticket sellers and cashiers. Behind them on the wall was a blackboard with the names of the horses and their odds. Savannah was there in the first race at 50 to 1.

"She's a risky bet," remarked Edith, staring at the board. "The bookies think she's unruly and may throw her rider or chase after a ghost."

"I'll bet they're wrong," Pamela remarked and placed a $1 bet on her to win.

Edith chuckled. "Aren't you brave! I must do no less." She also bet a dollar to win. Mrs. Dunn looked on with interest but abstained.

"That's a businesswoman accustomed to watching her pennies," Pamela said to herself.

At starting time for the first race, Virgil rejoined the party; he had also bet on Savannah to win. They moved to an area near the finish line reserved for wealthy owners. Edith was known there. The guards simply waved her party in. An usher brought them to seats with a clear view of the track. Several gentlemen tipped their hats to her and they exchanged opinions on the weather—it was pleasantly warm with a light breeze—and the condition of the dirt track, which was wet. Rain had fallen during the early-morning hours. Edith turned to Pamela. "This should be a muddy, untidy race. Savannah will enjoy it."

As the horses were led past the grandstand, the crowd's excitement grew to fever pitch. At the start the horses took off with Savannah a flighty third, the owner's horse leading the pack. Soon, Savannah figured out what she was supposed to do and put all her youthful energy into getting ahead of the others. At the halfway post she pulled into second place half a length behind the owner's Polly. Then Savannah put on a burst of speed and came abreast of her.

Going into the final stretch she and Polly were neck and neck. Walbaum's jockey lashed out with his whip to distract Savannah. This was clearly a foul. But the trick failed. Savannah kept her eye on the prize and won by a head.

She trotted to the barrier and nuzzled Edith in a touching gesture of affection. "I'm so proud of you!" Edith exclaimed, caressing the filly's head. An exultant smile lit up the woman's face like Pamela had not seen before. Edith's two years of dedicated work had come to fruition. And terrible memories seemed at least momentarily forgotten.

At the women's ring, Pamela and Edith collected on their bets. As they were leaving the grandstand, Pamela noticed Rachel Crake in her black silk widow's weeds, sitting partially hidden behind a large flower box of nasturtiums. A moment later, Robert Shaw sat down beside her. He looked wrathful, waved a ticket in her face, then tore it up. Sheltered by the flower box, Pamela drew as close as she dared to eavesdrop.

"What's the matter, Rob?" asked Rachel.

"I got skinned in that race. You told me to bet a thousand dollars on Polly to win. It was a sure thing, you said."

"That's what Mr. Walbaum told me. He should know. He owns the track, and Polly is his horse. I thought he would make sure she won. Well, he tried. You saw the trick his jockey pulled."

"It did me no good," Shaw complained. "I went back to Mitchell's den this morning and lost three thousand on the roulette wheel. At this rate, we'll soon be broke and can't afford to stay in our miserable boardinghouse."

"It's not my fault," she whined, "that Jed died *after* he signed the new will. Since then I've hocked most of my jewelry to pay your debts."

Shaw snorted, "You bring me bad luck. I shouldn't have risked my neck for you."

"Don't say that," she pleaded, then caressed him. "Cheer up. Maybe you'll have better luck in the second race. Walbaum has a horse there too."

"All right, I'll talk to the bookies. If I get a good tip, I'll lay down another thousand."

Pamela immediately began to walk away. At the same time, Shaw got up to leave and noticed her. Their eyes met. "Bitch!" he growled, his eyes dark with fury.

She hurried down the stairs to the lawn between the grandstand and the track. He started to follow her, but she met Virgil Crawford, who had waited for her. Shaw gave up the chase and turned toward the men's betting ring.

"So, what was that all about?" Virgil murmured.

"I eavesdropped and nearly got caught."

Virgil frowned. "Mr. Shaw is not a gentleman. Still, he wouldn't hurt you in broad daylight here in front of five thousand spectators. In the dark of night he might. So, be careful."

"I shall. Thank you."

"To judge from his angry reaction, you must have heard an intriguing conversation."

"Yes, I believe I did."

Unfortunately, Shaw's expression "risked my neck" was ambiguous, as well as intriguing. She would mull it over before drawing a conclusion and talking about it. She had also noticed the tension in Rachel's relationship with Shaw. That could lead to their breakup, and Rachel might then speak freely about her partner's role, if any, in Captain Crake's death.

As Pamela and Virgil walked toward Union Street and Edith's carriage, Pamela repeated Shaw's words silently: *"I shouldn't have risked my neck for you."* She wondered if he was using a common figure of speech for the risky bets he was making. Or, was he thinking of the electric chair?

# CHAPTER 21

## A Cold Grave

*New York City*
*Tuesday, July 24*

Tuesday morning at five, Harry Miller and Emil Schmidt waited in the Butchers Bar near Crake's meatpacking plants. Last night, Emil had mentioned that he often joined men from the cleaning crew for breakfast. They might have information that could be of use in retrieving Ruth Colt's body from the pork-processing plant.

A few minutes after five, the cleaning crew drifted in. Emil introduced his acquaintances to Harry. Someone mentioned that the shift was shorthanded. Harry winked at Emil. Here was an opportunity to see whether the old air duct was still bricked up.

A little later, the night manager arrived, another acquaintance.

"My friend and I could use some extra money," said Emil. "We're available for the night shift."

The manager thought for a moment. "I'm happy to find experienced workers, Emil. I'll pay you and your assistant by the hour. Come to the plant at seven o'clock this evening. I can use you in the cooling room until midnight."

After breakfast, Emil went back to work at the West Washington Market. Harry began looking for Sergeant White, the detective who initially investigated Crake's assaults on young women. After closing the investigation, Inspector Williams had assigned him to a petty crimes unit on the other side of Manhattan.

Harry found him off-duty at home with his wife and two young daughters in a warm apartment on Fourteenth Street near Union Square. It was lunchtime, and Mrs. White insisted on setting a place for Harry. After a tasty meal of potato salad, brown bread and cheese, and peaches, the table was cleared. Mrs. White brought iced tea to the men and withdrew with her daughters to another room.

Sergeant White asked, "What brings you here, Harry?"

"Do you recall that you investigated Ruth Colt's disappearance back in February?"

"Yes, the case was shut down when Captain Crake seemed involved."

"Well, I've come to tell you that after five months there has been a break in the case. A credible witness claims to know that Colt's body was hidden in Crake's pork-packing plant, a mile from here." Harry went on to describe the investigation up to now. "I need to check out the tip tonight. There's an outside chance that Crake might have later moved the body."

"Congratulations, Harry. What does this have to do with me?"

"If, in fact, I find the body, the police should be there to declare the site a crime scene and secure the evidence. Otherwise, the management might try to hide the body to avoid scandal."

"If I were to do this, wouldn't I first need permission from Inspector Williams?"

"I think so. He may like the idea better now than he did five months ago. Crake's death cut the financial connection between them. The police reformers are also badgering him. Solving the Colt case would make him look good."

"I'm interested, Harry. I think of that girl whenever I gaze at my daughters. When should the police move in?"

"Tonight at about midnight after the cleaning crew has left the building. The police should finish long before the plant opens again at five."

"Harry, I'll talk to the inspector this afternoon. He might refuse permission, but he just might do the right thing. Recently, he has seemed more thoughtful than usual, perhaps because he's nearing retirement and concerned about his pension. Shall we face him together?"

Harry shuddered at the prospect. Williams had been involved in sending him to Sing Sing. Nonetheless, he muttered, "Let's go."

At three in the afternoon, Harry and the sergeant walked into police headquarters on Mulberry Street and made their way to the detective department. Harry felt a surge of bitterness. He had earned a detective badge there, but it was shamefully snatched away. He tried now to put aside resentment and focus on the meeting with Williams.

A clerk showed them to the inspector's office. "Come in," said Williams in a detached voice, and gestured for them to sit facing him at his writing table. For a moment he assessed the two men without a flicker of a smile or any other sign of good will. "What's on your mind?" he said, gazing coolly at them.

Harry replied, "I have received a credible tip concerning the missing girl Ruth Colt. The person who helped Mr. Jed Crake hide her body has agreed to reveal its location. He has not come forward earlier because of Crake's threats to kill him. Since her body is prima facie evidence of a serious crime, I believe the police should be involved."

"Where's the body?"

"Hidden in one of Crake's plants, a short distance from where he killed her."

Williams leaned forward, arms resting on the table. "I know you, Miller, and your service in this department. I'll ignore the prison record. In Prescott's firm you've become a first-rate detective. I trust your judgment. What do you propose?"

For a long moment Harry was speechless. For whatever reason, Williams had affirmed him. Then he replied, "I'll check on the tip this evening. If it's true, as I expect, I'll call in Sergeant White and the police detail shortly past midnight when the plant is empty. Retrieving the body and examining the site shouldn't take them more than an hour or two and won't cause a mess. The plant will resume operation at five o'clock as usual. The body will be frozen and should go directly to the morgue."

"Why didn't you give your tip to Mr. Porter, the company manager?"

"The girl's body could be a nuisance, perhaps a scandal, for the company. If I gave the tip to Mr. Porter, he might choose to conceal or destroy the body. I didn't want to take that risk. The body is first and foremost evidence of a serious crime."

"I agree," said Williams. He turned to Sergeant White. "Go back to your original assignment, the investigation of the missing girl. Tonight, organize the police detail together with Mr. Miller and recover Miss Colt's body. I'll get a search warrant for you. Keep me informed. Early tomorrow morning, I'll explain to Mr. Porter what we've done. I'll also deal with the press. Good day, gentlemen."

Out in the hallway, Sergeant White exclaimed, "The inspector surprised me."

"Yes," Harry remarked dryly. "Williams said what any competent, right-minded inspector should. That frankly surprised me too. Tomorrow he'll take credit for neatly solving this case. Anyway, thank God for little favors. Let's get on with tonight's work."

At seven in the evening, Emil and Harry reported at the pork-packing plant for work. At Emil's request, the night manager assigned them to the cooling room. About 500 tightly packed carcasses hung there from a forest of hooks. Though already bled and cleaned, they still dripped and covered the floor with slippery gore. Cleaning the room would take hours.

From time to time workers came in with buckets of clear and soapy water and clean brushes and mops, and hauled away the waste. After a couple of hours, the pace of work slackened enough for Emil to inspect the closed duct.

"The patch appears just as I left it months ago," he told Harry. "But I'll try to pull out a few bricks to see if she's still there." A nearby bench allowed him to stand at eye level with the patch. From his pocket he pulled out a chisel and attacked the mortar in the lowest range of bricks. Meanwhile, Harry swept up the debris and continued cleaning the floor. With frequent interruptions, Emil managed to loosen six bricks, an area eighteen inches wide and six inches high.

He turned to Harry. "I'm ready to pull out the bricks. Bring the lantern. We'll see what's in here." He handed the bricks to Harry one by one. When the third brick was removed, Harry felt a rush of freezing air. When the last brick came out, the flow was strong and uncomfortable. Emil took the lantern and held it up to the hole.

For a moment he stood still and was reverently silent. Then he whispered, "She's there." He reached in. "Her body is frozen hard." He handed Harry the lantern. "Give me the bricks. I'll fit them in loosely, just in case."

He had just fitted the sixth brick when the night manager

walked up. "What do you think you're doing? Get down here and finish the floor."

"The old duct is blocked. The carcasses in this area aren't getting enough cold air in this hot weather."

"Let it be. I'll have a man look into the matter one of these days. The air feels cold enough to me."

They finished work as the bell rang announcing midnight and the end of the shift. At the exit, they lingered a few minutes until their companions went either to the next building or home. Then Harry signaled Sergeant White, who came running toward them.

"We found her," Harry said. "Bring the ice wagon up close. We want to keep her frozen for the autopsy. Follow us." He led the police into the packing plant, past a pair of bewildered watchmen and the night manager.

Late in the afternoon, Harry and Emil Schmidt waited for Sergeant White in Pete's Tavern on Irving Place. "It's my treat," Harry said when inviting the others. "We must celebrate solving the Colt case." The police had recovered the girl's frozen body and taken it to the morgue where her aunt identified it in the morning. Harry had wired a message to Pamela. It was nearly dawn when he fell into bed.

Sergeant White walked into the tavern, a broad smile on his face. "I've just left police headquarters. Inspector Williams is in a good mood, pleased with last night's operation. Here are the evening papers." He passed them to his companions.

In an interview with the *Mail and Express,* Williams reported that the police, acting on a tip, had recovered the body of Ruth Colt, a young murder victim. A coroner's inquest would make a final determination of the facts. A preliminary examination indicated a violent death by strangulation. Funeral arrangements would soon be announced.

In the *Evening Post,* speaking for the Crake Meatpacking

Company, Mr. Porter regretted the untimely, violent death of the girl and thanked the police for expeditiously removing the body with no damage to the company's property or its products.

Harry laid down his paper and asked his companions, "Have you noticed that neither Porter nor Williams has mentioned that the girl's suspected killer was the packing company's founder and chief executive?" He lifted up his glass and led the others in a toast. "To Ruth Colt. May she rest in peace. Finally."

# CHAPTER 22

## *Painful Revelation*

*Saratoga Springs*
*Wednesday, July 25*

Early that same day, Pamela sat down for breakfast in the hotel dining room. While she was reading the menu, her waiter came with a telegram.

> COLT'S BODY RECOVERED. CASE
> SOLVED.
> HARRY

Pamela breathed a sigh of relief, then felt a rush of satisfaction that justice had been served. Confused images and sounds of the packing plant surfaced unbeckoned in her mind. She grew eager to hear the precise details.

Then Virgil Crawford approached her table. "May I join you?" he asked with a slight bow.

"Please do," replied Pamela, and handed him the telegram. Her curiosity was piqued. Was it by chance that he came shortly after the telegram?

He read the terse message as if he, too, were trying to puzzle out the details. "Edith and James should be pleased. Our house-keeper, Mrs. Colt, will identify her niece and bury her, a painful duty, even though they were estranged." His jaw tightened in anger. "Unfortunately, Crake has escaped punishment again. But the court of inquiry and the press must at least tell the world that he was responsible for her death."

Pamela agreed, but she wondered skeptically whether the court would rise to its duty. Virgil gazed at her with a hint of admiration in his eyes. "You and your partner, Mr. Miller, have proved to be shrewd and tenacious investigators. You will also, I'm sure, solve the murder of Captain Crake . . . if anyone can."

An odd inflection in his final cautionary phrase puzzled Pamela. Was he teasing or taunting her?

After breakfast, Pamela walked to the spring in Congress Park and ordered a glass of water, hoping for a chance encounter with one of the suspects in the Crake murder. When a suspect's guard is down, he might unwittingly reveal his secrets. A few minutes later, James Crawford approached in the wheelchair pushed by Virgil. They smiled to Pamela but sat at a different table and ordered water. When they finished drinking, they lingered in quiet but intense conversation.

She wondered if Virgil had told his cousin the news concerning Ruth Colt. To judge from their frowns, they seemed to have something else on their mind. Pamela decided not to interrupt them and she rose to leave. Virgil rushed up to her. "Mrs. Thompson, could we meet discreetly in the park near the fountain? James would like to talk to you privately."

With a frisson of apprehension she agreed and set off into the park. At the fountain she looked for a secluded place, assuming they were to discuss a sensitive issue. The two men arrived shortly, and she led them to a bench hidden by a hedge.

"We are worried about Jason Dunn's erratic behavior," James began. Virgil took a step back but remained quietly engaged. "Since Edith had recommended him, the hotel management has approached her with its concerns. He recently seems distracted or preoccupied, and sometimes angry. His work has consequently suffered. He goes off on an errand and forgets what he was supposed to do. He resents constructive criticism and snaps at guests who complain."

"Why have you brought this problem to me?" Pamela asked. "Can I be helpful in some way?"

"Yes, I believe you can," James replied. "Since you are investigating Captain Crake's death, you have an interest in Jason. He was at the Victor Herbert concert on the seventh, so he is a potential suspect. You may also be aware of his animosity toward Crake, prompted apparently by the captain's flirtation with pretty chambermaids like Francesca Ricci." James hesitated, then met Pamela's eye. "Jason has recently also made threatening remarks about Edith. I fear he may harm her."

Pamela looked askance.

James persisted. "Jason claims she is his mother and accuses her of abandoning him as a baby. Therefore, it's her fault that he's been unhappy all his life." Pamela noticed the sardonic tone in James's voice. Her eyes drifted unbidden toward his wheelchair. Years of nearly constant pain appeared to have drained James's capacity for empathy. He had little left over for Jason's complaint.

"Why would she reject him?"

"She was ashamed of him. You see, from his youth, Mr. and Mrs. Dunn had led him to believe that his father was a brave Confederate officer who died in battle. His mother was his fiancée, who died in childbirth. Eventually, Jason doubted that story and searched for a factual one. Earlier this year on a visit to Charleston, he discovered Mrs. Dunn's secret diary and read a new, shocking version of his birth."

"And that is?"

"In April 1865, just as the war ended, my sister, Edith, arrived, pregnant, at the Dunns' hotel in Charleston, begging for secret lodging until she gave birth. Mrs. Dunn is our maternal aunt. The Dunns agreed to shelter her, promised to raise the child as their own, and concocted the melodramatic tale of the star-crossed lovers. At the time, Mrs. Dunn asked Edith about the baby's father and was told that he was a common soldier passing through Savannah. He had soon disappeared. Mrs. Dunn didn't pursue the matter any further."

"That's unfortunate," said Pamela. "Jason doesn't realize that Crake forced himself upon Edith. She still suffered from the lingering effects of a brutal beating and assault. The plantation was financially ruined, and her parents were dead. Her prospects for a suitable marriage were poor. Hence she reasonably felt that she couldn't raise the child herself. At least she put it into the hands of a decent, responsible couple. Many women in a similar situation might have left it on a church's doorstep."

"I agree," said James. "Unfortunately, Jason may believe that Edith gave herself willingly, even lusted for the soldier, a man scarcely more than a tramp. Virgil and I are both deeply concerned that Jason may have slid into a dangerously irrational frame of mind. We fear for Edith and perhaps for Mrs. Dunn. Could you look into this matter and perhaps suggest a solution?"

Pamela considered his request for a moment, then replied, "I could meet Jason and sound him out. He seems willing to talk to me. When I have a clearer impression of his state of mind, I'll contact you. We'll decide then what more could be done."

When Virgil and James left the park, Pamela moved to a bench overlooking the fountain and thought over what she had learned. Edith Crawford's awful secret was now likely to be exposed. Jason would probably tell anyone willing to listen. Could Edith live with that—literally? A short while ago she said she'd rather die.

What exactly was Jason's frame of mind? Had James Crawford intimated that Jason had unwittingly killed his father? If he realized what he'd done, he would likely also attempt to kill his mother. Pamela felt uneasy in her mind. Could James have been subtly trying to scapegoat Jason and steer the investigation away from himself and Virgil? After all, they were legitimate suspects in the case.

Pamela returned to the park's mineral spring in hopes of running into Mrs. Dunn. Her sour appearance could have to do with Jason's perusal of her diary. Faithful to the visitors' ritual, she soon arrived with Edith Crawford. They took a table and ordered glasses of the water. Both women appeared to be very upset. Edith waved a greeting to Pamela, hesitated for a moment, then beckoned her to the table and mentioned to Mrs. Dunn that Pamela was a private investigator.

"A challenging profession for a woman," said Mrs. Dunn through tight lips. "I understand from Edith and James that you have learned a great deal about the Crawfords and their kin—thanks in part to my disloyal foster son, Jason."

Pamela chose her words carefully. The older woman was breathing heavily. "Mrs. Dunn, I regret that he read your private diary without permission. If I were in your place, I would also be disappointed and angry with him. Unfortunately, he has coped poorly with his discovery and is mentally disturbed. He needs to learn that you and Edith have done the best you could for him under very difficult circumstances."

Mrs. Dunn stared hard at Pamela. "You have too much sympathy for that ungrateful young man. He will learn life's lessons the hard way." She signaled to Edith that she wanted to leave. The two women drank their water and left in the direction of the hotel.

Pamela waited a few minutes in reflection on the Crawfords, a family in crisis. Then she left the spring and returned to the hotel. Jason might be playing his flute in his free time.

Pamela found Jason in the cupola of the hotel's central tower, sitting near an open window, already dressed for his bellboy duties. His flute was on a table at his side. He was looking down at his feet, a scowl on his face.

Pamela approached him. "May I speak with you, Jason?"

"I'm busy," he said curtly, then looked up. "Oh, it's you, ma'am." He fetched an empty chair for her. "What do you want to talk about . . . as if I couldn't guess?"

"James Crawford has just told me that you discovered the identity of your real parents."

He shrugged. "I'm sorry that I read Mrs. Dunn's diary. I wouldn't know now that my mother dumped me with Mrs. Dunn, who raised me as a servant, not a son. When I grew curious about my parents, she told me a fantastic lie about a heroic officer's death in battle and his fiancée, who died giving birth to me. In fact, my mother slept with a soldier, like a common whore. I was the unfortunate result."

Pamela noticed that Jason seemed unaware of that soldier's identity. "Have you discovered your father's name?"

"It's not in Mrs. Dunn's diary. He must have been one of the thousands of Union or Confederate soldiers in Georgia in December 1864, when I was conceived. I wouldn't know where to start looking."

"What do you know about Edith Crawford's background?"

"A little. I met her occasionally in Charleston at the Dunns' hotel. She and her brother were raised on a plantation near Savannah. He was injured in the war. Afterward, they went into the shipping business and moved to New York. She's rich, smart, and good-looking. Doesn't smile much and keeps people at a distance."

Pamela searched Jason's face. How much of the Crawford family's tragedy could he bear to hear? The full truth could trigger a desperate, irrational reaction. He might throw himself out the window. Or, he could lash out at her. On the other hand, if the truth remained hidden, he would continue to search for his natural father's identity and grow increasingly obsessed and frustrated. Finally, she decided she should take the risk and tell him gently. If he were to heal, he needed to know.

"Jason," she began, "you will probably begin to feel better if you understand your mother's situation at the time."

Pamela then related what had happened on that December day in 1864 when Captain Crake and his foraging detachment descended on the Crawford plantation. As Pamela spoke of Crake's furious assault on Mrs. Crawford and Edith, Jason turned pale. Tears filled his eyes; his lips quivered.

"You were conceived, then, in your mother's extraordinary pain and anguish. She was severely injured, not only in body but also in spirit. Nonetheless, she didn't reject you but bore you to term. Unfortunately, she lacked the strength to raise you, so she placed you in the best hands that she knew, Mrs. Dunn's."

Jason was silent, his brow creased in conflicting emotions. Then his expression hardened. "Why did Mrs. Dunn lie to me all those years? My mother never contradicted her. Maybe she helped invent the lies. The two women must have agreed that my birth was shameful. How could a rich, prominent Southern lady like Edith Crawford show her face—and her bastard Yankee baby—in Savannah society! Ridicule is what they feared. That's the truth. It doesn't make me feel better."

Pamela gazed at Jason and felt inept, and began to regret that she had tried to enlighten him. He was mired in his misery. Could anyone free him? Hunched forward, he stared into space, his chin thrust out and rigid. For a long moment, they sat there together silently. Pamela couldn't find words that might lessen his bitterness and lift his spirit. He had stumbled onto a harsh reality from which there seemed to be no escape. After thirty years, society would still punish a bastard and his mother—all the more if they aspired to lofty heights of wealth and social prominence, like the Crawfords.

Eventually, Jason let out a long, slow breath and his shoulders relaxed. He turned his gaze toward Pamela. "There were thousands of men in Sherman's army near Savannah that December day. But Fate is a cruel bitch. She chose Captain Jed Crake to forage the Crawford plantation and meet my mother. Brutal, lecherous, and false, he's the man I've hated most in this world. And you tell me he's my father! I'm so happy I want to jump for joy—out of this window."

He rose from his chair and walked rapidly to the window. She followed him, her anxiety mounting with every step. The windowsill was waist high. She gasped as he leaned over the edge and stared down at Broadway six floors below.

"Come back, Jason." She spoke as firmly as she could. Her voice threatened to turn into a shriek. "You may hurt yourself and others."

He slowly drew back from the window, a malign smile on his face. "Why don't you try it? The view is great." He took a menacing step toward her, then another.

She stood her ground. "Another time, Jason. I'm not dressed for it today."

He stared at her. A confused expression came over his face, but he didn't insist. He turned toward the window, stretched out his arms, and asked in a high, piping voice, "I wonder how it would be to fly like a bird? Someday I'd like to try." He twirled round and round, flapping his arms.

She studied him closely. His eyes were unnaturally bright and unfocused. She wondered if he was taking drugs to ease his pain. When he tired, she led him downstairs.

# CHAPTER 23

## Kinship's Duty

*Wednesday, July 25*

Back in her room, Pamela wrote in her journal about this encounter with Jason Dunn. Clearly, his mental problems had deep roots in the past, but they had worsened and had to be addressed soon. Tom Winn might know a competent doctor willing to help. In the meantime, she hoped Jason wouldn't hurt himself or anyone else.

At the reception desk, she waited while the clerk was busy. Jason was standing off to a side. Usually his appearance was fastidious. Now his pale, drawn face was unshaven and his hair was tousled. The clerk glanced at him critically, then gave him a message to deliver. He ran off without noticing Pamela.

"Where's Tom Winn?" she asked the clerk.

"He's in his office. A short while ago, he was looking for you. His door is open."

"May I close the door?" Pamela asked as she entered Winn's office. "I need to speak privately about the bellboy Jason Dunn."

Winn frowned at her mention of Jason. Then he straightened his tie and pulled up a chair for her. "What's he done?"

"This morning, he threatened to jump out of the cupola onto Broadway six floors below. I believe he's mentally ill and dangerous." She sketched Jason's state of mind from his birth to the present but without mentioning names. "In a true sense," she concluded, "he's a war orphan, one of the uncounted casualties."

"Poor chap, I feel for him." Winn sighed. "But we can't have him killing himself and perhaps a passerby. The housekeeper lent him a key to the cupola so he could raise and lower the flag. He uses that opportunity to practice his flute. He's really very good at it. For a start, I must take away the key, though that might trigger a determination to kill himself. He could jump out of a sixth-floor window."

"Could the hotel put him in the care of a qualified medical person?"

"Possibly. From time to time, we have this kind of medical emergency. Recently, a gentleman gambled away a family fortune at Mitchell's den across the street and then tried to hang himself in one of our rooms. A chambermaid pulled him down. We called on Dr. Carson in town. He has a calming manner with desperate men and women, and runs a clinic for their recovery, but he's expensive and must be paid." Winn tilted his head in a doubting gesture.

Pamela acknowledged that the Grand Union was a commercial enterprise, not a philanthropic institution. "But there are hotel guests of means who are acquainted with Jason and concerned for his welfare. I'll approach them with this problem. In the meantime, he should be kept occupied. Could he be assigned to supervised duties on the ground floor? He's an experienced waiter. Perhaps he could work in the barroom."

"An excellent suggestion, Mrs. Thompson. I'll speak to the management. They are already worried about him."

\* \* \*

As Pamela hurried over to the Crawford suite, anxiety welled up in her mind. How would Edith deal with the idea of being responsible for her abandoned son? She could simply refuse to become involved and resent Pamela's interference in family problems.

In that case, perhaps Mrs. Dunn could assume the task as Jason's foster mother.

Unfortunately, her resources were limited and her health at seventy was doubtful. She and Jason also had a strained personal relationship. Years ago, she had gladly waved him good-bye when he left Charleston for New York. His search for his true parents had become irritating and embarrassing. Recently, his reading of her secret diary had angered her.

Nonetheless, something had to be done. And the Crawfords had to do it. Jason was one of them, even if they would rather forget it. His suicide would lie heavily on their consciences and expose their dark secret to the whole wide world.

At the Crawford suite, Pamela squared her shoulders and knocked. Virgil opened the door. Taken by surprise, he hesitated for a moment. "Oh, Mrs. Thompson, we were about to go to dinner. What can I do for you?"

"An urgent matter has come up that I should bring to the Crawford family's attention. I fear it might spoil your appetite."

"Bad news, then?"

"Distressing, I would say."

"Then come in. You should speak with James. I believe Edith is occupied in the final stage of her toilette. Mrs. Dunn is resting in her room."

Dressed in a light silk suit and tie, James was seated in his wheelchair, reading the *New York World.* "Good evening, Mrs. Thompson. What brings you here?" His tone was friendly but not cordial. He seemed to sense that she was bringing trouble.

"I must excuse myself for disturbing you at this time." She paused as he laid the paper aside. "Jason Dunn has become suicidal, perhaps homicidal as well. Something must be done for him before it's too late. The hotel management is fully aware of his condition and is willing to help, but the chief responsibility for him lies with the family."

A stunned silence filled the room. James spoke first. "Dinner must wait." He turned to Virgil. "Tell Edith and Mrs. Dunn to come. Mrs. Thompson will give us the details. Then we'll discuss what we must do, if anything."

Edith emerged fully coiffed and dressed for dinner, but her eyes were wide with apprehension. "What's happened?" she asked, pulling up a chair. Her eyes shifted back and forth between Pamela and James.

"Jason appears to have fallen into some sort of mental crisis," James replied. At that point, Mrs. Dunn came into the room, sleepy-eyed and sullen. James showed her to a chair, then glanced toward Pamela. "Go ahead, please."

She briefly described Jason's condition and the hotel's concern. "He's a danger to himself and to others. In his employment papers, Mrs. Dunn is listed as his next of kin in case of an emergency. This appears to be an emergency. The legal, and probably the only feasible solution is for Mrs. Dunn, with the support of the family, to commit him to Dr. Carson's care."

"What?" shrieked Mrs. Dunn, now fully alert. "He left me years ago. I owe him nothing. He's an ungrateful young man and the author of his own troubles. You don't know him, Mrs. Thompson. He's pretending to be sick in order to gain sympathy." She glared at Pamela. "Furthermore, don't you be telling me what I should do. This is none of your business."

"Now, now, Mrs. Dunn," said James, his tone soft but firm. "We face a crisis that has been long in coming. I'd rather hear the bad news from Mrs. Thompson than from the police or from scandalmongers. She's had years of experience dealing with family problems."

Through this exchange, Edith sat rigid, eyes wide, her hands pressed to her lips. Virgil stood poised as if to catch her, should she faint.

When everyone was quiet and a measure of calm had returned to the room, James took the lead. "We must do what we can to avert a tragedy and a scandal." He spoke to Pamela. "I, too, have noticed a change for the worse in Jason. I thank you for alerting us. He must be saved from himself. I can't think of a better solution than the one you have proposed. It also appears to be legal and has the hotel's backing. Behind the scene, I will assume the costs and act on Mrs. Dunn's behalf. She will experience a minimum of bother."

He surveyed those gathered around him. "Does anyone object or have a better plan?"

Mrs. Dunn sighed deeply and wrung her hands but remained silent. James was about to continue when Virgil spoke up. "I only wish to point out that Jason could object to this arrangement and refuse to be confined in a clinic under Dr. Carson's authority. He might think it's too much like being placed in prison and could engage a lawyer. Then Pandora's box might open."

"You are right, Virgil," said James. "We should first try to persuade him that this arrangement is in his best interest. That might be a difficult task since he's not acting like a fully rational person." He looked around at the others, then asked, "Does anyone here or elsewhere enjoy his trust and could talk to him?"

All eyes turned toward Pamela. For a moment she wished that she hadn't gotten involved with the Crawfords. "I'll try," she said. "God help us."

Back in her room, Pamela sat at her desk and reflected on her daunting task. Before going any further, she would visit Dr.

Carson and inspect his facility. She needed to be convinced it was suitable if she was to persuade Jason. He was likely to share the common view that treatment of the mentally ill was often ineffective and inhumane. The public asylums were overcrowded and poorly funded, and offered only custodial care.

The popular journalist Nellie Bly may have strengthened the public's negative attitude. A few years ago, Bly had feigned illness and was committed to a New York lunatic asylum. For ten days, she had suffered together with other inmates the most appalling abuse and deprivation. When she complained, an attendant doused her with pails of cold water. Her reports caused a national outcry of indignation. Pamela hoped that Dr. Carson offered an enlightened alternative.

Early in the evening, accompanied by James and Virgil Crawford, Pamela arrived at the gate of a large estate on the north edge of the village. Dr. Carson had agreed to see them. His porter was waiting and let them in.

Carson himself welcomed them at the front door. He remarked that the hotel proprietor, Mr. Wooley, had said their visit was to help one of his employees. "Let me show you what I can do."

Before going inside, he made a sweeping gesture over the property. "This estate was a wealthy woman's summer residence. When she died, she left it to us because we had cured her daughter's mental illness."

A low, decorative wall encircled the property. The grounds were landscaped in the informal English fashion, stretches of green lawn intermingled with groves of trees and flowerbeds. The clinic itself was a large, rambling, three-story, brown-shingled residence with a great porch stretching across the front side. Its rocking chairs were empty now. The patients were probably at supper.

Carson led Pamela and the Crawfords into a wood-paneled

foyer with a large fireplace and comfortable chairs. Off to the side was the door to his office. They entered and sat facing each other. A middle-aged man with thinning hair and gold-rimmed eyeglasses, Carson was unremarkable, except for the kindness and intelligence in his eyes.

"Mrs. Thompson, could you draw me a picture of the patient and his situation at the hotel? Mr. Wooley spoke in rather general terms."

Pamela identified Jason, sketched his life's history, and described the symptoms of his illness. She didn't mention the Crawfords by name.

Carson listened attentively, occasionally seeking a clarification. When she finished, he was briefly silent, a reflective expression on his face. "In layman's terms, Mr. Dunn appears to suffer from a personality disorder. As you realize, its roots reach back into his infancy. You are right to take his anger and his suicidal remarks seriously."

"Could you treat him?"

"I think so. We've had patients in the past with similar symptoms, and they responded well to our therapy. I should stress that it has been tested, going back a hundred years. At the time of the French Revolution, Dr. Philippe Pinel determined that depression and certain other mental illnesses were caused by traumas or similar profound distress to a person's character or spirit. Pinel devised a therapy to restore the damaged spirit to a healthy state. That's what we try to do here. Let me show you."

From his office they walked into a parlor where men and women were gathering for a concert. A young man sat at a piano. Carson whispered, "The pianist was scheduled to play at Carnegie Hall, a few months ago, when his health broke down. He has recovered well enough to play for us tonight. Music was part of his therapy."

They left the room quietly as the pianist began. Carson remarked, "Instead of tying a sick person to his or her bed, or worse yet, to the wall, as is too often the custom in asylums, we occupy the patient's mind with constructive activity, such as painting or woodcarving or playing a musical instrument."

They walked on into the dining room. Tables were being set for a meal. Each table had a vase of cut flowers on a white linen cover. A large window offered a charming, restful view of the distant Appalachian foothills.

"As you may recall," Carson said, "Miss Bly's New York asylum served her and the other patients thin gruel and rotten meat for dinner in a prison setting—as if they were criminal inmates. Our patients eat nourishing meals in a friendly, attractive environment. As always, the staff is nearby giving support and encouragement."

In the rear of the building were the baths. "Since at least Roman times," Carson remarked, "soaking the body in warm water has soothed the spirit. Massages are also helpful."

Behind the building were barns for horses, cows, and other animals. "Feeding and petting these creatures help our patients to engage with others and learn to care for them. For the same reason, there are also ducks and fish in the pond and cats, dogs, and birds in the house."

When the tour ended, Carson brought Pamela and the Crawfords back to his office. "What you've seen are merely our tools. Skillful, highly motivated, and well-paid hands make them effective. Our staff understands mental illness, empathizes with patients, prompts and directs them with questions, and listens carefully to what they say."

"What's your goal for the patients?" asked James Crawford.

"In a few words, we aim to bring patients to a lasting, healthy, realistic understanding of themselves and their relationship to others."

Throughout the tour James had seemed attentive and asked pertinent questions. Now, he thanked the doctor. "Your facilities and your method impress me. You will be hearing from those of us concerned for Jason's recovery." He gestured to Virgil that they were leaving and waved good-bye to Pamela.

Pamela remained behind and thanked the doctor. "Your approach seems appropriate for Mr. Dunn. I can imagine that the cost is high, but that's not an obstacle for his patron. I'll try to persuade Jason to meet you." She wished him good-bye and left.

As she walked back to the hotel, she felt encouraged. Still, the Crawford family's problems were daunting. Edith needed better mental health almost as much as Jason. The root cause of their illness was the same person, Captain Crake. Pamela had almost lost sight of her task to find his killer and free Francesca Ricci from prison. Jason was still a major suspect.

# CHAPTER 24

## A Reluctant Patient

*Wednesday, July 25*

Jason had disappeared. Pamela couldn't find him at the reception desk. He hadn't reported for duty in the evening. At the concert in the garden there was no sign of him. Pamela returned to the reception desk. The clerk she knew had just come on duty.

"Could you tell me where Jason might be? I'm concerned about him."

The clerk seemed embarrassed. "He's missing. On past evenings, I've noticed him on Washington Street, apparently looking for a female companion. Don't tell him that you heard it from me. He hates being spied on."

Pamela promised discretion. The clerk was a dependable source of information. She needed to keep his good will. She went to her room and changed to plain street clothes and scuffed shoes, and rearranged her hair into a simple bun.

She needed to be inconspicuous. Washington Street was a mixed, lower-class district to the south of the hotel on the far side of the tracks. The Metzgers and other hotel employees lived there, together with railroad workers and transients. Visitors of modest means frequented the inexpensive prostitutes living upstairs above the cheap taverns.

Jason was lounging on a street corner in the light of a gas lantern outside Mickey's, ogling young women going in and out. To judge from their low-cut blouses and heavy makeup, they were looking for customers. When he spoke to them, they either shook their heads or simply ignored him. Finally, he looked at his watch. An alarmed expression came over his face. He set off in a hurry in Pamela's direction. She slipped into an alley so he wouldn't see her. He continued on toward the Grand Union.

Pamela walked into the tavern looking for a familiar face. Erika Metzger from the laundry sat alone in a corner, staring at the glass of beer in her hands. To judge from her heavy-lidded eyes, it wasn't the first glass. "May I join you?" Pamela asked in German.

Erika looked up, surprised to hear her own language, then recognized Pamela, smiled, and replied in German, "Please do." She continued in German. "We live upstairs. It's not nice, but it's cheap. Right now the air's too warm, so I came down for a beer." She hesitated, but asked anyway, "What brings you to this part of the village?"

"I wanted to talk to Jason Dunn and was told he was here."

"He left just a minute ago. Said he was looking for my husband, Karl." She took a long drink of her beer. "This summer he and my Karl have been thick as thieves. Business, they tell me. They were supposed to meet here tonight."

Pamela showed interest.

"They talk a lot about Crake. He was trying to get Karl fired at the hotel and almost succeeded. That would have ruined us. Jason claimed he could help Karl. I don't know how. He's just a bellboy. But Karl seemed to appreciate the offer." She drank again, nearly emptying the glass. "Have you found out yet who killed Crake?"

"No, I'm still looking." But she felt she was now a step closer to the answer.

After Erika left the table, Pamela lingered for a few minutes, observing the tavern's patrons. She recognized waiters and maids from the hotel. A young woman named Molly, who worked in the hotel laundry, approached Pamela's table.

"Could we talk?" she asked.

Pamela recalled that the woman had just spoken with Jason at the tavern door. "Yes, then may I buy you a drink? I'd like one."

Molly agreed to a beer. Pamela signaled a waiter for two glasses. Molly began, "I've seen you talking to Erika Metzger in the laundry and again here. I don't understand German, but I heard Jason's name. Why are you interested in him?"

"As you may know, I'm investigating the death of Captain Crake and have to speak to all the people connected to him. That includes Jason. What can you tell me?"

"I've gone out with him a few times and listened to his flute. He's strange and recently getting worse. Tonight, he came to my room and tried to get me into bed with him. I refused. The girls say he's very rough and is likely to kill one of them. Well, he kept on asking and offering me money. I became really annoyed and I insulted him."

She stopped when the waiter arrived with the beer. When he left, Pamela pressed Molly. "What did you say to Jason?"

"If the truth must be told, I said, 'I'd rather sleep with a jackass than with you.' Jason grew red in the face and warned I'd be sorry. He'd get even with me like he did with Francesca Ricci. I said he was a liar and just making things up. He grew angry and shouted, 'Who do you think told the police he had seen her leaving Crake's cottage the night he was killed?' He pointed to himself. 'As far as I'm concerned,' he said, 'she can hang or rot in jail for the rest of her life.'

"I asked him, 'So, did you kill the captain?' Jason stared at me in his odd way. Then he said in a low, nasty voice, 'Wouldn't you like to know?' "

Pamela walked back to the hotel, puzzled by Jason's behavior. The garden concert had ended. Many of the men had scattered into the barroom and the billiards room. Other men and women had settled into the rocking chairs on the porches, or had left the hotel for Canfield's Casino or any one of a dozen gambling dens on Broadway. Winn was standing at the reception desk talking to a clerk.

He looked tired and worried, but he became alert when he noticed Pamela approaching. Before she could even greet him and mention her concern, he said, "We have a problem with Jason Dunn. The management fired him privately this evening for reporting late to work, that coming on top of other recent poor performance. He began raving incoherently about his misfortunes and abuse. Dr. Carson sedated him, and we put him into a secure room for the night. I delayed moving him to Dr. Carson's clinic until I heard from you. Will his acquaintances agree to commit him and pay the costs?"

"I'll go to them immediately and find out."

The Crawfords had attended the hotel's evening concert. When it was over, they had remained in the garden to enjoy the fresh summer-evening breezes. They had just returned to their suite when Pamela knocked on the door.

Virgil opened, glanced at Pamela, and murmured, "Trouble again?"

"I'm afraid so." She added, "I may have found a solution as well."

"I've just served an herbal tea and toast. Would you join us?"

"Yes, my message can be discussed over tea."

She followed him to the parlor. Mrs. Dunn had already gone

to her room, but Edith and James were seated by a tea table with cups in their hands. As Pamela entered the room, they turned toward her and gasped in unison, brows furrowed.

"What have we now?" exclaimed Edith.

James motioned to Virgil to pull a chair up to the table, then turned in his wheelchair to face Pamela. "At this late hour, you must have news to do with Jason."

"Correct. The hotel has fired him, and he has had a mental breakdown. At present, he is sedated and resting in a secure room. The time has come to decide what should be done for him. Do you wish to bring Mrs. Dunn into this conversation?"

"No," James replied. "It would only upset her. She has left the matter in my hands."

"This afternoon, you saw Dr. Carson's clinic and the therapy that it offers to patients. Were you satisfied?"

"Yes, indeed. He inspires confidence and respect. Could you give us an idea of the commitment we would have to make?"

"The first step is to agree to move Jason to the clinic. His initial examination would then begin tomorrow and could take from a few days to a week. During that time, you could become more familiar with the doctor, his clinic, and his therapy. At the end of the examination, he should tell you whether he could treat Jason and, if so, what the treatment would involve."

Edith waved a warning hand. Her voice was high-pitched and strained. "James, we must ask ourselves, Why are we getting more deeply involved with Jason Dunn? He's kin only in the most vulgar, physical sense, due to a dreadful accident in my life. And Mrs. Dunn is right: He's the author of his own misery. I say, let the state of New York care for him. Otherwise, he'll be fretting us for the rest of our lives."

James gazed at her, his eyes beginning to tear. "I share your concern, Edith. But I still believe that healing Jason is possible and is the best outcome for us. Untreated, Jason could bring his complaints to the public. Inevitably, our tragedy would be tied to Crake's murder and become front-page news. I simply can't bear to see you unfairly maligned, the butt of snide remarks."

Edith sank back in her chair, a defeated expression on her pallid face.

Virgil reached out a hand as if to console her but checked himself and drew it back. His face was creased with sorrow.

James turned to Pamela. "We should proceed with Jason's initial examination. When we understand his condition and the prospects for the future, we'll come to a decision. What's the next step?"

Pamela replied, "Tom Winn will contact you tomorrow morning about the legal issues. With your approval, he'll make the arrangements for moving Jason to Dr. Carson's clinic. Then let's hope for the best."

Virgil escorted her to the door.

"I fear for Edith," said Pamela. "She may hurt herself. Watch her closely."

# CHAPTER 25

## A Conspiracy?

*Thursday, July 26*

Edith Crawford stood alone on a desolate beach, pale and haggard, tearing at her hair, screaming silently. Then she waded out into the dark water until only her hair was floating on the surface. Pamela woke in a sweat, heart pounding. She jumped out of bed and paced the floor for several minutes. The crisis in the Crawford family was beginning to obsess her. Finally, she banished her fears with the thought that Virgil could be trusted to look after Edith.

After breakfast, Pamela made the ritual visit to the Congress Park spring to pick up useful gossip about her suspects. Helen Fisk soon arrived with Yvette on a leash. "I must thank you, my dear, for Birgitta, my new Swedish maid. She's a jewel. Her massages make me feel years younger."

Pamela was pleased to hear good news for a change. Then she noticed a petite woman in a black silk widow's garb, her face concealed by a black lace veil. "Look, Helen, I believe that's Rachel Crake."

Helen frowned. "The fact that she's alone and veiled tells me that something is amiss. Last night on the front porch, I heard that Shaw lost heavily at the track yesterday and declared he'd win it all back at Canfield's Casino if he had to bet until dawn."

Pamela added, "I saw him at the track on Tuesday. He had lost a thousand by the time I left after the first race. His mood was already ugly. He blamed Rachel for his bad luck. Perhaps she sees through him now and may help us investigate him."

With a shaky hand, Rachel lifted her veil to drink a glass of the spring water. Then she spoke briefly with the young black waiter and walked out into the park.

Helen whispered, "Follow her, Pamela. I'll have another glass of water and pick up a few more bits of news here. We'll meet later in my rooms. Watch out for Shaw. Keep him at a distance."

Rachel walked as far as the decorative fountain and sat on a bench. After glancing left and right, and seeing no one near, she folded the veil back, closed her eyes, and exposed her face to the sun's rays and a light breeze.

Pamela had followed her from a distance. She waited a few minutes, then quietly walked up to the young widow. Her once-pretty face was swollen and discolored with bruises. Pamela softly gasped. Rachel woke with a start. Pamela apologized, but added, "You shouldn't allow him to beat you. It will only get worse. Leave him."

Rachel pouted. "You've no right to sneak up on me like that." In the next second, she began to sob. "What can I do, Mrs. Thompson? I've given him my money, and he has lost it all. We can't pay the rent or buy food. The police won't let us leave town. Their spies follow us wherever we go."

"Where's Shaw?"

"With our last dollar he went to breakfast on Phila Street. He said he's going to borrow money and go back to Mitchell's den. Maybe he'll leave town. If I complain to the police, he'll track me down and break my neck."

"How do you feel about him after all this?"

"I hate him. Look what he's done." She lightly touched her bruised face. "It's not the first time. And he's leaving me without a cent. I couldn't even pay the waiter at the spring just now. He looked at my face, saw me crying, and said, 'Forget it. The water is on me.' I felt so miserable that I didn't even thank him."

"I'll arrange protection for you, Rachel; then I'll alert the police to his assault. Later, when you feel safe, we'll have a conversation about Mr. Shaw."

Pamela left Rachel in the care of Helen Fisk and went searching for Tom Winn. She met him as he returned to his office in the hotel. He and James Crawford had just arranged Jason's transport to the Carson clinic. James had remained in the background out of sight. Winn had accompanied Jason in a coach.

Pamela was surprised. "Didn't Jason resist? I thought I'd have to persuade him."

"No, I told him that the hotel management thought he wasn't feeling good and needed help. Jason hadn't objected. His mind is quite confused, and his mood is now passive and depressed."

"That's reassuring," she said. "At least he's in capable hands. Now I'm on my way to the police station. Shaw has beaten Rachel and I must report him. Who knows if he might flee to New York and disappear into the underworld?"

"Right," Winn replied. "We need to hold him here."

At midmorning, Pamela found Brophy enjoying a cigar in his office. The room was full of pungent smoke. He laid the cigar aside and gestured her to a chair facing him. His mood seemed relaxed and friendly for a change. Following her report on Shaw's assault on Mrs. Crake, he said, "I'm not surprised that Shaw might try to skip town. He's a clever rascal and often eludes my spies. I'll charge him with assaulting Mrs. Crake and put him behind bars. First, I'll take a look at her face and have her sign a complaint."

Pamela then related the comments of Molly, the laundry worker, on Jason. "In a moment of unsound mind, he seems to have admitted to falsely implicating Miss Ricci in Crake's death."

"Sounds plausible," Brophy remarked. "I'll talk to Molly and get a statement for the record. When we question him, we may have to make allowance for his mental state. He might be delusional."

Early in the afternoon, Pamela went to Helen Fisk's suite. Birgitta let her into a small parlor and closed the door. "While Mrs. Fisk is away visiting friends and acquaintances, she has left me in charge of Rachel. Can you imagine it?"

Pamela was amused.

Birgitta smiled and crossed her fingers. "For the moment she's docile. Of course, that won't last. Late this morning, Detective Brophy came here to question her and saw the swelling on her face. She gave him the details of the beating and signed a complaint. After a massage, she now appears to be in good spirits."

Pamela followed Birgitta to the breakfast room, where Rachel sat by a window overlooking the hotel garden. "Mrs. Thompson has come for tea," said Birgitta, and set an extra place at the table. Rachel smiled a welcome, but her eyes were wary. The women raised their cups in a toast.

"Rachel," Pamela began gently, "you told the police that Shaw was gambling at Canfield's Casino the night of your husband's murder and that you joined him at about eight. During the rest of the evening, was he ever out of your sight?"

"I didn't see him when he went to the bathroom or to Mr. Canfield's office on business." She hesitated. "Seriously, it was a warm night. The casino was crowded, the air very stuffy. Rob said he needed fresh air, so we stepped outside. He left me standing by the door and walked into the park. I can't tell you exactly when he returned. I might not have seen him right away."

"But in the police report, Rachel, you said, 'Rob was with me at the casino all evening.' Why didn't you tell the truth?"

Rachel's face took on an expression of wounded innocence. "Rob told me that I shouldn't mention his walk in the park. It would only complicate matters." She paused. "Anyway, the police didn't pursue the point. Frankly, I think they were already convinced that the Italian girl had killed the captain."

"Have you ever thought that maybe Rob killed Crake?"

Again, she didn't take offense. "I didn't suspect him at first. He wasn't a violent man for as long as I had known him—that's about five years. He behaved like a clever, amusing gentleman. He took alcohol in moderation and didn't smoke nasty cigars or pipes, just an occasional cigarette. He liked to gamble for high stakes, but so did the captain and I. At that time, Rob was lucky and usually won."

"When did you change your mind?"

"Eventually, his luck turned bad, and so did his attitude. He began to call me stupid and a whore. About the same time, the captain became suspicious of Rob and me, and threatened to cut me from his will. Rob said to me, 'Crake should watch his step. He knows that I've killed a man before.' "

"What could he have meant by that?" Pamela asked. "Was he referring to the black men he killed during Britain's war with the Zulus in South Africa?"

Rachel shook her head. "He was warning Crake that he had once killed a white man like himself at a gambling den in Kimberley, near the gold fields, in a quarrel over a woman."

Pamela addressed both women. "Did Shaw ever say that he killed the captain?"

They exchanged glances. Then Birgitta shook her head. Rachel spoke tentatively. "You heard him say at the race track that he had risked his neck to get Crake's money for me. I asked him what he meant by that remark. Had he done something that he could be hanged for? He looked worried. 'Oh, it's nothing,' he said. 'I lost my temper. Forget I ever said it.' Then he saw that you had heard him and he ran after you.'"

Pamela left Rachel in Birgitta's care and returned to her room in an agitated mood. She paced back and forth, realizing that Rachel was a cunning young woman who knew how to play the role of an innocent victim. Under questioning, she had subtly shifted any responsibility for her husband's death onto Shaw. In fact, she had believed she would gain by her husband's death and could have told Shaw where he could be found.

Shaw emerged as a major suspect with a strong motive: to secure Crake's money for Rachel—and himself. He also had access through Jason or Metzger to a boning knife. And finally, when he left the casino and walked into the adjacent park, he could have hurried to the rear of the hotel and into the garden, then sneaked into Crake's suite during the concert. Jason could have given him a key as well as a knife.

So, Pamela began to see that a conspiracy of his enemies might have killed Crake. Fate had brought Shaw, Metzger, and Jason Dunn together with the captain in the summer at Saratoga Springs. Their individual roles, however, were obscure.

Metzger had the most convenient access to the alleged murder weapon, and he was expert in using it, though only on the carcasses of animals. However, he would be concerned that the knife could be traced back to him. Moreover, he was unfamiliar with the victim's rooms and his movements.

As a bellboy, Jason had easy access to almost any place in the hotel. While attending the evening concert in the garden, he was aware of the victim's movements. However, he would have had to borrow or steal the murder weapon from Metzger. Since he had worked with Metzger in a meatpacking plant, he had experience using boning knives on animals, but he had not yet killed a man.

Shaw, in contrast, was an expert swordsman and a trained, experienced killer. He could quickly and precisely deal the fatal blow even in a dark room and with an unfamiliar weapon. However, like Metzger, he would not know the victim's location or his movements unless Jason or someone else told him. Finally, someone—either Metzger or Jason—had to put the boning knife in his hands.

It was now late in the afternoon. Pamela threw herself into a chair. She hadn't eaten since breakfast. Tired and hungry, she stared at the wall. A telephone hung there. Prescott had insisted that she have a room with one. It was time to consult him about the next step.

It took a while. Prescott's cabin didn't have a phone. Pamela finally reached him through the Curtis Hotel in Lenox, a short distance from the cabin. She gave him a brief account of the investigation since he left.

When he heard her theory of a conspiracy to kill Crake, he remarked, "Good work. This is plausible speculation. I'll return to Saratoga Springs on Saturday at noon. Harry Miller will join us later in the afternoon."

"How are things in Lenox?" She left it to him to bring up his family problems.

"We'll talk about them when we meet on Saturday. I'm looking forward to seeing you then. It's good to hear you."

She slowly returned the receiver to its hook, trying to hold on to the sound of his voice as it faded in her mind.

# CHAPTER 26

## *Friend or Killer*

*Friday, July 27*

Early in the morning before breakfast, Pamela received a message from Tom Winn.

> The police arrested Robert Shaw late yesterday in
> his boardinghouse and lodged him in the town jail.
> Brophy will charge him with battery on Rachel
> Crake. Unfortunately, a magistrate will soon set
> him free on bail. Caution Mrs. Crake.

Pamela breakfasted with Birgitta and Rachel in the dining hall and repeated the warning from the police. Rachel listened intently. "Robert must fear that I've exposed him. I can imagine his mood. When he's angry, he becomes very quiet. Right now, he's plotting how to get out of prison and kill me. Then he'll flee to South America or wherever, change his name, and go on gambling."

"Don't worry," said Pamela. "He can't touch you if you remain in the hotel with Birgitta."

When Pamela returned to her room, a message lay on the floor.

> Mrs. Thompson, would you care to visit Saratoga
> Lake with me this afternoon? If you are so inclined,
> you can reach me at the Crawford suite.

The message was signed, "*Virgil.*"

Pamela sat down to consider his request. Did Virgil wish to become a male friend, the fourth after Prescott, Harry Miller, and Peter Yates? Why not? She and Virgil were both honestly employed, had no lofty social ambitions, and were happy to serve others. They shared an appreciation of music and the arts. She was a widow; Virgil was a widower. However, he was among the potential suspects of a murder she was investigating. That could become a problem only if she were to lose her objectivity.

She rose and began pacing the floor. What would Prescott say? He was a special friend. She admitted that his reaction would concern her. But why should it? They didn't have exclusive rights over each other. He dined and danced with female friends. Granted, society held men and women to different rules of behavior. Nonetheless, why shouldn't she go for a boat ride with Virgil on a fine summer afternoon? Besides, he was an attractive man, and she liked his kind, gentle spirit. She was pleased that he had asked her.

Granted, certain men and women might raise an eyebrow because of his race—he considered himself a black man. To begin with, how could they tell? In a boat on the lake he would appear as "white" as any man in Saratoga Springs. In view of his other qualities, why should his race matter? True, he was born a slave. But his servile origin was due to a social evil that all decent men and women had repudiated. It had been abolished thirty years ago at great cost.

She sat down at her writing table and wrote that she'd be delighted to go to the lake with him. They could meet in the foyer in half an hour.

He was waiting near a window, leaning lightly on his sword cane and looking out over the front porch toward Broadway. In a tan silk suit, his shirt open at the neck, a straw hat on his head, his slender, supple body was poised to move. He must have heard her footsteps on the marble floor, for he turned, removed his hat, and greeted her. She was wearing a simple yellow silk gown, her hair in a chignon. His appraising glance quickly turned to approval.

As they left the hotel, he pointed to the sky with his cane and announced, "The weather is sunny, but its heat is tempered by a moderate southerly breeze. The boating should be good."

The ride to the lake was itself a joy. At the livery stable behind the hotel, the Crawfords had rented a simple but comfortable carriage for the season. Its canvas roof now sheltered Virgil and Pamela from the midday July sun. Two fine horses pulled them in steady traffic on Union Avenue, past several great mansions and the thoroughbred racetrack, and through a few miles of pretty farmland to the north end of the lake. At a marina, Virgil rented a canoe, and they joined dozens of small boats and sailboats milling about on the water. On this day, a section of the lake was set aside for college men in long, narrow racing shells practicing for the national regattas to be held here later in the summer.

Heat shimmered over the water, its surface rippling in a light, cool breeze. Pamela raised a parasol to ward off the sun's rays. Virgil took off his coat and straw hat, and laid the cane by his side. He paddled effortlessly to the center of the lake, a large oval about six miles long and almost two miles wide. Then he stowed the paddle, put his hat back on, and let the canoe drift.

Pamela took out her opera glass and handed it to him.

"How clever! It has a swivel lens that gives a diagonal perspective, just what every professional investigator should have. A suspect wouldn't realize she was being observed." He aimed the glass toward the shore but turned the lens toward her. "Charming," he murmured and returned the glass. "Worthy of its owner. Have you used it?"

"Thus far, only at the opera. Prescott gave it to me as a reward following a successful investigation last summer in the Berkshires."

They continued to drift. Faint bursts of friendly shouts from other boats skipped across the water. Waves lapped against the canoe. The air was clean and fresh. Puffy white cumulus clouds moved slowly through the sky like a flock of sheep.

Pamela savored the moment, eyes closed. Then she gazed at Virgil as he looked toward the distant mountains, a hint of melancholy on his face.

"Are you sad?" she asked.

"Sorry. A passing sentiment. I shouldn't let it spoil your pleasure."

"You didn't, I assure you."

"I used to share moments like this with my wife, Mary. I miss her." He brought forth a bright, kindly smile. "And I'm happy now to share them with you."

After a moment of reflection, she remarked, "I'm struck by how close—in the best sense of the word—you three Crawfords are."

He explained sagely, "As you've learned in your own experience, adversity brings out the best or the worst in human nature. We Crawfords went through hell during the war. In the horror of it all, God has taught us how to love each other. That has simply become our way of life. Each of us—Edith, James, and I—has been wounded, so we must care for each other."

He brought a teasing smile to his lips. "You've discovered much about the Crawfords. Now would you reveal yourself? I know very little except that you call yourself a widow and a private investigator. You are obviously much more."

She gave him a brief account of her life—privileged childhood, education in a women's college, travel abroad, social work in city slums—up to the crisis in her marriage to a banker, Jack Thompson. "We had grown apart," was all she could bring herself to say about his suicide a few years ago.

His eyes were sympathetic. "I read the story of his death in the newspapers. I can scarcely even imagine how much it must have hurt you."

"Fortunately, true friendships and fulfilling work have helped to heal my spirit."

"What led you into private investigation? It's not regarded as women's work."

"I'm not the first female detective. Thirty years ago, Allan Pinkerton hired a young widow, Mrs. Kate Warne, as one of his operatives. She helped him thwart a plot to assassinate President Lincoln. I began at St. Barnabas Mission by investigating the dire conditions of children in poor families in the slums of Lower Manhattan. The next step was to investigate my own husband's fraudulent behavior. Finally, my lawyer, Mr. Jeremiah Prescott, took me on as an apprentice, trained me in techniques of investigation, and sent me to guard Macy's jewelry."

"Do you enjoy your work?"

"I enjoy outwitting thieves, but my greatest satisfaction lies in helping someone like Francesca Ricci, a poor Italian immigrant, or anyone else, for that matter, who is wrongly suspected or accused of a crime. Prescott usually indulges me."

For a moment Virgil appeared withdrawn, reflecting on her remarks. Then he picked up the paddle. The canoe had drifted near to shore. "Shall we have a lemonade on the terrace and watch a boat race?"

She agreed gladly. He paddled into the marina and tied up the canoe.

Nearby was a hotel with a terrace overlooking the lake. They took a table with a view and ordered drinks. Below them on the water, two racing shells were lining up for a practice run, four oarsmen and a coxswain in each boat. In the crowd that had gathered on the terrace, young and old alike were furiously placing bets.

"Am I correct?" she asked Virgil, as their drinks arrived. "The young oarsmen in crimson shirts are from Harvard, the blue from Yale?"

"That's what I've been told," he replied. "I've never been to college." He added softly, "When I grew up, no college in the North or South would have me."

"You must have had an excellent tutor at home. You are a truly educated man."

"Mr. Dawson was his name. To this day, I recall him fondly. He laid the foundation, a love of language, beginning with Greek and Latin. Thereafter, James, Edith, and I have tutored each other. I feel very fortunate to have packed a great store of knowledge into my poor head."

A shout interrupted their conversation. She took out her opera glass again and gazed at the sight. The two college boats were now speeding out into the lake toward an official boat a half mile away. They made a wide turn around the boat and hurried back. Harvard beat Yale by a length, and bets were then settled.

A group of fashionable women at a nearby table, who had keenly watched the race and had bet heavily, stood up to leave, still chattering on about it. One of them was so absorbed that she failed to notice a gold coin fall from her purse. She and her companions walked away, leaving the coin on the floor. Both Pamela and Virgil had observed the scene. But before either of them could react, a young waiter dashed to the lady's table, scooped up the coin, and furtively put it into his pocket. Instead of going after the lady, he quickly cleaned the table, then started off in the opposite direction toward the far end of the terrace. The victim was still in sight and still chattering away, oblivious to her lost coin.

Virgil leaped up, seized his cane, and confronted the waiter. "Are you going to return that coin, young man?"

The waiter put on a defiant face. "What coin?" he snarled. "And who are you?"

Virgil raised the cane. "Hold your bad mouth or I'll give you a taste of this stick and haul you to the manager. You'll be in jail within the hour. Go to the lady. Now!"

A terrified look came over the waiter's face. He pulled the coin from his pocket and threw it on the floor. "I ain't got no coin," he whimpered.

"Then I'll deal with you later." Virgil picked up the coin, excused himself to Pamela, and hurried after the victim. At first startled, she thanked him profusely and tucked the coin into her purse.

When he returned to the table, Pamela asked what he would do about the waiter.

"On the way out, I'll tell the manager that he may have a thief on his staff. If the manager asks, I'll give him the details." He glanced at the sky. "The sun is low in the west. Shall we dine? I know one of Saratoga's best-kept secrets, an authentic French restaurant. The owner is a friend."

"I'd be delighted." She had a sense that she was being courted, and she enjoyed it.

Le Chat Qui Dort was in an old brick building up an alley off Caroline Street. The sign over the entrance depicted a sleeping cat. Pamela and Virgil were welcomed by the cat, wide awake and curious, and by a red-faced, sturdy, middle-aged woman.

"Monsieur Crawford, *bon soir.*" She wiped her hands on a towel, then glanced a question at Pamela.

"A friend, Mrs. Pamela Thompson," he replied. "We have come to sample your husband's cuisine and your pastry."

When they were seated, Virgil explained that the chef, Jean-Luc Beaudry, owned a much larger gourmet restaurant in New York City. He closed during the summer and moved to this small one in Saratoga, open five nights a week in the tourist season. He and his wife lived upstairs.

"Why Saratoga?" Pamela asked. "He could have chosen Newport with its ocean views and rich patrons."

"Saratoga fulfills Jean-Luc's idea of a heavenly vacation. He delights in its mild summer weather and mineral springs, its thoroughbred track, and Canfield's Casino. And he's among friends. Many waiters from his New York restaurant work for Canfield in the summer."

The interior reminded Pamela of a French country inn with its white plastered walls and exposed oak beams, wooden tables and chairs, and rustic crockery and tableware.

"How charming!" she exclaimed.

Virgil smiled. "From New York, Jean-Luc brings a selection of his finest French wines. We'll order a meal and follow his recommendation for the wine."

"Are we going to be his only patrons this evening?"

"We're early and his first. In a few hours this room will be full, and the prices will go up. Diamond Jim Brady and Lillian Russell and other celebrities might come. We'll be gone by then."

In a few minutes Jean-Luc came out of the kitchen. He and Virgil entered into a brief discussion in French about the meal. Pamela had earlier mentioned that she would prefer something light and tasty in modest portions. Virgil had agreed. With advice from Madame Beaudry, the two men chose a cold cherry soup, a garden salad, and a vegetable omelet. The dessert would be her gooseberry tartlet and the wine, a Loire white from Saumur.

"This is a simple meal and should arrive shortly," Virgil said. "For the more elaborate productions, Jean-Luc needs a day's notice. He would have to shop in Albany."

Madame Beaudry returned with a bottle and poured into a glass. Virgil swirled the wine, sniffed from the glass, and drank a thoughtful sip.

"That will do nicely," he said. She filled their glasses, and they toasted each other.

Then he leaned back, cocked his head, and asked Pamela, "Would you tell me what you did during the war?"

His interest seemed genuine and pleased her. "In the early years, my parents shielded me from its violence. Father thought I was too young and impressionable. Mother, however, believed I should have a taste of it. She herself was deeply involved. Her family came from Virginia. Many relatives still lived there and supported the Southern cause. Almost from the beginning she volunteered as a nurse in military hospitals. After Gettysburg in sixty-three, she took me along to visit the thousands of Confederate wounded left behind by Lee's retreating army. Her cousin, an officer, was among them. Because he had been blinded, Mother managed to save him from prison and brought him to our home on parole. For the rest of the war, I helped care for him. He was a thoughtful patient and taught me how to deal with suffering. I've been caring for people in need ever since."

"Then we have something else in common. My cousin James is also an exemplary patient. He rarely complains and is grateful for services and mindful of others. Captain Crake and Sergeant Tower nearly killed his body, but that only strengthened his spirit. He is determined to make the most out of life and disdains revenge, a primitive passion."

"So what does he think of Crake?"

"A man of unsound mind, perhaps marginally insane but functional enough to run a large business and earn a lot of money. Speaking like a scientist, James would say that Crake suffered from diminished ability to control a deep, abiding, irrational anger at whatever opposed his will. In less scientific moments, James likens Crake to a rabid dog."

"Might James consent to putting Crake down, as a menace to society?"

"Yes, I imagine he would. And I would agree. After the plundering of the Crawford plantation, Crake went with Sherman's army to Columbia, South Carolina, where he joined other soldiers in attacking black women. To the end of his life he remained free to commit similar crimes. A few months ago, you discovered that he killed Ruth Colt. Beyond a doubt, he had committed many assaults and rapes in New York City against young female employees and prostitutes. In a few cases, he may have killed his victims and destroyed their bodies. To avoid arrest, he either paid off the victims or threatened them with reprisals, and they refused to testify against him. Or, he paid off the police and they refused to investigate."

"You've raised a serious question. May a private person presume to eliminate such a menace?"

His expression darkened. "I think so, if the public authorities are unwilling or unable to do it. I would have killed Crake years ago, but James disapproved. Instead, he hired the Prescott agency in the hope that you could gather sufficient evidence to send Crake to the gallows. That effort failed. Fortunately, on July seventh, someone tried and succeeded." He glanced toward the kitchen and his eyes brightened.

Madame Beaudry approached with the cold cherry soup. Pamela murmured to Virgil, "We must now honor the chef and not allow Crake to spoil our supper."

The meal was worthy of the chef's reputation. The conversation was pleasant. After the omelet, Pamela proposed a toast to the chef. The freshly baked gooseberry tartlet arrived, followed by coffee. The room began to fill up as they left.

"A concert will soon begin in the hotel garden. Are you game for it?" Virgil helped Pamela into the carriage.

"Jean-Luc has restored my energy. I would enjoy the concert. Victor Herbert will conduct—again. Do you realize that it's nearly three weeks since Crake died during one of Herbert's concerts?"

"I hadn't made that connection. Is it unseemly?"

"It needn't be. Mr. Herbert isn't likely to allude to it. The hotel management would prefer that we all thought of something else."

"Then we'll return the carriage to the livery stable. We can walk the short distance to the garden's rear entrance."

As they sat down, the orchestra was already on the platform and tuning their instruments. Victor Herbert simply welcomed everyone and announced: "To open the program, we'll give you 'Garry Owen,' the ever popular march of New York's own 'Fighting Sixty-ninth.' You may clap with the music when I give the signal." The following tunes were equally lively, putting the audience into a joyous, carefree mood.

Pamela enjoyed the concert as much as anyone. Still, part of her was mindful of Crake's murder in an adjacent cottage during a similar concert. She couldn't detect any similar concern, much less guilt, in her companion. Virgil seemed caught up in the music, tapping his feet to the orchestra's beat, an expression of simple pleasure on his face. He and she exchanged amused glances during the ticktock in "Grandfather's Clock."

As the sun set, gas lanterns were lit. The garden turned into a magical world of strange, shifting shadows. In a thin silk dress, Pamela felt chilled and began to shiver. Virgil noticed and gallantly laid his coat over her shoulders. She tried to demur, but he whispered, "Humor me, I'm pretending to be a Southern gentleman."

When the concert ended and the audience dispersed, Pamela realized that her opera glass was missing. "I would hate to lose it," she exclaimed. "It must be in the livery stable. I had it when we left the lake and I haven't used it since. Perhaps I dropped it while climbing out of the carriage."

"The stable is open until midnight. We'll go back there. Someone may have found it."

They hurried through the garden to the hotel's back entrance and out into the street. It was narrow, poorly lighted, and almost deserted, creating an eerie atmosphere. The livery stable's door was half shut. Virgil and Pamela slipped inside and called out for the stableman. Finally, he came on wobbly legs, carrying a lantern, and giving off a strong scent of cheap whiskey. He stared stupidly at Pamela while she explained her problem.

"We'll have to look for ourselves," exclaimed Virgil, seizing the stableman's lantern. "Let's find our carriage."

That was difficult. The stable was large, crowded, and dark. Finally, they found the carriage room and then the Crawford carriage. The search took a while, but eventually Pamela lifted a seat cushion and there was the opera glass. She breathed a sigh of relief. It was now quite late. They made their way back to the entrance, Virgil holding the lantern.

The stableman was leaning against a wall near the door. Virgil stiffened. "I smell a rat," he whispered to Pamela and handed the lantern to her. With his right hand, he gripped his cane; with his left, he suddenly seized the stableman by the scruff of the neck and forced him through the opening in the doorway.

From outside, a large club fell upon the man and he sank to the ground. Virgil pulled the sword from his cane just as a ruffian holding a club jumped over the stableman's body and burst into the stable. Virgil slashed the man's arm. He screamed and dropped the club. Pamela kicked it out of reach.

"Halt or I'll kill you." Virgil held the blade to within an inch of the man's throat.

Pamela stared anxiously at Virgil. His jaw jutted out, his eyes seemed to burn in their sockets. The ruffian was a tall, thin man, dirty, bearded, and toothless. He cowered and began to babble and to weep. For a moment Pamela held her breath, fearing that Virgil would shove the blade into the man's jugular vein.

Then Virgil seemed to relax. He deftly sliced the man's suspenders. His trousers dropped around his ankles. Virgil ordered him to lie on his stomach; then he seized a length of rope and tied him hand and foot.

Meanwhile, Pamela held the lantern, an astounded witness of this spectacle.

Virgil wrapped the ruffian's bleeding arm, then turned to her with a troubled expression. "I'm truly sorry that our delightful outing ended in this sordid way. I must escort you back to the hotel and report to the police. Tomorrow morning, I'll tell you of any complications. Detective Brophy might want to question us."

"Don't worry about me, Virgil. I have no regrets. You've been enjoyable company and a perfect gentleman."

On the way out, Virgil stepped over the stableman's prostrate body, called to Pamela for the lantern, and examined him. "He'll live. The police can deal with him. I suspect that he wasn't drunk, just pretending. He and the ruffian were in league, waiting to rob a couple like us who arrived late at night."

Back in her room, Pamela felt fatigued, but her mind was too agitated for sleep. She changed to nightclothes and brushed her hair but still wasn't sleepy. She paced the floor, trying to sort out her thoughts.

Tomorrow, Prescott would return. What would she say to him? The dramatic events at the stable would be broadcast on the porches of the Grand Union, at the springs in the town, and in the saloons. And what would be gained by trying to conceal the trip to the lake and the supper at the French restaurant? She ran both hands through her hair. Why was she even raising these questions with herself?

She and Virgil had behaved properly. These worries were, in fact, insulting to Prescott. He was a reasonable man and a sophisticated gentleman. Why would he be upset?

Well, for a start, Virgil Crawford was one of Prescott's potential suspects, though up to now not among the most important. Still, Prescott might fault her for drawing so close to a suspect that her judgment might be impaired.

Prior to today, Pamela had thought that Virgil's character was too peaceable and kindly for murderous action. At the stable a few minutes ago, however, he was bold and clever in the face of danger and skilled in the use of force. She could now imagine him killing Crake in retaliation for the unpunished crimes he had committed at the Crawford plantation and elsewhere.

As a veteran chef, Virgil would surely know how to use a boning knife. A friendly, engaging man, he was familiar with the hotel's kitchens and could have secretly borrowed or stolen a knife. Or, he could have used his sword cane. Its blade was thin, narrow, and single-edged, and would match Crake's wound. Finally, he and Edith shared a strong desire for justice or revenge.

They only needed an opportunity. And they had one at Victor Herbert's concert in the hotel garden, the evening of July 7. Virgil could easily have slipped away from the audience, killed Crake, and returned to his place next to James.

Pamela sighed, unhappy with her reasoning, in particular with her conclusion. It seemed out of character for the Crawfords to slaughter an old, sick, unarmed man in the dark, even if he were once a villain. Justice would not be served in that way. Brother James would have to know of the plan and, as a man of honor, would normally disapprove. But even James must acknowledge that sometimes a man must act out of character, as in war, and do evil in order to prevent greater evil.

# CHAPTER 27

## *Prescott Returns*

*Saturday, July 28*

After breakfast, Pamela went directly to the police station. Virgil Crawford had been there earlier. Detective Brophy took her testimony about the incident at the stable, then brought her to the jail and had her confirm the identity of the stableman and the assailant. The former had a fresh bandage on his head; the latter, on his arm.

At the stable she and Brophy talked through the incident. He seemed so matter-of-fact that she asked, "Is violence like this common in Saratoga?"

"It happens often enough," he replied dryly. "Times are tough. Late at night, desperate, unemployed men gather near the tracks and the stables. They get their money any way they can. We play down the problem. Otherwise, hotel guests would be too frightened to go out at night. But they really needn't worry. Broadway and the hotels are safe. We chase away all the sturdy beggars, tramps, petty thieves, and common drunks, as well as the whores. That's ninety-five percent of our business."

"What do you know about the two villains who attacked us?" Pamela was beginning to feel pity for them.

"They're typical west-side Saratoga criminals," Brophy said with a shrug. "The stableman has been arrested elsewhere in the county for burglary and gave false references to the hotel to conceal his criminal record. The tall, thin man is a penniless, unemployed railroad worker. This is probably his first criminal offense. Later in the day, I'll ship them to the courthouse in Ballston Spa for trial and catch a couple more like them tonight."

Pamela walked the short distance from the stable to the station and joined a large, milling crowd of expectant friends and relatives, baggage porters, and hucksters with signs and loud voices soliciting guests for the village's dozens of hotels and boardinghouses. Since the thoroughbred track began offering daily races a few days ago, the railroad companies had put more trains into service. Tourists were pouring into Saratoga Springs, boosting its population from near 10,000 to close to 50,000.

At noon, Prescott's train slowly pulled into the station, its arrival announced by jets of steam, screeching brakes, and the station bell's insistent clanging. Pamela felt her heartbeat begin to race, but she resisted the urge to join the crowd pressing toward the train. She didn't wish to appear eager but would welcome Prescott in a proper, friendly way. She reproached herself for thinking like a silly schoolgirl. After all, he had been away less than a week. And he was her friend, not her lover.

He usually traveled in a parlor car at the end of the train. The crowd was thinner there, so she could draw closer. He slowly stepped down from the car, searching the crowd, his face drawn and gray. When he spotted Pamela, he brightened. They shook hands and greeted each other. He let a porter take his bag.

As they walked toward the Grand Union Hotel, she asked how he felt. He didn't look well.

"We'll talk about it later. I'll be all right."

When they reached the room he had reserved, he asked her

in for a few words. "The stress of dealing with my wife, Gloria, has kept me from a restful sleep. That triggered nightmares from the war. Perhaps now they will go away." He gazed at her with a disarming smile. "You are a good influence on me."

"Why don't you eat something and then rest for a while. Let me know when you are ready. We'll meet downstairs and walk to Congress Park. Fresh air will be good for you. There we can talk."

He bowed to her advice. "I'll be ready and eager."

At four o'clock, Pamela's phone rang. Prescott's voice sounded strong. "Shall we meet in the foyer?"

"I'll be there in ten minutes."

When they arrived, Tom Winn drew them off to a side and quietly said, "A magistrate released Shaw on bail late this afternoon. At the hearing, he sounded contrite and promised to remain in Saratoga and be available for questioning. Still, I thought I should warn both of you."

"Do you know where he might be at this time?" asked Prescott.

"Surely he's in one of Saratoga's gambling dens, trying to rebuild his fortune."

In a shaded, secluded part of Congress Park, Pamela began the conversation diplomatically. "Tell me about your son, Edward."

"We had a good visit. He has a decent room of his own upstairs in the porter's cottage and eats with the family. His work is healthy and rewarding, an excellent break from his studies. Mr. Huss, the master gardener, generously shares his knowledge and seems to look upon Edward as a disciple."

"And how was Gloria?"

"Difficult. As I told you earlier, she and I differ on Edward's upbringing. At Ventfort she continued to insist that gardening was wrong for Edward. If he has to be with me in the Berkshires for this summer, as our legal separation agreement requires, he should behave like a young gentleman, not a farmer."

"What does she want the young man to do for two months?" Pamela tried not to sound sardonic.

"She says he should join the boat club on Lake Mahkeenac, improve his tennis game, and play golf. Above all, he must not hide himself away in a porter's house at Ventfort. He needs to get invited to John Sloane's magnificent new cottage, Wyndhurst. He should also pay social visits to the Schermerhorns and other rich families, go to parties in their great cottages, and mingle with young men and women of his own class."

"And what good will that do him?"

"According to Gloria, he would make influential contacts. When he leaves college, he'll need them. How else will he marry well and get ahead socially and in business. He should leave gardening to the servants."

"So, Gloria spoke her mind. Any harm done?"

"She carried on in the same vein with Edward. He listened politely but told her he would continue to go his own way. Unfortunately, she became annoyed. Without telling Edward, or me, she brought her concerns to Mrs. Morgan and insisted that she tell Edward that his services were no longer needed at Ventfort."

"What nerve!" Pamela exclaimed.

"I agree," Prescott added. "Fortunately, Mrs. Morgan reminded Gloria of Mr. Morgan's high regard for gardening. He had personally hired young Edward Prescott, encouraged his ambition, and certainly wouldn't tell him to leave."

"Gloria appears to have badly miscalculated."

"Yes, indeed. Over a game of billiards, Mr. Morgan hinted as much to Mr. Fisher, Gloria's banker friend and escort. At supper that evening, Fisher announced a change of plans. He and Gloria would leave for New York on the morning train. I was seated across the table from her. She shot me a venomous look."

"How can her wrath hurt you?"

"In our future divorce proceedings she will further blacken my reputation with false accusations of spousal abuse and infidelity. She may also seek sole custody of Edward. Finally, she may claim a large monetary settlement."

Pamela reminded him that Edward would soon be his own man. "You can probably tolerate or fend off her other blows. But do you really think that Fisher will go ahead with her plan to divorce and remarry? This incident at Ventfort should serve as a warning to him. With a shrew's reputation, she wouldn't be as useful as he hoped. Since her beauty is also fading, she has little else to offer him. It seems to me that she's becoming a toothless tiger."

Prescott smiled wryly. "But even without teeth, a tiger can scratch and draw blood. Now, tell me about your investigation."

She briefly described Jason's decline into mental illness. "Dr. Carson has had him for less than three days. It may be premature to visit him today. Perhaps tomorrow we should at least speak to Carson. He may tell us if Jason can be restored to a sound mind and give us a credible account of what happened to Captain Crake on the night of July seventh."

Pamela went on to speak of Rachel Crake and Robert Shaw. "Rachel's living temporarily with Helen Fisk, frightened and cautious. But she might eventually tell us more about Shaw. In my conspiracy theory, he might be the killer. Either she or Jason was well placed to guide him to Crake at the moment when he was most vulnerable. Perhaps we should also speak to the butcher Metzger. He might have supplied the alleged weapon for the murder."

Prescott reflected for a moment. "Your theory is supported by the fact that these three men knew each other and shared similar grievances against Crake. At some point, they may have realized that individually none of them could safely kill Crake, but together they could manage. We might get one of them to confess and implicate the others."

He rose to leave. "Shall we return to the hotel for supper?"

She shook her head. "First, I must tell you about my adventure yesterday." He sat down, looking a bit startled. She began with Virgil Crawford's invitation and their visit to Saratoga Lake, moved on to their supper at the French restaurant, and finished with the evening concert at the hotel. Prescott listened, relaxed, with a slight smile on his lips.

She went on to describe how she and Virgil had gone back to the stable to retrieve her opera glass from the carriage and were attacked.

Prescott's smile vanished. "That could have ended badly," he exclaimed. "Crawford shouldn't have allowed you to go there after dark."

"It was safer for us to go together." She spoke gently to avoid provoking him. "In any case, the danger seemed small. The stable's neighborhood is seedy, but it isn't a hellish slum like Mulberry Bend in Lower Manhattan."

He relented. "I'm pleased, of course, that neither of you was injured." He hesitated. "Did you learn anything about Virgil in that incident that might relate to Crake's death?"

"Yes, he has the physical ability, the mental agility, and the moral courage to have killed Crake. But I'm left feeling that it's not in his character. He could easily have killed our assailant, or left him to bleed to death in the stable. Instead, he bound the man's wounded arm and reported the incident immediately to the police."

"That speaks to his humanity. However, there's a major difference in his attitude. He's personally indifferent to these villains, but he hated Crake with a special passion."

"That's true," she granted. "But he would defer to his

cousins, Edith and James. They appear to respect the spirit as well as the letter of the law. They could have hired assassins to murder Crake years ago in New York. Instead, they engaged us, hoping to build a legal case against him. Someone killed him before they could confront him in court."

Prescott nodded thoughtfully. "I take your point."

"It's nearly time for supper. Shall we leave?"

Prescott gazed at her. "Would you be willing to take the evening off from crime? After supper, I'll meet Harry at the station and take him to the boardinghouse where Rob Shaw is staying. Harry will spy on him. Then you and I will go to the hotel ballroom for a dance—they call it a hop."

"I'd be delighted. Who knows, a clue could turn up in the most unexpected moment."

After supper, Pamela went to her room to prepare for the dance. Prescott walked to the station to meet Harry's train. When Harry stepped onto the platform, Prescott hardly recognized him. He was wearing a beard and a moustache, and had darkened his hair.

He proudly stroked the beard. "After you phoned that I'd be following Robert Shaw, I realized that he and I hadn't met face-to-face. Still, he might have seen me from a distance and would recognize me. In our office, I found the beard and the moustache worn by George Allen, the jewel thief we caught last summer. I dyed my hair to match."

"You fooled me," remarked Prescott, then noticed the initials *H.M.* on Harry's luggage. "Would Shaw recognize your name?"

Harry reflected for a moment. "I doubt that he would. Miller is a common name. I've also deliberately kept out of the limelight."

Prescott picked up one of Harry's bags and started for the street. "We'll take a cab to Shaw's boardinghouse. I've reserved a room for you. Mrs. Taylor, the landlady, is a friend. She's aware of your mission and agrees to cooperate. Shaw doesn't know that."

"I see," said Harry. "Tom Winn deliberately placed Shaw and Rachel in a house where he could safely spy on them."

"Right," said Prescott. "Now, when you've settled into your room and have had something to eat, I would like you to search his room. The landlady agrees. Hopefully you'll find a clue to his part in the death of Captain Crake. Also, keep track of where Shaw goes and whom he meets this evening. He was most recently seen gambling at Mitchell's saloon and will probably finish the evening at Canfield's Casino."

Prescott knew Mrs. Taylor from previous visits to Saratoga Springs, and had recommended guests to her. She was a sturdy, sharp-eyed matron, about fifty, the widow of an invalided Civil War sergeant who had died of old wounds a few years ago. Prescott helped disabled veterans like Taylor with their legal problems and had won a modest pension for him. Mrs. Taylor now lived on that pension and the income from her lodgers.

She came to the door, gestured to a boy to take Harry's bags, then heartily shook Prescott's hand. "We'll take good care of your friend, Captain." She knew Prescott had been wounded in the war and referred to his rank to honor his sacrifice. He personally avoided any reference to his service, but he respected Mrs. Taylor's gesture since it came from the heart.

She turned to Harry with a smile and welcomed him, then led him into a parlor, briefly laid down the rules of the house, and showed him to his room.

Meanwhile, Prescott remained in the background, studying the house, a big, rambling, wooden building. Soon, Prescott grew anxious that Shaw might return and recognize him. So he bid Harry good-bye and good luck. They would keep in touch by courier, a dependable boy employed by Mrs. Taylor.

\* \* \*

Harry quickly settled into his room, ate the soup, bread, and salad that Mrs. Taylor served him on a tray, and devised a plan to search Shaw's room. He could return at any time. A search could require at least a half hour. If he were to come unexpected, Harry would need a few minutes' warning. He would have to involve Mrs. Taylor.

She was in the kitchen with a scullery maid, cleaning the iron stove in the final stage of closing down for the night. She looked tired and was probably hoping to get off her feet.

Harry knocked lightly on the door to get her attention. "May I have a word with you, ma'am. It's important."

She took off her apron and led him into the tiny anteroom of her apartment. "Captain Prescott said you had work to do here. How can I help?"

Harry thanked her for being willing. "All I'll ask of you, ma'am, is to lend me the key to Shaw's room. Ring a bell if he returns in the next hour while I'm searching his things."

She agreed. He hastened up the stairs to Shaw's room on the top floor, opened the lock, and stepped inside. It was large, simply furnished with two wooden chairs and a table, and offered few opportunities for concealing things. Mrs. Taylor didn't take smokers, so the air was fresh, except for a faint scent of female perfume in the bedding, presumably left by Rachel two days ago. Otherwise, she had left no trace.

Shaw was a tidy man, a habit left over from years of service in a regiment of the British army. His clothes hung neatly in a row in a closet. His boots stood at attention on a mat by the door, cleaned and polished. A pencil and a pad of paper were perfectly centered on the table.

When Harry began to search the room, he didn't have a specific goal in mind. But he assumed that Shaw would lock up anything valuable or compromising. A stout trunk stood in a corner. Its lock was more secure than most and took several precious minutes to pick. Harry rapidly fingered his way through underclothes, toiletries, file boxes, and account books. At the bottom of the trunk he found a small, loaded pistol and a dagger. There was nothing else of pressing interest.

There were no letters. Odd, Harry thought. They must be hidden elsewhere. By this time, he feared that Shaw might return at any moment. He glanced up at the ceiling's unevenly plastered surface and noticed a hole where a lighting fixture must have once hung. He hurried out of the room, locking the door behind him, and ran upstairs to the attic. After removing a few loose planks, he found the hole. With the aid of a spyglass, he could view most of Shaw's room below. A few minutes later, he heard the bell and waited.

As a clock was striking nine in the evening, Shaw entered his room, sat at the table, and drew fistfuls of money out of his portfolio. Lady luck had been with him in Mitchell's gambling den. For a few minutes he played like a child with the money; then he opened the trunk, stuffed the money into a large bag, and closed the trunk. He quickly wrote a message, rang for the errand boy, and ordered him to take the message to the front desk at the Grand Union Hotel and bring back the reply.

Twenty minutes later, the boy returned with a message and received a tip, a generous one, to judge from the broad smile that lit up his face. When Shaw was alone, he quickly read the message, left it lying on the table, and hurried to the trunk. He pulled out the pistol, checked the bullets in the chamber, and thrust the pistol into his pocket. He raised his trouser leg and strapped the dagger to his calf. Then he hastened from the room, locking it behind him. Harry heard him running down the stairs and slamming the front door behind him.

Harry hurried to Shaw's room, opened the lock again, and dashed to the message lying on the table. It was from Rachel: She was pleased by his good fortune and looked forward to being with him again. "*With all my love and many kisses, Rachel.*"

Uncertain where Shaw was headed and whether to try to follow him, Harry thought of the missing letters. He would enlist Mrs. Taylor in the search. She might have a different perspective on Shaw and could figure out where he would hide things.

Harry went to her parlor and approached her straightforward. "Ma'am, I strongly suspect that Mr. Shaw has killed Captain Crake and is about to kill his widow. Will you help me search his room?"

She looked him up and down with a playful smile and said, "Mr. Shaw has a sly manner and shifty eyes. He's off gambling now. Are you looking for anything in particular?"

"Letters, ma'am. Hidden letters from Mrs. Crake." They climbed upstairs to Shaw's room, and they began to search. Almost immediately, Mrs. Taylor discovered a packet of letters exchanged between Shaw and Rachel, hidden in a large Bible. Shaw had cut away the pages to form a receptacle.

Harry asked Mrs. Taylor how she found it so quickly.

"Shaw is a smart aleck," she replied. "From experience with his kind, I know how his mind works. His greatest joy in life is to fool other people and feel superior. Most people respect the Bible, even if they don't follow its precepts. I heard him speak of it with contempt. Yet, he kept a copy in his room. I wondered why. When you mentioned his missing correspondence with Mrs. Crake—another man's wife, mind you—I realized that he would think the Bible was the most appropriate place for it. He could insult the holy book, deceive other people, and feel superior in the bargain."

Harry thanked Mrs. Taylor, took the letters to his own room, and sat down to read them. He had hardly begun when he realized that they were written in code. He would have to decipher them, quickly.

\* \* \*

Pamela was eagerly waiting outside the hotel's ballroom when Prescott returned from Mrs. Taylor's boardinghouse. He whispered to her, "Hopefully, Harry will penetrate Shaw's secrets. Now, shall we dance?"

They walked into the ballroom. Helen Fisk was already there, moving gracefully about the room, chatting with virtually everyone, introducing Birgitta as her friend from Sweden, not only an expert in the latest scientific massage therapy but also an excellent dancer. That she was an attractive woman was obvious. Birgitta had quickly grown in Helen's estimation to become a friend as well as a valuable servant.

A few minutes later, Rachel arrived in her black silk gown and thin black veil, but that was the only mark of widowhood about her. As she entered, she drew the veil back. Summer guests near her appeared to titter, but many others smiled encouragement, overlooking her cunning and self-serving character.

Prescott noticed this, then turned to Pamela. "You have to grant that she's a witty, charming companion, eager to have fun and to share it with others."

Pamela agreed. "I'm amazed. Saratoga in the summer is more tolerant than any other place I know."

Rachel sat with a pair of courtesans whom Pamela recognized from Canfield's Casino. She observed them with a skeptical eye.

"Rachel is keeping bad company," she said to Helen Fisk, who had just joined her.

"I share your concern." Helen frowned. "Shortly before we came to the ballroom, she wrote a message. When I offered to send it for her, she became very agitated. So, I suspect she's up to her old tricks. She's hinted that she'd like a suite of her own—and have me pay for it. I told her flat out that I wouldn't consider it."

The musicians had assembled on the podium and now began

to tune their instruments. Helen moved on to chat with acquaintances and Pamela joined Prescott. She had just enough time to warn him about Rachel's message. The master of ceremonies announced the first schottische. The orchestra struck up a tune. Pamela and Prescott started out, hopping, then twirling together, an arm behind each other's back.

They had danced before in New York, but only infrequently. Now she was reminded how good he was. At the end, he bowed smartly. His face slightly pink from the exertion, his eyes shimmering with pleasure, he had shed ten years in his appearance.

The next dance was a waltz. Prescott paired with Birgitta. As Pamela turned to a new partner, she found herself facing Virgil Crawford.

"May I have this dance?" he asked politely.

"I would be delighted," she replied, and she meant it, recalling the pleasure of yesterday's visit to the lake, the supper at Beaudry's, and the concert. His attentive manner brought out feelings of self-worth that she thought she had lost when her late husband had betrayed her. Then she noticed Edith and James Crawford in the front row of spectators, watching and smiling with approval.

Virgil was light on his feet, had an excellent sense of rhythm, and waltzed like a prince.

During the waltz their conversation was limited to brief, scattered comments mostly on the music. So, in the midst of a whirl, Pamela was startled when Virgil asked, "Have you and Prescott tracked down Crake's killer yet?"

She shook her head. "Not yet. We're still looking." At the dance's conclusion, an intermission was called. Pamela sensed that Virgil wanted to pursue the topic. At that moment, she suddenly recalled Harry Miller's observation that a guilty person can become obsessed with his or her crime and thus prone to bring it up at odd or inappropriate times. Was that the case with Virgil's question? In her thinking about suspects in Crake's murder, she had come to focus on the possible conspiracy of Metzger, Dunn, and Shaw. She had lost sight of the Crawfords, whose motive for revenge was probably the most compelling of all.

This train of thought annoyed her. She liked the Crawfords and had pushed back the idea that they could have murdered Crake. She also had come to this dance for pleasure. If anyone was obsessed by crime, it was she. Still, the urge to pursue this question dogged her and she followed Virgil to the spectators' section.

Edith and James welcomed her while Virgil brought her a chair and then took his place behind James. "We see that Mr. Prescott has returned," Edith began. "Has anything developed in the Crake case?"

James added, "We were also wondering about Jason. Do you know how he is doing?"

"I've nothing dramatic to report about the case. We know a great deal more than when we began. Mr. Prescott is looking over the evidence that I've recently gathered. Tomorrow, we'll visit Dr. Carson's clinic and hope to learn about Jason's prospects for healing." She added, "If he recovers his health, he may shed new light on the case. During the evening of Crake's death, Jason was uniquely positioned to observe what happened."

While Pamela spoke, she studied the Crawford sister and brother. They seemed apprehensive. Were they concerned what a healthy Jason might say?

Pamela sat next to James. He leaned toward her and asked softly, "Would you or Mr. Prescott mind if Virgil and I went with you to speak with Dr. Carson?" He hesitated. "Edith would prefer to stay here. Perhaps she could be involved later."

Pamela thought the request seemed reasonable. James was facing a large bill for Jason's therapy and should know what he would be getting for his money. Next to Edith, James was also Jason's closest blood relative.

"I think it would be a good idea," Pamela replied. "But I'd better speak to Prescott."

The intermission had ended and Prescott was now waltzing with Birgitta. When they finished, Pamela excused herself and asked for a few words with him. A young man already had Birgitta in his sights and was waiting to speak to her.

Prescott walked off the floor with Pamela. She passed James's request on to him and gave her reasons for agreeing with it.

"I share your opinion," Prescott said. "At the first opportunity, I'll ask Dr. Carson if he wants Jason's family involved somehow in his therapy. Let's visit with the Crawfords now. I'll speak with James."

"Afterward, we'll continue with the hop, right?"

He smiled eagerly.

# CHAPTER 28

## Search

Saturday, July 28

As they started walking toward the Crawfords, Pamela cast a glance over her shoulder and grew alarmed. She surveyed the hall and her heart sank. She tapped Prescott on the shoulder.

"Unfortunately, the Crawfords must wait. Rachel Crake has disappeared. We must find her."

Her companions, the two courtesans, were still in their seats. Pamela hastened over to them and remarked, "I'm surprised that Rachel Crake left suddenly. Was she ill?"

"Oh no!" exclaimed one of the courtesans. "Rachel got a message and became ecstatic. She told us, 'My friend just broke the bank at Mitchell's Saloon.' Then, she smiled like a little girl. 'I've been naughty. I wasn't supposed to tell.' "

At that moment, Helen entered the ballroom, a distracted look on her face. She hurried up to Pamela. "I've been looking for Rachel Crake. She has gone!"

"I've just noticed that," Pamela replied. "What have you learned?"

"Not much," she replied. During the hop Helen had kept an eye on Rachel. After the first schottische she had received a message. A few minutes later, she left the ballroom. When she didn't return, Helen went searching for her. Eventually, a chambermaid reported that Rachel had been to Helen's suite with a bellboy, threw her things into a trunk, and left bright-eyed and smiling.

"Of her own free will," Helen concluded, "the foolish young woman has apparently gone back to Shaw."

Pamela and Prescott started a search. The night clerk at the front desk said that Jimmy Cochrane, the young courier from Mrs. Taylor's boardinghouse, had delivered to the desk a message addressed to Rachel. The bellboy brought it to her in the ballroom, then assisted her to a side exit where a carriage from Dempsey's Livery was waiting. The coachman loaded her trunk on the rear rack, helped her into the carriage, and drove off.

"Shaw was carefully covering his tracks," muttered Prescott. "Thus far we can only suspect that he's involved in her disappearance."

Pamela was alarmed. "Why would he hide his face unless he intended to harm her?"

"I fear for her," Prescott replied. "We should pick up Harry and then visit Brophy at the police station."

At the Taylor boardinghouse, they quickly gathered Harry into the carriage. He reported that Rachel was trying to extort money from Shaw. "In a packet of recent letters she threatened to tell the police that she had overheard him plotting with a couple of men to kill Crake. If the deed could be done before he changed the chief beneficiary in his will, he would give them $5,000 apiece and the satisfaction of killing the man whom they all hated."

"According to Rachel, who were Shaw's accomplices?" asked Pamela, fearing that her suspicions would be confirmed.

"Metzger, the German butcher, was one. He hated Crake from their battles in the New York packinghouse and now feared that Crake would persuade Mr. Wooley to fire him. The other was Jason Dunn. His reasons were obscure to me, having to do with Crake's brutal treatment of women."

"What did Rachel try to extract from Shaw in return for her silence?"

"The money he won at Canfield's Casino and an apartment on Union Square in New York City."

"Apparently," surmised Prescott, "Shaw has lured her from the ballroom and her safe room in the hotel. In his message he seems to have agreed to her terms and promised to send her safely back to New York. Her joy will soon be deceived, foolish woman."

Within a few minutes their carriage reached the police station. They were fortunate to find Detective Brophy. He was at the door about to leave, his face lined with stress, his eyes dull with fatigue. Keeping the peace in Saratoga on a Saturday night had apparently stretched him and the rest of the police force to its limit.

"I'm on my way to a saloon brawl," he growled. "Pickpockets and whores are back in business on Broadway. Just an hour ago, I arrested a few and chased the others away. So what do you want?"

"Rachel Crake has gone missing," replied Prescott, and added the vital details. "We think her life is in danger."

Brophy blew out a loud sigh of exasperation. "You just told me she left the dance in good spirits. That means freely. In this country, we let people disappear if they want to. I need evidence that her life is at risk." He tipped his hat to Pamela and rushed past them into a waiting coach.

As they watched him drive off, Prescott remarked to Pamela and Harry, "We can't count on the police. They don't have time for Rachel. Pamela and I will search the town for her." He turned to Harry. "Keep close track of Shaw. You will probably find him at Canfield's Casino. We'll meet you there."

244 / Charles O'Brien

* * *

They searched for Rachel throughout the town. Finding her seemed hopeless. This was now high season in Saratoga Springs. Guests filled all the hotel porches and occupied every rocking chair. Carriages and pedestrians flooded Broadway and moved at a snail's pace. The restaurants and saloons were packed, and the gambling dens were doing a furious business.

At Mitchell's Saloon, Prescott found a waiter who could tell him that Shaw had come early in the evening and had persuaded Mitchell to give him a $100 credit.

"Can you believe it?" the waiter exclaimed. "That rascal Shaw then walked into the back room, played roulette for an hour, and walked out with over a thousand dollars."

"Just in time to inform Rachel of his good fortune and entice her out of the hotel," Prescott remarked to Pamela.

She added, "At that point, Shaw needed a carriage to pick up Rachel." Dempsey's livery stable was behind Mitchell's Saloon. The stableman glanced at Pamela's sketch of Shaw, and said that he had rented a carriage and driven it out of the stable in the direction of Broadway. He returned it an hour later. The stableman pointed to Shaw's name in the register.

From the stable they went to Canfield's Casino and joined Harry. While Pamela and Harry studied the guest list in the entrance, Prescott found Shaw observing a poker game. He drew him aside and asked about Rachel. "You rented a carriage from Dempsey's livery stable, picked her up at the hotel's side door, and drove away. Where did you take her?"

With an impatient sigh, he replied, "If you must know, I took her and her trunk to the railroad station. A friend was supposed to pick her up, entertain her for a few hours, and send her off on the night train to New York. I gave her money to tide her over and checked her trunk through to the city. She said she was going back to the brothel where we first met. Then

I returned the carriage and went back to the casino. I don't know where she is now."

"Have you forgotten that the police ordered her, as well as you, to remain in Saratoga Springs?"

Shaw shrugged and turned back to the poker game.

Prescott returned to his assistants in the entrance hall. "Pamela, come with me. Harry, you follow Robert Shaw like a flea on his back. He may feel cornered and will be dangerous. Find out his hiding place and whether Rachel Crake is there. If he is Crake's killer, she most likely knows how he did it and is our best potential witness. The sooner we find her, the more likely she'll be alive. Are you armed?"

Harry smiled and pulled a blackjack from his pocket.

As they left the casino, Pamela suggested, "In a half hour the night train to New York should arrive. We may find Rachel at the station. In any case, we could check Shaw's story with the station master."

The station's platform was empty. Inside the hall, a single electric bulb cast a feeble light. A few tourists rested on the wooden benches, eyes shut. The telegraph office was closed. A light was on in the ticket office, but no one was there. Prescott rang the bell for service, jarring the tourists awake. A clerk appeared, looking cross.

"What do you want?" he asked.

Prescott showed his papers. "We're searching for a missing person, Mrs. Rachel Crake, who was supposed to take the night train to New York. She was here at about ten-thirty tonight with a man. He is said to have bought a one-way ticket and checked her trunk through to New York City. Have you seen them?"

From her bag, Pamela pulled her sketched portraits of Rachel and Shaw, and showed them to the clerk.

He held the pictures up to the light. "I remember them now.

The man had an accent and inquired about the train being on time. You're right. He bought a one-way ticket for the woman and checked in a trunk. They'd come back, he said, in time for her to catch the train."

"You should know," said Prescott, "that both of them are under police orders not to leave Saratoga Springs. We'll wait for them. If they don't arrive, can you hold the trunk here?"

The clerk frowned, then stammered, "I don't know if I can. The man didn't say that it absolutely had to go out tonight. But . . ."

Prescott asked calmly, "May I use your phone to call for a constable?"

The flustered clerk replied, "Yes, of course."

The constable arrived in a carriage just as the train pulled into the station from the north. Pamela and Prescott identified themselves. "We are waiting for Mrs. Crake. She intended to leave Saratoga Springs in violation of a police restraint. Could you prevent her trunk from being loaded onto the train?"

He nodded. "Detective Brophy said I should take the trunk back to the police station. He also instructed me to prevent her from leaving, if she shows up."

They waited on the platform while passengers left the train amidst the usual clamor and hustle of the porters and hotel agents. As departing passengers boarded the train, Pamela, Prescott, and the constable stood close to the coaches to see if Rachel might have disguised herself. None of the passengers resembled her. The constable put her trunk onto the rack of his carriage.

"Could we ride with you, Constable?" Prescott asked. "We'd like Detective Brophy to open the trunk and allow us to look at its contents."

The constable nodded. "He said he wanted a word with you."

* * *

"So, she didn't show up." Brophy was chewing on his cigar, feet up high on his desk, hat tilted back on his head. "Why would she leave her trunk at the station? Something's fishy there."

"Open the trunk," Pamela suggested. "You might find a clue."

"I should've thought of that myself, ma'am, though there's probably a law against it." Brophy gestured to the constable, who fingered through a rack of keys and found one that might open half the trunks in Saratoga. It worked. He lifted the lid.

It had obviously been packed in a hurry. Rachel hadn't folded her gowns before throwing them helter-skelter into the trunk on top of a mixed pile of shoes, gloves, and underclothing.

Brophy announced to Prescott, "The constable and I must go out on the street for an hour to help rich drunks find their way back to their hotels and boardinghouses. You and Mrs. Thompson may search the trunk. The night officer will keep an eye on you."

When Brophy and the constable had gone, Prescott said to Pamela, "It's well past midnight. Shall we give a half hour to the search and then go back to the hotel?"

"Fair enough," she replied. "I'll be looking for a diary or other hidden papers." She picked up a silk gown, quickly patted it in vain for secret pockets, and laid it aside. Prescott did the same with other clothing. They soon reached the bottom of the trunk. The remaining items were toiletries, brushes, handkerchiefs, and the like. Pamela fingered through them, then shook her head. "We haven't found any jewelry or money yet. She must have packed them. Where?"

"In the trunk itself," Prescott replied. "We'll check it for hidden compartments."

For a few minutes, they explored the trunk, a common,

sturdy, traveler's chest with a rounded lid. "It has a false bottom," he exclaimed, and pulled it out. Small cases of jewelry lay interspersed with a diary and packets of letters. "We should study the most recent entries now. The rest can wait."

The diary frequently referred to a secret place where Rachel and Shaw hid from her husband during romantic trysts.

"I know it's late," Prescott granted, "but let's take a quick look before going back to the hotel." They borrowed a lantern, caught a cab, and found the small cottage in a grove at the end of an alley off Circular Street, a five-minute ride from the Grand Union Hotel.

The grove was dark. The eerie screech of an owl pierced the early-morning silence. Pamela wondered if Shaw might be spending the night inside with Rachel. No lights or sounds came from the cottage.

Prescott knocked on the door several times with increasing vehemence. No one could have slept through it.

Pamela asked, "May I try to pick the lock?"

Prescott glanced at her with surprise.

"Harry has taught me. I can open simple locks with a hairpin."

"Then try your skill on this one. I'll hold the lantern."

It was an easy lock. Pamela picked it in a few minutes. Prescott pulled the door open, first a crack, then all the way. He held up the lantern and illuminated a small, fully furnished parlor. They stepped inside. Pamela detected the strong scent of Rachel's perfume in an upholstered chair and more of it in the drapes. Rachel and Shaw had used the cottage within the last few hours.

Off to one side behind the parlor was a small bedroom; on the other side, a tiny kitchen and a WC. There was no electricity and no telephone in the building, but it was clean and orderly. There was no sign of violence or conflict.

Prescott lit a kerosene lamp and knelt down to check the parlor's varnished hardwood floor. None of the boards seemed loose. The same was true in the bedroom. He opened a chest of women's clothes and sorted through them. "What's this?" he called out to Pamela. Among the dresses he had found a chambermaid's apron and bonnet.

She studied them carefully. "They must be the female disguise that Shaw wore as he left Crake's cottage, misleading Jason to think it was Francesca. She and Shaw are about the same size."

Prescott added, "He came here from the casino, changed, then hurried to the hotel and killed Crake. He ran back to the cottage, changed again, and returned to the casino—all in the space of an hour."

They returned to the parlor and continued searching. She lifted a pillow on the upholstered chair and found a fancy handkerchief, initialed *RC.* "It's wet with drops of red wine. Rachel has used it this evening."

Prescott worked his way to the kitchen floor. He called Pamela. "There are drops of a liquid on the floor and a wet, wine-stained towel on the rack."

She joined him. "And here's a half-empty bottle of red wine in the cabinet and two empty glasses in the sink."

"We'll need a chemical test on their residue." Prescott sniffed the glasses. "But it's certain that Shaw brought Rachel here from the Grand Union a few hours ago. He poured red wine into two glasses in the kitchen. They drank from them in the parlor. Afterward, he or she put them in the sink without rinsing them."

"So, what happened next?" asked Pamela. "There's still no sign of violence. The bed hasn't been disturbed. They must have left."

"They couldn't have gone far. Shaw returned to gamble at the casino within an hour of the time he left Mitchell's."

As Pamela was leaving the kitchen, puzzling over these new clues to Rachel's disappearance, the front door suddenly opened. Robert Shaw stood in the entrance, glaring at her, a pistol in his hand.

# CHAPTER 29

## *The Pit*

*Sunday, July 29*

Shaw stepped inside. "What do we have here?" he asked in a mocking tone. "Breaking and entry and burglary are still crimes in New York, I believe. The law also allows me to use lethal force to protect my property." His lips pressed tightly together. His gaze was as cold as ice. He raised the weapon.

Suddenly, a dark figure reared up behind him and swung a blackjack at his head. The gun fell to the floor. For a moment Shaw stood dazed, then crumpled.

Harry picked up the gun and stuck it in his pocket; then he searched the prostrate man for other weapons and found the dagger strapped to the calf of his leg.

"Shaw must have heard almost everything you said," said Harry, taking charge. "He was outside watching you through the window. Rachel should be nearby, either dead or in danger of dying. We must act quickly. One of the town constables has a bloodhound that finds lost children, hikers, and wandering elderly folks. He lives only a few steps away. I'll wake him up. We'll be back shortly."

Pamela found rope, and Prescott tied up the still-unconscious man. Soon he began to stir and to open his eyes. At first they didn't focus, but eventually he stared at Prescott. "You and your lady friend haven't found any proof of wrongdoing. You're more likely to go to prison than I."

"Don't fret," said Prescott. "We're bringing a bloodhound into this investigation. Finding Rachel should be child's play for him. You had better pray that he finds her alive; otherwise, you will burn in the electric chair like the unfortunate Mr. William Kemmler."

For the first time since Pamela set eyes on Shaw, his lips trembled with fear.

Soon, Harry appeared, followed by Blue, a large black and tan bloodhound with a black, wrinkled snout and long, flapping ears. His big, gentle eyes calmly surveyed the humans gathered in the room while he waited for instructions from a sleepy-eyed constable. He turned to Pamela. "Ma'am, can you give Blue a scent of the missing woman?"

Pamela pointed to the pillow that reeked of Rachel's perfume.

The constable led the dog to the pillow. He inhaled the scent and was instantly eager to begin tracking. At his handler's command, he started sniffing through the rooms, then out the door to the rear of the cottage and up to the edge of the grove to a pile of brush. There he stopped and pointed still as a statue. While Pamela held up a lantern, Harry and Prescott pulled the brush away to reveal a trapdoor. Blue advanced a step closer. There was no doubt in his mind.

For a moment they stood around the trapdoor, silently gazing down at it with respect and even sorrow, as if it were a person's newly dug grave. Then Harry sighed and pulled open the door, revealing a large pit. Blue strained at his leash. Pamela stepped forward and held the lantern over the opening.

The pit was stonewalled and about six feet deep. On the bottom lay a figure in a canvas sack. Harry and the constable climbed down a ladder, lifted the sack over their heads, and placed it on the ground at the edge of the pit. Prescott opened the sack, revealing Rachel's head. Pamela brought her lantern up close.

"Has she been strangled?" she asked.

"I can't see any marks," he replied.

The constable climbed out of the pit and glanced at the body. "It looks like murder." The words sounded so inadequate. He turned to Harry, who had followed him out of the pit. "Bring Detective Brophy here to study the scene while it's fresh. We'll need a coach for the woman's body and for Mr. Shaw. I must take Blue home, then I'll come right back." As he was leaving, he said to Prescott with a teasing smile, "I'm putting you in charge while I'm gone."

While these arrangements were being made, Pamela held the lantern close to Rachel's face. The pert, lively expression, so characteristic of the woman, was gone. A deep sorrow came over Pamela at the thought of a young life so brutally ended. It didn't help to reflect that Rachel had foolishly gone back to Shaw and tried to extort money from him. He denied her any chance to turn her life around.

Prescott approached. "I'd better check on Shaw in the cottage. Will you be all right out here alone?"

"Yes," she replied, "it may sound odd, even morbid, but I feel I should stand by her side."

He gazed at her for a long moment. "I understand."

A short while later, Prescott joined her. "Shaw is secure, locked in his thoughts. He refused to speak." For several minutes, Pamela and Prescott stood quietly by the body, absorbed in reflection. Then the stillness of the night was broken. Detective Brophy trudged out of the darkness, followed by Harry.

Brophy addressed Pamela and Prescott: "I'll take charge of the investigation now. It'll soon be dawn. You'd better get some sleep. Come to my office in the afternoon and give me your statements. Too bad we've lost her, the key to her husband's death."

Pamela cast a last glance at the body and gasped, then dropped to her knees for a closer look. "Her eyelids flickered," she shouted.

Prescott knelt beside her and felt the artery in Rachel's neck. "There's a very faint pulse. She must still be alive."

In a few minutes, a medical examiner arrived. For a moment he stood by the woman, confused. He had expected a corpse. Then he pulled smelling salts from his bag and brought them to her nose. She began to stir and half-opened her eyes.

"Rachel," Pamela said loudly into the woman's ear. Her lips moved.

"Amazing," said the examiner. "I've never seen the likes of this. She may have overdosed on a drug. We'll take her to the hospital immediately."

Pamela and Prescott walked back to their carriage. Harry remained behind with Brophy and the constable to study the scene and to question Shaw. When Pamela climbed into the carriage, a profound weakness overcame her. "Thank God for Harry," she said. "Without him, this night could have had a sad ending."

Prescott closed the carriage door. "We owe him a great deal. It was a close call. Shaw was preparing to shoot."

Pamela added, "And had he shot us, who would then have known that Rachel was buried in the pit?"

# CHAPTER 30

## *Aftermath*

*Sunday, July 29*

At midmorning, Pamela awoke fatigued, having tossed and turned during the night. Her mind had churned up a lurid vision of a dark pit, and Rachel's sightless eyes had stared at her. For a moment she felt that criminal investigation could be unhealthy for her. Then rays of sunlight slanting through the window banished her demons.

There was a knock on her door. Pamela opened it; it was Birgitta. "Mr. Prescott has just told Mrs. Fisk and me what happened last night. I thought you might need a lift. I'll draw a bath for you. It'll soak the fatigue out of your body. Then I'll give you a massage and bring you breakfast."

Pamela felt greatly relieved. "Birgitta, you are an angel from Heaven."

She shook her head. "I really enjoy helping people feel better. By the way, I asked Mrs. Fisk about getting into medical school. Would it be difficult for me, a woman? She said, 'Don't worry. I'll help you.' "

\* \* \*

Early in the afternoon, Pamela and Prescott were shown into Brophy's office. It was stiflingly warm. He sat behind his desk in shirtsleeves and without a collar. His coat and hat hung on a hook on the wall; his cigar lay in a tray off to one side. He hadn't shaved or slept. Pamela feared that he might be irritable and difficult to deal with. To judge from the high pink color of his face, he risked having a stroke.

But he greeted them with a broad smile and gestured to a couple of chairs. For a moment, he gazed at them, then said, "Good work. You arrived at the cottage just in time and saved Mrs. Crake's life. The medical examiner figured that she probably wouldn't have lived through the night."

"What happened to her?" Pamela asked.

"Shaw insists he didn't try to kill her. His story, for what it's worth, is that they were drinking wine in the parlor and she suddenly stopped breathing. When he couldn't find her pulse, he thought she had died and he'd be blamed. So he hid her in the pit and went back to the casino to win more money. He planned to take the early train to New York and catch the first boat to any place where he could make a living at gambling."

"What do the medical doctors say about her?"

"She may have suffered a reaction from mixing a patent medicine and the wine. Shaw claims she often indulged in a tincture of laudanum. They say she should recover."

"It might have been accidental," said Prescott. "But Shaw could have done it to rid himself of her. She threatened him."

"I agree," Brophy said. "Would you like to interrogate him while I listen in?" He glanced at Pamela. "Mrs. Thompson can join us. A constable will take notes. You could touch on Shaw's role in the death of Captain Crake as well."

"A good idea," Prescott replied. "I look forward to dueling with Shaw."

\*　\*　\*

The interrogation room's walls were whitewashed and plain. A pair of high windows let sunlight into one side of the room. The other side was shadowed. Prescott sat at a wooden table in the sunlight; the constable scribe sat next to him. Pamela and Brophy remained in the shadows.

Shaw appeared at the door in plain, shapeless prison garb, his hands and feet in irons. A constable led him to the table, set him down, and sat behind him. His brow appeared still creased with pain from the blow that Harry had given him. Nonetheless, he looked confident and ready for battle.

Prescott began, "Tell us, sir, how Rachel Crake came to be in a cottage you rented and was found near death in a concealed pit on the property?"

"She wanted to return to New York. As I told you earlier, I drove her from the hotel to the railroad station, bought her a one-way ticket, and checked her trunk."

"I recall that part of your story. I assume you're about to change the rest."

His eyes flickered momentarily, possibly with embarrassment. "Rather than wait two hours in the station hall, we went to my cottage, drank wine, and chatted. She decided not to go to New York after all. I said she could stay in the cottage as long as she liked. I would go to the casino for a couple of hours of poker. At that point, she collapsed and looked dead. She must have slipped too much laudanum into her wine. I feared the police would blame me, so I hid her body."

Prescott observed, "Your story is implausible. By trying to hide her body from the police, you've implicitly admitted your guilt. In fact, you attempted to kill her with a lethal mixture of wine and a patent medicine containing laudanum, ingredients that are readily available."

"Why should I want to kill her? We were lovers."

"Partners in crime would be closer to the truth. You and she conspired to kill her husband for his inheritance. That's clear in the messages you hid in the Bible at Mrs. Taylor's boarding-house. My assistant, Harry Miller, has deciphered them, including the one in which Rachel demands a large sum of money in return for her silence about your role in the conspiracy. At first, she supported your alibi that you were gambling at the casino on the evening of July seventh. Recently, however, she stated before two witnesses that you left the casino for at least an hour, time enough to kill Captain Crake. We've also found the chambermaid's apron and bonnet that you wore. Which of Rachel's stories is true?"

"Her recent version is a lie. We had quarreled, so she was punishing me."

"If her demand for money was based on a lie, why did you agree to her terms?"

"I thought if I paid her, she would stop spreading lies about me. Victims of extortion sometimes find it more convenient to pay off the extortioner."

Throughout Prescott's indictment, Shaw remained calm and collected, his head tilted slightly at a skeptical angle. At the end, he remarked, "I'll refute you in court. I did not kill Crake. I have nothing more to say."

After Shaw was led out of the room, Brophy remarked, "Shaw is sure that his luck will change and that he'll wiggle out of this situation as he has throughout his life. I'll charge him now with Mrs. Crake's attempted murder and move him to the jail in Ballston Spa."

Pamela asked, "Will you now charge Rachel? Messages between her and Shaw reveal that they conspired to kill the captain."

Brophy looked skeptical. "Was Rachel actually involved in the killing?"

"Yes, she was," Pamela replied. "Rachel, not Jason, told Shaw that Crake had retired to the cottage. She, better than anyone, knew that he would take a drug and soon be incapable of defending himself. She provided Shaw with the chambermaid disguise. Metzger the butcher wasn't involved, either. Shaw used his own dagger, rather than a boning knife. And finally, Francesca Ricci had nothing to do with Crake's death. At the least, could we get her out on bail?"

"I agree," Brophy replied. "We need to revisit Captain Crake's murder. When I deliver Shaw to the county jail, I'll talk to the judge about your girl."

Pamela saw a glimmer of hope for Francesca.

At supper that evening in the hotel dining hall, Harry joined Pamela and Prescott at their table. He had helped the town police prepare a report for the district attorney.

Pamela asked, "Was Brophy apologetic for charging Francesca with the death of Captain Crake?"

"The short answer is no," Harry replied with a wry smile. "And I resisted the temptation to make him eat crow. Brophy knows he must do the investigation right this time. I made myself useful, and he seems grateful."

At that moment, the waiter arrived to take their orders.

"Steak and potatoes for me," Harry said, then added, "and a pint of Ruppert's ale." Prescott ordered the same. Pamela chose broiled cod and white wine.

When the waiter left, Harry turned to Prescott. "To strengthen our case against Shaw, we'll have to address thorny legal issues. Your search of Rachel's trunk and later your forced entry into Shaw's cottage could be considered illegal. In each instance, you lacked a warrant to search private property. Shaw's attorney will most likely ask the judge to dismiss all charges."

Pamela objected, "The idea that Shaw could escape punishment for murder is outrageous." She turned to Prescott. "How do you think we should respond?"

Prescott replied, "I respect the Common Law and understand the need for a search warrant under ordinary circumstances. Last night, however, you and I rightly believed that Rachel was in imminent danger. We didn't have time to hunt for a magistrate and ask for a warrant. If challenged in court, I would invoke the law's principle of 'exigent necessity,' which means simply that saving a person's life overruled respect for private property. I'm sure that the district attorney is familiar with the idea."

"In view of that legal principle," Pamela asked Harry, "how did you manage to find Shaw's messages from Rachel?"

"When I couldn't find them myself, I asked Mrs. Taylor to help me."

"Did she faint? Or order you out of the house?"

"Not at all." He winked at Prescott. "I had charmed her. She quickly found them hidden in a Bible."

Pamela turned to Prescott. "In this instance, do we have a legal problem?"

"No," he replied, "as the property owner, Mrs. Taylor has the right to search a suspicious renter's room and his things."

"What will happen to Rachel, assuming she recovers?"

"In return for testifying against Shaw, she should be held less responsible than he, but she must not be exonerated. Otherwise, as Crake's widow, she could challenge his recent will and claim half of his estate."

Harry asked, "How deeply, if at all, were the butcher Karl Metzger and the bellboy Jason Dunn implicated in Crake's death?"

"We'd better find out," Prescott replied. "Shaw might try to shift the blame to them, as well as to Rachel."

Since coming to Saratoga Springs, Harry had cultivated the acquaintance of the German butcher, sometimes drinking beer with him in neighborhood taverns. On Sunday evening, as the news of Rachel Crake's nearly fatal experience spread throughout the town, Harry wondered how Metzger was reacting. In her messages, Rachel had named him as a coconspirator in her husband's death.

Harry found him at his customary table in Mickey's. His companions were trading opinions about the incident. Karl seemed preoccupied and had little to say. Soon his companions moved on to another table and Karl sat alone, staring into his beer.

Harry approached with his usual "Mind if I join you?"

Karl lifted his gaze and grunted a tepid assent. Harry ordered a beer and asked softly, "What's the matter, Karl?"

"I can't bring myself to talk about it, Harry. Help me to get my mind on something else. Let's talk baseball. Did my favorites, the Baltimore Orioles, win this afternoon?"

Harry quickly shifted into his role as a baseball fan. His interest was genuine but not centered on a single team. He loved the game itself for its drama and the speed and skill of its players. In Sing Sing, a fellow convict, who had played briefly in the National League, was amused when Harry had asked if stealing bases was a felony? By the time Harry was released, his mind held a rich treasury of baseball lore. He had even learned to pitch a curve ball.

Harry put on a doleful face. "Sad to say, Karl, the Boston Beaneaters beat the Orioles again, this time eight to four. It was the Orioles' sixth loss in a row. They will also play Boston on Monday and should win. Do you want to bet?"

Metzger dug into his pocket and put a penny on the table. "The Orioles by four points or more!"

Harry put up a penny. "I'll bet they don't. You hold the stakes."

Karl was now in a better mood. They chatted baseball and drank beer for an hour.

Harry was tempted to bring up Rachel Crake, but he sensed Metzger was still skittish. "I'll be going back to the hotel, Karl. Will I see you tomorrow?"

Metzger appeared to reflect for a moment. "Would you join Erika and me at an old-fashioned German festival behind our clubhouse tomorrow evening?"

"Sure, I'll see you then."

# CHAPTER 31

## *The Past Examined*

*Monday, July 30*

At breakfast in the hotel dining hall, Pamela and Prescott ran into the Crawfords, and they agreed to eat together. Almost immediately, James asked Prescott, "What can you tell us about Robert Shaw's attack on Rachel Crake? The police have released scant information. Still, the news has spread throughout the town in garbled versions."

Prescott gave the Crawfords a careful account, Pamela adding a detail here and there.

"Well," declared Edith, "Rachel Crake was foolish to go back to a man who was untrustworthy and had beaten her."

"But why did he try to kill her?" James asked Prescott.

"She threatened to tell the police that she had heard Shaw conspire with two men to kill her husband. She demanded money for her silence. Shaw pretended to agree, lured her from the hotel ballroom to his secret cottage, and attempted to silence her forever."

"And did she name the two men?" asked Edith, her voice trembling.

"Yes," Prescott replied. "Jason, sorry to say, and Karl Metzger. But, of course, we only have her word for that. She also didn't claim to know their roles, if any, in actually killing Crake."

James gazed calmly at Prescott. "The circumstances of his death are still murky. You and Mrs. Thompson will have to help the police sort them out." He smiled cheerfully. "But we have a more pleasant task before us. How shall we amuse ourselves today? The weather promises to be beautiful. I suggest that we visit Mount McGregor. It's only a thirty-five-minute train ride from here and offers an outstanding view of the area. We could lunch at Hotel Balmoral and then visit our late President Grant's summer cottage."

Virgil added, "Since he died there nine years ago, it has become almost a shrine. Hundreds of his admirers visit it every day at this time of the year."

"I'd be happy to go for the meal and the view," said Edith dryly. "You men are welcome to the general. I had enough of him thirty years ago." She turned to Prescott. "What do you say, Captain? Didn't you serve under his command in the war?"

Pamela grew concerned how Prescott would react. He rarely mentioned his military service or rank, and never to glorify it. Thirty years later, he still suffered from the physical and mental wounds of combat.

He nonetheless smiled at Edith. "In the last year of the war, I occasionally saw General Grant, but only at a distance. He was a shabby-looking man with a reputation for hard drinking and outstanding horsemanship. Appearances can be deceptive. He was brilliant in the art of making war. Many say that his single-minded, ruthless, aggressive strategy brought the war to an end. In his cottage we might see him in a different light."

He glanced toward Pamela with a teasing smile. "And what do you say, madame?"

"I'm intrigued. His military feats are much praised. But his record as president is judged to be paltry, even shamefully corrupt. Still, I admire him for writing a thick memoir to pay off his debts while dying of throat cancer in that cottage. I'd like to spend a few minutes there with him."

For a moment, they were all silent. Then James said, "It's settled. We'll catch the ten o'clock train on North Broadway."

The ride began well. With ease, Virgil and Prescott lifted James and his wheelchair into a railroad carriage. For thirty-five minutes the train chugged past farms and hamlets in the foothills of the Adirondacks. The train struggled through the last few uphill miles, but eased onto the level ground at the top of McGregor and discharged its passengers in front of the Hotel Balmoral.

They ate lunch on the hotel's wide, shaded terrace, enjoying the view over the Hudson River valley below. A short walk on a smooth path brought them to Grant's cottage, a plain, two-story wood frame structure with a large front porch. The cottage's simplicity, Pamela thought, somehow suited the man. The two-volume memoir was his monument.

Their guide pointed to a chair on the porch. "The general wrote much of the time here, with a pencil on a lined, yellow legal pad. When he became too weak to write, he dictated to a stenographer. Mind you, Grant had throat cancer. It was torture for him to speak. Toward the end, his voice grew so weak the stenographer had to put his ear to the general's mouth."

They were led inside Grant's bedroom. The guide gestured to a bed by the window. "There he died, three days after writing the last line of his memoir." He showed them a fancy clock on the mantel of the fireplace. "His son stopped the clock at eight minutes after eight on the morning of July 23, 1885."

While the men continued to speak with the guide about Grant and his military achievements, Pamela and Edith walked to an outlook near the cottage. The air was crisp and clear. They had a magnificent view of the Adirondack Mountains to the north and the Catskills to the south. In the broad valley below, the Hudson flowed toward Albany and New York City.

After several minutes of quiet pleasure, Pamela asked about Mrs. Dunn. "We haven't seen her much since she arrived. Is she well?"

Edith shrugged. "She complains of aches and pains, but nothing serious. She will leave tomorrow for New York City for a week with a cousin and then return home to Charleston."

"Has she shown any concern for Jason?"

"None at all. When speaking with her we avoid the subject." There was a hint of regret in Edith's face.

"Has she always had that attitude?"

"I'm afraid so. Unfortunately, my situation at Jason's birth seemed so desperate that even her grudging willingness to take him was welcome. I didn't foresee the loveless misery ahead for him. When I began to notice his unhappiness with Mr. and Mrs. Dunn, it seemed too late for any practical remedy. I've often reproached myself for a lack of understanding and courage. Now I fear that Jason has fallen into bad company with that gambler Shaw and the German butcher Metzger."

"Do you suspect that Jason was involved in Crake's death?"

"Don't you?"

"Not really. But, if he were involved, his mental illness might mitigate his responsibility. I see grounds for hope. I'm going to propose to your brother, James, that he visit the clinic with Prescott and me tomorrow. We'll learn what several days of therapy may have accomplished."

She threw Edith a glance.

"I'm not ready yet."

The men soon joined them on the outlook and admired the view. "So, what have you learned, James?" asked his sister.

"A bit of wisdom," he replied. "Grant chose a good place to end his days, high above the petty, mundane concerns of most lives. Undistracted, he could go back three decades and consider what he and others in blue and gray wrought, for better or worse. He's remarkably fair-minded, I think."

Pamela addressed Prescott. "What will you take away from this visit?"

"Apart from the pleasure of the present company, I leave with many questions. How shall I reconcile Grant the military butcher and Grant the gentle, private person? As a general, more than most, he was prodigal of men's lives. Did he ever shudder at the slaughter? Did he ever weep for the countless widows and orphans his orders were creating? I doubt it, but I might be wrong. As a private person, he was generous to a fault and a kind father to his children. He loved animals, especially horses, and tried to prevent their abuse. Frankly, his mind is a mystery to me."

Prescott asked Virgil, "Any surprises?" As was his custom, he had remained in the background, observing the others, as well as the view.

"Nothing has surprised me," he replied. "I've read about Grant. Our visit reminds me that he put an end to slavery, as much as any man then alive, but at a terrible cost. France, Britain, and other countries, like Brazil recently, did it without bloodshed. As president, Grant left the work of emancipation, at best, half done."

James gazed thoughtfully at Virgil, then addressed the others. "This has been a delightful and rewarding visit for both mind and body. We should now return to the Balmoral for something to drink and then catch the last train to Saratoga."

As they waited for their drinks, Pamela brought up the idea of a visit to Dr. Carson's clinic. "After several days of therapy, the doctor should be able to tell us whether it seems to be working for Jason."

All of them but Edith agreed to go. She smiled sadly. "Perhaps on another occasion."

\* \* \*

Back in Saratoga Springs in the early evening, Harry and the Metzgers went out to the grassy lot behind the German clubhouse. The atmosphere was genial. Men and women with steins of foaming beer in their hands gathered around a brass band and sang to its robust marches and sentimental waltzes. Afterward, a meal of grilled bratwurst, noodles, and pickled beets was served under a tent. A dessert of cherry strudel was followed by coffee.

Harry knew little German, but most of these people were fluent in English. There were sack and egg races for children, croquet for women, and a horseshoe toss for men. Harry could throw with the best of them. Karl was his partner. Together, they shared a prize, a pair of beer steins.

As they walked away from the pitch, Karl looked as if he had something weighing on his mind. He motioned Harry to the side.

"I'd like a word, Harry, when the festival is over. Where could we meet?"

"Come to my room in the hotel. Ask for me at the front desk. I'll leave a message."

"I'll be there." The burly German was close to tears.

Shortly after nine, Harry showed Metzger into the room. Though the windows were open, the air inside was warm and still. Metzger had hurried up the stairs and was sweating profusely. Harry offered him a towel, a fan, and a glass of cold water. "We'll talk, Karl, when you've cooled down."

After he had mopped his face and fanned himself, he drank the water. "Thanks," he said, and put the glass aside. Harry refilled it.

"Did you like the bratwurst, Harry?"

"Does a child like candy?" Harry replied. The German was reluctant and for good reason.

Metzger stared into the glass for a long moment, then began hesitantly. "Ever since I heard the news about Rachel Crake, I can't stop thinking. I don't doubt that Shaw tried to kill her. She knew too much and couldn't keep her mouth shut. I'm trying to figure out if I encouraged him to kill old Captain Crake."

Harry raised a hand. "Start from the beginning. Tell me how you might have helped him."

"Since the season began here in June, Shaw has joined Jason Dunn and me in Mickey's for penny ante poker or for a throw of the dice. We often complained to each other about the captain. Over the years, he had angered all three of us, one way or another. Jason resented how he generally abused women and was trying to seduce Francesca. Shaw claimed he cheated at cards and was unfair to Rachel. I had long hated him for forcing me out of the meatpacking business. I knew that he was a guest at the hotel, but I kept out of his sight. I didn't want trouble. It would cost me my job."

Metzger again patted sweat away from his forehead and drank from the glass. "Then, in the morning of July seventh, my boss brought Crake into the meat department on a visit. By accident, he and I met. He flared up and ordered my boss to get rid of me. If necessary, he would complain to Mr. Wooley, the proprietor."

Metzger paused again, breathing heavily. His face was red.

"Take it easy, Karl," Harry said. "You rightly feared that if you were fired, you'd have no prospect of work, especially during the country's present economic depression."

"As I look back now, Harry, I see that a surge of anger carried me away. I felt I had to stop Crake. Shaw saw my anger. He urged us to act together. He would kill Crake if Jason and I would help. He asked me to lend him the new boning knife. He had earlier admired it. He said it would make a small, neat, but fatal wound and no mess. I could claim it was stolen. I would otherwise not get involved. In the evening of July seventh, Jason would keep track of Crake and guide Shaw to the right place at the right time for the killing."

"Who did you think would be blamed for the murder?"

"I asked Shaw. He said the police would suspect that a tramp stole my knife and broke into the cottage to steal money or jewelry. Crake surprised him and was killed. We didn't know that Crake had given Francesca Ricci the bracelet. I'm sorry the police arrested her. That's bothered me. I want to clear her."

"You're taking the right steps, Karl. So, Shaw came up with a plan to kill Crake involving the three of you. But I know it didn't work out that way. Tell me what happened next."

"Jason and I said we needed an hour to think it over. By one o'clock, I had decided the scheme was too risky. In any case, I didn't want my knife to kill anyone, not even Crake. Jason felt the same. Shaw heard us out, smiled, and said he'd drop the idea."

"What did you think when you heard that Crake was murdered and Francesca was arrested?"

"At first, I didn't know what to make of it all. Had Shaw hired the girl? Or was the killing an odd coincidence unrelated to Shaw's plan? What most disturbed me was hearing that the murder weapon was a boning knife. The police seemed to suspect that I was careless or even let the girl have the knife."

"Unfortunately," said Harry, "in the secret messages I've discovered, Rachel has implicated you and Jason, as well as Shaw. When she recovers, she'll claim she wasn't involved."

He glared at Harry. "Rachel's a liar! It was her idea from the beginning. She was always in the background, egging Shaw on. What do you think will happen?"

"That you are coming forward with the truth should work

in your favor. Sometime tomorrow, Brophy will call you into his office and ask you to explain. I recommend that first thing tomorrow morning you hire a lawyer. Brophy's not a bad sort. Still, he's a cop. Don't trust a cop to be kind or fair or forgiving." Harry leaned forward and measured his words. "I speak from experience."

# CHAPTER 32

## *Hope*

*Tuesday, July 31*

Pamela and Prescott were eating breakfast in the dining hall when Harry arrived late and sat down with them. "What did you learn from Metzger last night?" Pamela asked as a waiter approached.

Harry placed an order and reported briefly on the German's confession. Then he added, "I'm concerned that Shaw's lawyer will try to shift at least part of the blame for Crake's death onto Karl. I'll make sure he gets a good lawyer."

Pamela asked, "Could Shaw argue that Crake's death was due to a conspiracy of Jason and Metzger and Rachel?"

"That sounds farfetched to me," replied Prescott, "but lawyers sometimes have to make things up."

At midmorning, Pamela and Prescott rode with James and Virgil in the Crawford carriage to Dr. Carson's clinic for a conversation about Jason's condition. Edith went by herself to the exercise track to ride Savannah.

Carson had chosen a time when Jason would be engaged with a nurse and wouldn't encounter the visitors. They sat congenially at a conference table in the doctor's office.

Pamela began, "After nearly six days of examination, Doctor, have you reached a preliminary assessment of Jason's condition?"

"Yes," he replied. "Fortunately, his condition is treatable. He has adjusted well to our clinic's routine and accepts our procedures. We encourage him to speak of the past. As you already know, he has a deep-seated need to know who he is and where he comes from. For most of his young life that need was frustrated, causing resentment toward his family. He grew up with little appreciation or respect from the people in charge of him, and that led to self-doubt and then to self-loathing. When his condition recently became acute, he was tempted to seek release in suicide."

No surprises thus far, Pamela thought. Her companions seemed to agree. She asked, "Are there grounds for hope?"

"Yes," Carson replied. "Fortunately, Jason has strengths we can build upon, his musical talent, for example. We offer him many opportunities to perform. He also responds eagerly when we prompt him to speak his mind and then explore his complaints. It helps also that his physical condition is good. In contrast, some of our patients arrive here suffering from years of poor diet, lack of exercise, and neglected hygiene. Their recovery is much slower than I expect Jason's to be."

"Do you think the therapy will heal his mental illness?" James asked.

"I'm optimistic. The therapy has worked well on more desperate cases than his."

James addressed the doctor tactfully. "Your medical colleagues and your patients assure me that you are competent and trustworthy, so I'm prepared to enter into an agreement for Jason's treatment. We'll hope for the best."

As the visitors stood at the door out of the clinic, Pamela asked Carson if he could foresee any complications. He gazed at them with an eye steeped in family secrets, then said, "Mr.

Dunn may try to keep certain aspects of his past hidden from us to avoid being treated. That happens occasionally in cases of severe trauma like his. If he has any secrets, my nurses are trained to discover them and will pry them open."

Pamela asked herself, was Carson perhaps alluding to a secret as traumatic as killing one's father? She glanced at the two Crawfords. Their expressions were opaque.

She had an afterthought and drew Carson to the side. "Doctor," she said softly, "we learned late yesterday that Mr. Robert Shaw, a notorious gambler in this town and a suspect in Captain Crake's murder, was arrested over the weekend and charged with attempting to kill Mrs. Rachel Crake, his former mistress. If he is released on bail, perhaps as early as today, I urge you to keep him away from the clinic. He may attempt to harm Mr. Dunn, who possibly holds secrets that incriminate him."

Dr. Carson thanked her for the warning. "I know Mr. Shaw by reputation, and I've heard of Mrs. Crake's misfortune, but I wasn't aware of a connection to Jason. I'll alert the nurses. By the way, could you come back this afternoon? I'd like you to visit Jason. You are one of the few persons he trusts. You might catch a significance in his remarks that my nurses miss."

That afternoon, Pamela returned to the clinic. From Carson's darkened office through a one-way window, she watched Jason in the foyer while the doctor stood by her side. The brightly lighted foyer served as a gathering place after the noon meal. Nurses and patients were similarly dressed in casual summer clothes. Carson remarked, "We encourage patients to wear whatever they wish within a reasonable range of decency."

Most of the patients formed small groups and chatted normally with each other. Jason sat with a young female nurse and engaged in a rather strained conversation. "She's giving him advice on behavior with women," said Carson. "He's quite awkward on that score due to a history of unhealthy sexual experiences." Soon a female patient joined the pair and then a male. Introductions were made, followed by an exchange of teasing that produced a smile on Jason's face. "In a few more days, he'll be more at ease," Carson added.

Jason reached for an instrument case by his side and pulled out his flute. The stressed look on his face vanished as he heard a request for a tune. The gathering quieted down and Jason played "Drink to Me Only with Thine Eyes." The others listened raptly. At the end, they asked him to play it again. This time a slender, attractive young female patient with a sweet soprano voice sang Ben Jonson's lyrics.

> "Drink to me only with thine eyes,
> And I will pledge with mine;
> Or leave a kiss but in the cup
> And I'll not look for wine."

At the end, they bowed to the audience and then to each other. For a moment, Jason gazed fondly at the singer. His face filled with a tenderness Pamela hadn't noticed before.

When the gathering broke up, Carson led Pamela up to Jason. "Mrs. Thompson has come to visit you," he announced. "Please show her your garden."

Jason reacted with an embarrassed smile and a shrug of his shoulders, then slipped into the role of a bellboy. "Come with me, ma'am," he said to Pamela, as if she were a guest at the Grand Union Hotel.

She put on her straw hat and they walked through rows of roses in bloom next to a berry patch. "Tomorrow, I'll feed the horses. Today, I must pick a couple of quarts of raspberries for supper."

"May I help?" she asked.

He glanced critically at her white linen dress. "You must be *very* careful."

"You're right," she granted. "I'll only pick a few for the taste."

The berries were large, sun ripened, and delicious. Jason quickly picked two quarts and delivered them to the kitchen.

"Shall we find a shady bench and chat for a few minutes?" she asked.

"I've nothing else to do," he replied curtly, but his voice betrayed pleasure at the suggestion. He led her to a shaded bench overlooking the pond.

"This is my favorite spot," he remarked. "I love the sounds of the flute on the water." He glanced at her for a sign of interest. She replied, "I would like very much to hear it."

He began to play what resembled an endless variety of bird songs, subtly echoed by the pond.

Pamela gazed at Jason with astonishment. "I've never heard anything so beautiful in all my life."

"I listen to the birds at different times of the day and learn their songs. They bring me close to God—closer than people do."

"This place is good for you, Jason. You'll meet people with the uplifting spirit of birds, and they will help you find a way into happiness."

He stared at her doubtfully. "And who is paying for this?" He waved his hand over the estate.

"Your uncle, James." She had to be truthful with Jason. Lies had nearly ruined his life. She continued. "James is a kind, generous man. This is his way to acknowledge that you and he are kin. He's also a smart, successful businessman who believes you are a promising investment, rich in potential satisfaction for both of you."

"I would like to believe you, Mrs. Thompson. Maybe one day I shall."

Pamela rose from the bench. "I'll be leaving now. May I come again for a concert by the pond?"

"Please do. I'd like that." He remained seated. "There's

something I'd like to say to you." She sat down again by his side, wondering what was on his mind.

"I've heard that Rachel Crake is in the hospital, and they've arrested Robert Shaw. I'm pleased. He's one of the devil's minions. When I say that, I'm not talking crazy. A little over three weeks ago, he tried to suck me and Karl Metzger into his scheme to kill the captain."

Pamela was now paying close attention and urged him to continue. He looked out over the pond and described essentially the same conspiracy as Metzger with similar regret that it led to Francesca Ricci being blamed for Crake's murder.

"But," he concluded, "I see things much clearer now. Crake was a bad man and deserved to be punished. I'm not sorry he's dead. Still, I regret now that I encouraged Shaw to kill him."

"Did you actually help him on the night of July seventh?"

"No, earlier on that day I thought it over and told him that I didn't have enough nerve. I'd only mess up his plan. He didn't object and said he'd drop the idea. Somehow, he managed without me. The whole incident left me feeling distressed and unable to manage my life."

"When did you begin to change for the better?"

"After a few days in this clinic, I feel more comfortable about myself and others, and look at everything more clearly. I still have much to learn. I wish I had come here earlier." He hesitated. "But then I couldn't afford it, could I?" His eyes filled with tears.

Pamela gave him a handkerchief and urged him to continue.

He dabbed at his eyes. "While we were looking out over the pond and I was playing the flute, I thought of my mother, Edith, with affection for the first time, just for an instant, as if a little bird had flown by. And now I'm thinking of her again. How she must have suffered back in Georgia in sixty-four."

He began to tremble as if he were having a fit. Pamela grew concerned.

Jason seemed to sense her reaction. "Captain Crake has come back into my mind again and is taunting me while he violates a young woman. I'd like to tear him to pieces." Jason looked piteously at Pamela. "I don't feel well, ma'am. I need to go inside and see a nurse. You and I will talk again another time."

Pamela kept the Crawfords posted on Jason's progress. Then, one morning early in August, as Pamela was preparing to visit the clinic for the last time before returning to work in New York, Virgil Crawford came to her office. "Edith and James would like to go with you to the clinic," he said. "Do you think Jason is ready to meet them?"

"I think he is, but I'll check. I can telephone you from the clinic."

Early that afternoon, Pamela found Jason by the pond, playing his flute. His girlfriend, the young soprano, was at his side. When he finished the piece, Pamela approached. Jason welcomed her. His girlfriend excused herself and left. Pamela asked about his health. He responded that he felt encouraged. That morning, his nurse had recommended a gradual transition to the "real" world.

That same nurse had also encouraged Pamela to suggest to Jason that he meet his mother and uncle. So, Pamela now posed the idea to him. He didn't seem surprised or resentful. For a long moment, he quietly reflected. Then he gazed at Pamela, and said, "I think it's about time."

# CHAPTER 33

## *Deliverance*

*Monday, August 6*

Later that afternoon, when Pamela returned to the hotel, a message from Prescott was waiting for her.

> Detective Brophy wants to see you in his office.
> Harry and I are already talking to him.

She left immediately for the police station.

As she walked through the door, she felt a tense atmosphere in the room. Brophy sat at his desk. His coat and hat hung on a hook. He was again collarless. Sweat stained his shirt. He was chewing on his cigar. Next to him was seated Mr. John Person, the district attorney. Pamela had met him briefly at Francesca's arraignment in the county courthouse in Ballston Spa.

Prescott pulled up a chair for her, and said, "We're discussing the case against Robert Shaw. He now admits going to Crake's cottage the night of July seventh, disguised as a chambermaid, to persuade him to leave Rachel in his will. But, he insists that Crake was already dead. He also claims that Metzger and Dunn must have killed Crake, though he had earlier tried to dissuade them."

Pamela shook her head. "How does he explain Rachel's message identifying him as the killer?"

"He says she shouldn't be trusted since she acted out of spite and in order to extort money from him. For good measure, he continues to insist that Rachel's overdose was an accident."

Harry added, "We've also questioned Metzger. This morning, he came here with a lawyer, who advised him to say only that he didn't kill Crake. He wouldn't comment on the passages in Rachel's message that seemed to implicate him."

Brophy put aside his cigar and asked, "What can you tell us, Mrs. Thompson, concerning Jason Dunn's role in this crime?"

"I've spoken candidly with him. He admits having discussed the murder but decided against it. He accuses Shaw of the crime. I should add that Jason's mental condition is still fragile, but his remarks to me were credible."

Mr. Person thanked her politely, then spoke with the assurance of an experienced prosecutor. "The preponderance of the evidence indicates that Shaw killed Crake with Rachel's assistance to prevent him from cutting her out of his will. They had expected to share the inheritance. He tried to kill Rachel to prevent her from testifying against him. Both Crake's murder and the attempt on Rachel's life appear to be premeditated. I conclude that Shaw deserves the death penalty."

"I agree that's what happened," said Prescott. "At trial, however, Shaw's attorney will attack the credibility of Rachel's messages. They are obviously self-serving. She also implicated Metzger and Dunn. According to her, they conspired with Shaw to murder Crake. Shaw's attorney will try to shift at least some responsibility to them."

"That could be difficult to determine in court," the district attorney admitted. "Dunn could plead that he was acting under the influence of severe mental illness. Moreover, if I charge them with aiding and abetting a murder, they might refuse to cooperate. That could weaken my case against Shaw." He threw up his hands. "How is justice best served?"

Prescott came up with a suggestion. "Persuade Shaw to change his story in return for life in prison instead of the death sentence. Threaten him with the electric chair. He would have to admit to confronting Crake, but only in order to persuade him to write his will in Rachel's favor. Crake refused and cursed him. Shaw lost his temper and killed him. Shaw never intended to kill Rachel, but their quarrel got out of hand. Shaw's new story would not implicate Metzger and Jason in Crake's death."

This discussion annoyed Pamela. She had been long enough in Prescott's law firm to understand that the legal system was as messy as a sausage factory and often achieved much less than perfect justice. Over a span of thirty years, Captain Crake had committed several serious crimes, including Edith's rape, but was never charged because he was rich, powerful, and clever enough to evade responsibility. Now at least Crake was no longer a threat to others.

Still, a nagging doubt disturbed her peace of mind. No one had seen Shaw kill Crake, and he would confess only under the threat of the electric chair. He might indeed have discovered Crake's bloody corpse and panicked. All the evidence against him was circumstantial. The testimony of Rachel, Jason, and Metzger could be dismissed as self-serving.

If not Shaw, then who else could have killed Crake? It would have to be a very clever man with opportunity and motive.

A few days later, when the district attorney had formally charged Shaw with Crake's murder, Harry Miller felt it was time to deal with another piece of unfinished business, Karl Metzger. Misleading reports of his alleged role in the Crake murder had put his job at the hotel in jeopardy. If he were fired, he faced unemployment, homelessness, and destitution. Wooley thought Metzger had been too friendly with Shaw and had carelessly mislaid the boning knife that Shaw had then stolen.

Harry went to Mr. Wooley, the hotel proprietor, and explained that the murder weapon was not Metzger's boning knife but Shaw's dagger. The manager of the meat department, who accompanied Harry, praised Metzger's skill and pointed out that it would be hard to replace him at the peak of the tourist season.

"Mrs. Thompson and I," Harry concluded, "have observed Karl Metzger and can attest that he's an honorable, hardworking man. The Crake affair has taught him to choose more carefully his drinking companions. He's happy in his job at the hotel. Contrary to Captain Crake's assertions, he has no intention to stir up trouble."

The meat manager seconded Harry's argument. Wooley looked skeptical, but in the end he said Metzger could stay.

The last unfinished business fell to Pamela. For a month, she had worked to free Francesca Ricci from prison and clear her name. When Shaw was formally charged, the district attorney petitioned the court in Ballston Spa to quash the charges against Francesca and to release her. That procedure was cumbersome and took several days while Pamela waited impatiently.

Finally, August 10, the day of the girl's release, Pamela drove to the prison. At the appointed hour, Francesca was led out, dressed in the frock she wore when she entered. Pamela was stunned to see how she had changed in a month. The heedless look of a young madcap was gone, replaced by dull eyes and sagging shoulders. Pamela worried that the change might be irreversible.

They climbed into the carriage and began the ride back to Saratoga Springs. The air was warm, the sky blue. Cows grazed in lush meadows. Birds twittered in the trees. Children played in hamlets along the road. Francesca began to brighten. By the time they reached Saratoga Springs, she was humming an Italian folk tune, her feet tapping to the beat.

She turned to Pamela with a big smile. "It's good to be free."

# CHAPTER 34

## *Finale*

*New York City*
*Wednesday, August 29*

Pamela was chatting with the office clerk when Prescott arrived, refreshed and tanned. She asked, "How was camping in the Adirondacks?" He had just returned from two weeks of canoeing, fishing, swimming, and hiking with his son, Edward.

"Splendid!" he replied, leading her into his private office. "Have you heard from Harry?" Miller was away on vacation with Sergeant Larry White and his family at a cottage on Long Island.

"He met Larry's sister-in-law and fell into a budding romance."

"Good for him! She might sweeten his disposition. What else happened while I was gone?"

"A few days ago, Robert Shaw began a life sentence in Dannemora. He had accepted the district attorney's plea bargain. I'm sure he hopes that lady luck will eventually smile on him."

"And what's happened to Rachel?"

"She was convicted of conspiracy in her husband's death and

sentenced to six years in Mount Pleasant, the women's prison on the grounds of Sing Sing."

"I pity her," said Prescott. "Life there will be harsh and degrading for a beautiful young courtesan." He asked tentatively, "Any personal news?"

"Yes, according to local gossip, the Morgans at Ventfort have excused your wife Gloria's social blunder as due to a parent's misguided but well-meaning concern. Gloria and her banker friend, Mr. Fisher, are still together. . . ." Pamela searched his eyes.

Prescott frowned. "And what else?'

"She has sued you for divorce in Connecticut, accusing you of mental cruelty and infidelity."

Prescott let out an exasperated sigh and pointed to a heaping basket of correspondence. "My lawyer's letter is probably in there, together with a summons to appear in court."

"But there's also heartwarming news," Pamela added. "Jason will stay with the Crawfords in the city for a week, then return to Saratoga Springs and work through September at the hotel. Signor Teti has employed him as a part-time handyman and will give him music lessons. For the time being, he'll continue to live at Carson's clinic."

The clerk appeared at the door. "Mr. Virgil Crawford to see you, sir, concerning recent business."

"Show him in." Prescott glanced at Pamela with a look of surprise.

Before she could reply, Virgil entered and handed Prescott a check. "This concludes the Ruth Colt case. A coroner's jury has ruled that Captain Crake was responsible for Miss Colt's murder. Her aunt has properly buried her. This is as much justice as we can expect in an imperfect world. I would have preferred to see him convicted and hanged. Hopefully, a Higher Court will give him his due."

"Tell me about Jason," Prescott asked. "I understand he has drawn closer to his mother."

"Yes, thanks to Savannah. It's touching to watch Jason and Edith grooming her together. So, we have reasons to celebrate. I'm authorized to invite you and Mrs. Thompson to dinner Friday evening at the Crawford home on Washington Square. The party will be you two, the family, and a half-dozen congenial acquaintances. Dress semiformal. As family chef, I'll arrange a memorable meal."

Prescott glanced at Pamela, and she agreed. He said, "I accept gladly. This offers an opportunity for a gesture that I've been thinking about." He took down the military sword hanging on the wall behind him and handed it to Virgil. "It came from Gettysburg and may have belonged to your cousin Arthur Crawford."

Virgil held the sword at various angles to the light and studied it through a magnifying glass. Finally, he met Prescott's eye. "Sir, I can assure you that this sword once belonged to my cousin Arthur." He pointed to tiny letters faintly engraved on the hilt: TUTUM TE ROBORE REDDAM. "That's Latin for the Crawford family motto: 'With my strength I'll make you safe.' As he was leaving home to join his regiment, he raised the sword to express his devotion to our family, our country, and our way of life."

"Would your family like it back?" Prescott asked. "Or, would it be too painful a reminder of your great losses in the war?"

Virgil replied, "James will answer for us. But I can safely say to bring the sword with you to dinner tomorrow evening."

As their coach approached the Crawford home, Pamela felt uneasy, not knowing precisely what to expect. The burden of the family's tragic past always seemed present in Edith's haunted look, in James's stoic suffering, in Jason's resentful eyes, in Virgil's gracious, freely offered servitude. Besides the reconciliation of Jason and his mother, what else were they supposed to celebrate? Captain Crake's death?

She cast Prescott a side glance. The sword lay in its scabbard on his lap. For comfort in the late August heat he had chosen a light gray dinner jacket, white shirt, gray bow tie, and dark gray trousers. His figure was still athletic and trim at fifty-two. Pamela felt pleased beside him in a red short-sleeved silk gown and a pearl necklace.

Virgil met them at the door, hung the sword on a hook, and then showed them into a parlor. Edith joined them and broke into a delighted smile as Pamela presented her with a bouquet of freesias. The other guests arrived, mostly cultivated Southerners, to judge from their accent. While Virgil disappeared to check on the meal, James welcomed them all in his study. Over aperitifs they admired his collection of antique ivory chessmen and his large library of Greek and Latin literature with modern illustrations. From the study they went to the music room. Jason was there with his flute. When the guests were seated, Virgil came with a cello, and Edith moved to the piano.

At a gesture from Edith, they began the Irish folk tune "The Londonderry Air." Pamela listened rapt as the trio poured their own painful sense of suffering and loss, and their yearnings for happiness into the bittersweet melody. As the music soared, Pamela's lost daughter, Julia, slipped unbeckoned into her mind, lovely as in life. "I miss you so," came soundlessly from Pamela's lips.

She feared she would break into tears and spoil the party. Fortunately, Virgil announced, "To put us in a festive mood for the dinner table, we'll close the music with 'Gaudeamus Igitur,' from the finale of Johannes Brahms's *Academic Festival Overture.* James will sing the original Latin. Sing along if you know it." He gave a nod and the trio set out at a lively tempo.

*"Gaudeamus igitur juvenes dum sumus . . ."* ("Let us rejoice while we are young . . .")

James's voice was a strong, clear baritone. Prescott joined him in perfect harmony. The mood in the room lightened. At the song's conclusion, Virgil showed them into the dining room, where an oval table was set for ten. Virgil and Jason retreated to the kitchen.

The room's modest size, its polished hardwood floors, pastel yellow walls and green drapes, potted plants in the corners, and flower boxes on the window ledges created an impression of intimate elegance. Compared with the Morgans, Astors, and Vanderbilts, the Crawfords entertained on a small scale, consistent with their restrained social ambitions.

In a waiter's black suit and white gloves, Jason served lobster bisque, followed by broiled striped bass and anchovy sauce with new potatoes. The meat course was stuffed veal with fresh roasted vegetables. Edam and Roquefort cheese and fresh fruit came next, and for dessert crème brûlée. With each course he offered the appropriate wine. Pamela took small portions and barely sipped the wine. Afterward, Jason and Virgil served coffee and liqueur in the drawing room, then remained with the company.

Over the mantel was the large portrait of Arthur Crawford in his officer's uniform, flanked by portraits of his mother and father. A miniature of the painting stood on the mantel beneath the portrait.

Virgil came with the sword, handed it to Prescott, and said, "I believe we are ready." The guests gathered around him.

With heightened feeling in his voice, James addressed Prescott. "Captain, tell us the story of that sword."

Prescott bowed to James, then recounted the events of that fateful day in July at Gettysburg: the Georgia infantry's advance through the wheat field, the young officer falling, the Georgians retreating.

"When I reached him, he lay dead from a wound to the heart. Death was instant. I doubt that he suffered. I picked up his sword, intending to return it to his family. But before I could determine his identity, the Georgians rallied and drove us back. I was wounded. Months later, after my recovery, I searched unsuccessfully for the family. Years later, I mounted the sword on my office wall as a memorial to an unknown victim of the war. Since I've learned his identity, I believe the sword belongs here."

He presented the sword to James. James drew it from the scabbard, read aloud the Crawford motto, and said, "It's Arthur's. In the confusion following the battle, his body disappeared into an unmarked grave. This sword is all we have of him, and, of course, the memories and the paintings." He glanced up at the large portrait over the mantel. "We'll place the sword beneath it."

Virgil had prepared the spot and now hung the sword and stepped back.

James shook Prescott's hand. "Thank you, Captain, you've brought a bitter chapter of our family's history to an honorable conclusion."

They gathered in front of the fireplace and gazed at the sword. There was a moment of silence and a few tears, then a collective sigh of relief. "Finally," said James, "we've put frustrated anger and resentment behind us and are free to live."

While the others enjoyed their drinks and continued to reminisce, Pamela drifted away, looking at other portraits in the room. Her gaze fixed on a small painting of Virgil in the prime of life, seated with his right hand gripping his cane. The artist caught him in a grim mood, eyes hooded. Unwelcome suspicions raced to Pamela's mind.

She slipped out of the room and into the entrance hall. Virgil's cane stood in a rack. She drew out the sword and closely examined its blade. In tiny letters was etched the inscription: FIAT JUSTITIA RUANT COELI. ("Let justice prevail though the Heavens fall.") Suddenly, the pieces of the Crake murder puzzle fell into place. She heard soft footsteps behind her.

"You won't find blood, Pamela. I cleaned the blade." Virgil gently took the sword from her hands and slid it back into the cane. He motioned her into his parlor. "We'll talk better here," he said, while studying her face, reading her mind.

"I see you have concluded that I killed Captain Crake. I do regret that Miss Ricci spent a month in prison. That was not in the plan. She would never have gone to trial."

"Don't be concerned, Virgil. She has recovered and has actually gained from the experience."

"I have no regret for Rob Shaw's life term in prison. British authorities want to hang him for a murder in South Africa, so he's fortunate to be in Dannemora. We are all better off for having one less parasite in our midst. Rachel Crake was rightly convicted of conspiring with him to kill her husband. Six years in Mount Pleasant might improve her character."

"So, why was Crake killed?"

"Certain crimes cry out to Heaven for righteous vengeance. Crake's reached that level. In such cases, when the civil authorities fail to act or, worse yet, are complicit, then the duty falls to anyone who is able to perform it."

"Private vengeance is risky, Virgil. The state calls it criminal and prescribes a severe punishment."

"True, there is that risk." His tone was sardonic. "But it's lessened by our country's long tradition of popular or vigilante justice. As we speak, a black man is probably being lynched somewhere, and not only in the South."

Pamela flinched at his bitter irony. "How did it happen, Virgil?"

"When Rachel Crake left the concert to gamble at the casino, I knew that Crake would be alone and drugged. I slipped into his room and stabbed him. As fate would have it, while I was wiping his blood from my blade, I heard someone at the door. I hid in a cabinet. Rob Shaw stole into the room in a chambermaid's bonnet and apron, dagger drawn. The light was low. He crept close to Crake on the sofa and raised the weapon. Suddenly, he saw that the man was already dead. Cursing God, he fled from the room."

"Were Edith and James involved in the killing in any way?"

"No, not at all. I told them only after the fact. Edith was pleased with what I had done. James refused to pass judgment. We are still best friends."

"Have you felt any remorse?"

"Yes, I feel soiled and unsatisfied, all the more because my deed was unnecessary. Shaw would have done it." Tears pooled in his eyes. He gazed at her with yearning. "Do you think less of me now?"

She shook her head. "I surely do not judge you, Virgil. I feel only compassion. I believe that even righteous vengeance takes a terrible toll of one's humanity, and you are suffering. I'm not obliged to report to anyone what you've told me. I hope you find peace." She caressed his cheek. "Shall we join the others in the sitting room?"

Choked up, he gazed at her for a moment, then returned the cane to the rack. They waited while he grew calm. Then he said, "Thank you, Pamela, I'll check on things in the kitchen."

Back in the sitting room, Pamela asked Prescott, "Shall we thank our hosts and leave now?"

"Yes, they seem reconciled with each other and with their past."

# Author's Notes

For a readable account of Saratoga Springs in the Gilded Age, go to George Waller's *Saratoga: Saga of an Impious Era* (Prentice-Hall, Englewood Cliffs, NJ, 1966). On the social background of Saratoga Springs, see Thomas A. Chambers's *Drinking the Waters: Creating an American Leisure Class at Nineteenth-Century Mineral Springs* (Smithsonian Institution Scholarly Press, Washington, DC, 2002). Chambers compares and contrasts Saratoga Springs and White Sulphur Springs, Virginia. For racial issues in Saratoga Springs, consult Myra B. Young Armstead's *"Lord, Please Don't Take Me in August": African-Americans in Newport and Saratoga Springs, 1870–1930* (University of Illinois Press, Urbana, IL, 1999). Edward Hotaling tells the Gilded Age story of the Saratoga Springs thoroughbred racing track in *They're Off! Horse Racing at Saratoga* (Syracuse University Press, Syracuse, NY, 1995). For images and text describing the city's remarkable Gilded Age buildings, see Stephen S. Prokopoff and Joan C. Siegfried Prokopoff's *The Nineteenth-Century Architecture of Saratoga Springs: Architecture Worth Saving in New York State* (New York State Council on the Arts, New York, 1970).

In 1894, the Grand Union Hotel was at its peak among the world's greatest hotels. Its six floors occupied almost an entire city block and could accommodate 2,000 guests. It had hot and cold running water in every guest room, as well as indoor plumbing and electricity throughout the building and an elevator to the upper floors. Its furnishings and cuisine were luxurious. In the rear courtyard was a large park, shaded by tall elm trees and illuminated by gaslight. Concerts were regularly held there. In the twentieth century, the hotel's fortunes declined and it was demolished in the 1950s. Canfield's Casino, however, has survived to become a splendid witness to the Gilded Age and the site of the Historical Society of Saratoga Springs.

For the Gilded Age's memory of Sherman's March to the Sea, consult Wesley Moody's *Demon of the Lost Cause: Sherman and Civil War History* (University of Missouri, Columbus, MO, 2011). Concerning the atrocities blamed on Sherman's army, read Lee B. Kennett's *Marching Through Georgia: The Story of Soldiers and Civilians During Sherman's Campaign* (Harper Perennial, New York, 1995) for a careful analysis of accusations of rape of white women by Union soldiers. He concludes that it happened, as in the fictional case at the Crawford plantation, but it was contrary to military law and Sherman's orders, and doesn't appear to have been widespread. James Marten, in his *Sing Not War: The Lives of Union and Confederate Veterans in Gilded Age America* (University of North Carolina Press, Chapel Hill, NC, 2011), describes how white, chiefly Northern veterans coped with civilian life and how their pension demands were ambivalently regarded by the larger society. For a detailed, readable account of Sherman's campaign, including the Ninth Pennsylvania Cavalry's foraging south of Savannah, consult Noah A. Trudeau's *Southern Storm: Sherman's March to the Sea* (Harper Perennial, New York, 2008).

For dependable information on NYPD police inspector "Clubber" Williams (1839–1917) and the reform of policing in late-nineteenth-century New York City, consult James F. Richardson's *The New York Police: Colonial Times to 1901* (Oxford University Press, New York, 1970).

Conditions in Crake's meatpacking plants on Fourteenth Street in Manhattan resemble those in the much larger Union Stockyard in Chicago, as depicted in Upton Sinclair's influential muckraking novel, *The Jungle* (1906; ed. by C.V. Eby, NY, 2003).

Popular music in the Gilded Age was sometimes imported. "Funiculì, Funiculà" was composed in Naples in 1880 by Luigi Denza. In 1888, the lyrics were freely translated by the English songwriter and librettist Edward Oxenford. Ben Jonson's "Drink to Me Only with Thine Eyes" came from his poem "Song to Celia," in 1616, and has been a favorite for centuries.